PRAIS
THE YELLOV

"Warning: do not start reading *The Yellow Lantern* unless you've got plenty of time! You will not want to stop reading. With a page-turning style that will keep the reader on the edge of her seat, Dicken's twists and turns will have you guessing until the very end. Highly recommended!"

–Kathleen Y'Barbo, author of the bestselling
The Pirate Bride and *The Alamo Bride*

"Body snatchers, sabotage, and two people who are trying to rise above the darkness and deception shrouding their worlds. Angie Dicken's newest novel, *The Yellow Lantern*, is rife with fantastic historical details, enough intrigue to tickle the fancy of suspense lovers, and it evokes the compelling question—what lengths would we explore to rescue someone we love? Pick up this interesting and unique tale about a shadowy and intriguing part of our country's history."

–Pepper Basham, author of *My Heart Belongs in the Blue Ridge* and
the Mitchell's Crossroads series

"Angie Dicken has created a story replete with the historical details and nuances that pull me into a world I don't want to leave. Josie is in an impossible predicament, but she's someone I loved spending time with. This book has it all: compelling characters, historical setting that is a character in its own right, and writing that is lyrical and beautiful. It's a perfect read for those who love a good historical romance!"

–Cara Putman, award-winning author of
Shadowed by Grace and *Delayed Justice*

the YELLOW LANTERN

Angie Dicken

BARBOUR BOOKS

An Imprint of Barbour Publishing, Inc.

©2019 by Angie Dicken

Print ISBN 978-1-64352-083-4

eBook Editions:
Adobe Digital Edition (.epub) 978-1-64352-085-8
Kindle and MobiPocket Edition (.prc) 978-1-64352-084-1

All scripture quotations are taken from the King James Version of the Bible.

This book is a work of fiction. Names, characters, places, and incidents are either products of the author's imagination or used fictitiously. Any similarity to actual people, organizations, and/or events is purely coincidental.

Cover Image: Buffy Cooper / Trevillion Images

Published by Barbour Books, an imprint of Barbour Publishing, Inc., 1810 Barbour Drive, Uhrichsville, Ohio 44683, www.barbourbooks.com

Our mission is to inspire the world with the life-changing message of the Bible.

Member of the
Evangelical Christian
Publishers Association

Printed in the United States of America.

Dedication

To all my Proverbs 17:17 sisters out there—
thank you for being my friends.

Chapter One

1824

Heaven stank of tallow and shone a honey glow. Her eyes could not adjust beyond a blur. An unsteady drip plucked against a thick silence, prodding her skin to crawl with gooseflesh. Where was she? No, this could not be—

No lightness, no feathery existence.

She tried to sit up, but her head was as heavy as her father's felling ax. She could hardly drag it through the stale air. Panic swarmed within her. Perhaps death had not just stolen her breath but her salvation?

Josephine Clayton had not been afraid of dying. Mourning had taught her that living proved more difficult. The last moment she remembered was her father's watery eyes while he begged her to live. She was overjoyed he'd been freed from debtors' prison, yet the fever was raging, and she'd felt her breath slipping from her infected lungs. Her wages had set Father free. Now all she could pray was for death to come quickly.

Had her prayer been answered?

The celestial bed where she'd slept clung to her, wrapping her in an unforgiving grip. A smudged-out figure stole away the light and stood above her. Her heart raced with fear. A glint sparked in the shadows, and her eyes focused at last.

Dr. Chadwick stood above her with his knife raised and his usual coat of dried blood and bile brushing against her arm.

"No!" Her body lurched upward, but she was trapped.

The man's eyes widened, and the clatter of his tool against the hard floor pinged about the room. He shuffled out of view and came forward again; a blue bottle in his hand trembled as he pressed it against her lips. Josephine's breaths, no matter how much they hurt against her chest, were a wild stampede. She knew what he was doing. Would he force her to sleep?

"Sir, please! I am alive!" She jerked her head to the side. Her body writhed like a worm hanging from the clutches of a wren. "You cannot—"

"Josephine, you are weak and incurable. Let me help you now." Help? Like he had with the last patient?

Josephine had convinced herself that all hope was lost after Mr. Baldwin's fever never broke. She was sure that Dr. Chadwick used wise judgment in giving him the elixir that would bring on a deep sleep. But she had wondered if he'd mistakenly given too much to Ainsley's oldest man. And she was irritated by the quickness of Dr. Chadwick's transfer from the sickbed to the operating table. Josephine was hardly done with a prayer over the dead body when Dr. Chadwick had prepared his tools.

"Take care, my daughter, that you respect the doctor," her father had advised after she was hired as the doctor's assistant. Even though her mother often despised Dr. Chadwick's visits, in her last days he had seemed a comfort to the family, assuring them that he was giving her the best treatment he knew how.

But now? Josephine's head swam with doubt.

"This shan't hurt. There is nothing else to be done for you." His Adam's apple bobbed above his stiff collar, and his eyes reflected the same uncertainty she felt.

Josephine stared hard at him, lifting her head no matter how much it hurt. "I am alive, sir," she whispered. "I am weak, but I will grow strong again."

The doctor grimaced. His gray eyes were cast upon her, but she'd seen that look—one where she was just a resting place for his gaze, yet his mind was somewhere else. "I did not detect a heartbeat. . . these things do happen, though."

"Sir, please unstrap me."

"Nobody can survive what you've been through." He licked his lips, his grimace deepened, and now he avoided her gaze entirely.

"Josephine, all have mourned you. You've been dead for twenty-four hours."

"What?"

"Your father sat beside you at your viewing. His grief is full on. Even if I tried to make you well, your life will never be the same."

"Doctor, release me this moment." She tried to speak with force, but her body was near-lifeless. Her wrists burned against the ropes. "Please—" Tears should have fallen, but she had none. Her mouth was as dry as if it had been coated by the dust of a grave. "I am thirsty."

"Settle back. Let me give you something to calm you." He still did not look at her. His icy fingers encircled her arm.

"Wouldn't you rather my father know it was a mistake than induce my. . .my death?"

His eyes flashed, and he groaned. "You've been around here long enough."

She had agreed to assist in remedies and ailments. The messy business of exploring stolen bodies for clues and cures was something she'd not expected. But when her father was taken to debtors' prison, she had no choice but to stay and earn his way out.

The doctor ran his hand through his hair. "Josephine, you were not just set out for all to see. You were buried."

"Buried?" Her chest seemed to collapse, and she could not find enough air to fill it. "How—how did I—survive?"

The door flung open behind the doctor. Alvin appeared with his sinister brow and a muddied shovel slung across his shoulder. "Doctor—" His face paled when he saw Josephine. He rushed to the table, looking into her eyes with horror. "She—she lives?" He covered his mouth and pulled his dirtied knuckles across his chin.

"Not for long." Dr. Chadwick pushed his sleeves up, slid one hand behind her head, and brought the bottle into view again.

Alvin licked his lips, his gaze darting about as fast as Josephine's heartbeat. "Wait!" He clutched at the doctor's wrist. "I came to tell you, people are talking. The empty graves. People have discovered them. I cannot work alone. That fool has crippled us both." Blackness crept from the corner of Josephine's eyes. Alvin was trusted by her father and had helped Josephine secure this position with the doctor. Yet, when she discovered the work Alvin had taken on after leaving her father's farm, her disgust grew for him more and more. Even so, as much as she disliked him, it appeared he was at least trying to prevent her murder.

"Have they discovered hers?" Chadwick whipped his white mane in Josephine's direction. Alvin gave a quick shake of his head, casting his eyes down with a perplexed grimace. Dr. Chadwick breathed in deeply and cleared his throat. "Well then. We continue."

The blackness grew wide and long and wrapped itself around Josephine's vision.

"Wait!" A gargling yelp from Alvin delayed the fainting spell that threatened. The determination in his whitened knuckles around the doctor's wrist was the last thing she saw before her eyes closed. "I have a plan," he said, then the spell grew in full force. All was dark.

Would she awake from this nightmare, or had it just begun?

Dust hung in the sunbeam above the bed where Josephine lay. She'd begged Alvin to take her home to her own bed, but the doctor refused to let her go. He demanded she recover here, in his cellar among hanging garlic and onions and sacks of earth-scented potatoes. 'Twas better than being on his table among dirty tools. Yet straw poked through her thin nightdress, and the blanket was as coarse as the potato sacks. The stones in the copper bed warmer beneath the linen hardly held their heat through the night. She shifted away from the cooling metal.

Josephine pulled the blanket up to her chin as best as she could. Her elbows ached with weakness, and her fingers were numb with cold. She eyed the narrow staircase across the square room where a ribbon of golden light shone beneath the door at the top.

"Do not make a sound," the doctor had seethed as he situated her on the pallet that first night. "The kitchen servant does not know you are here, and nobody else for that matter." He filled the bed warmer with hot stones in the morning and in the evening. He would leave her a meal three times each day on the stand beside her small box of remedies. Otherwise, Josephine's care for her healing was her own. The day dragged on, and she fell in and out of sleep. How many days had it been?

She'd not grown as strong as she'd hoped. Upon this last waking, her body refused to return to sleep and at least forget awhile. As the daylight hours waned, giving way to a grim dusk, her tears fell to her pillow. The dark corners of the cellar played tricks on her with ever-brimming shadows and echoes of mice scurrying along the stone floor. She had begged God to prove that this was not some sort of hell—to assure her that she was indeed alive.

The lock on the door rattled with a key. Josephine clutched at her covers, her knuckles aching with the cold.

Boots appeared and descended the stairs with an uneven gait.

"Father?" Her voice was hoarse. She glanced at her empty mug and dry pitcher.

"Josephine, it is I." The familiar tone of her father blanketed her in a warmth she had yet to feel in this strange fate.

"Oh Father, I am so. . .so scared." Her lip trembled. His crooked shoulders and rounded face blurred as her eyes filled with tears.

"My sweet Josephine." He limped toward her then fell to his knees and gathered her hands. "You are alive, dear one. You are here with me." His cheeks and nose were pink, and his bright blue eyes glistened with the love she'd always known. "Your hands are ice, child." He squeezed her fingers in his warm palms and kissed her knuckles.

"Father, must I recover here?" Josephine sniffled. "Please, take me home."

Her father fell back and sat on his heels, slowly slipping his hands from hers. "Oh, my sweet one, how I wish I could do that." Folds of worry stacked upon his brow. Her eyes filled even more.

"You are better off here."

"How?" Her voice cracked. The soreness from coughing had lessened, but the exertion of using her voice irritated her throat. She swallowed past the pain. "How, Father? How am I better off with that doctor so close? I fear every morsel he gives me. What stops him from killing me?"

"Dear one, do not fear. We have an agreement with Dr. Chadwick." Her father flicked a nervous glance up toward the closed cellar door.

"We?" Josephine's memory was clouded, but upon waking that first time, she remembered a man who was nearly as unwelcome as the doctor. "Alvin?"

"Aye. Alvin has saved you from death."

"Alvin steals the dead. Why would he care for my own life?"

Her father slouched and hung his head. "He is a friend to me, Josephine."

"Father, he left your farm and employ for illegal deeds."

"Josephine." He licked his lips. His nostrils flared. He snatched his hat from his balding head and wrung it ferociously. "You must not think ill of Alvin." He squeezed his eyes tight. A tear slipped down his cheek. "When you are well, you must listen to Alvin. His plan will get us out of this mess. Will get me out of this mess." He lowered his gaze to the dry mug beside her bed.

She'd worked hard to free him from his debt. But she'd been ill, without pay for some time. What trouble had found him now? "Father, if I can get well, I will work and keep you away from prison. Do not depend on Alvin." Josephine carefully propped herself on her elbows. "Please, let me get you out of debt."

His shoulders slumped, and he wagged his head. "Oh, my dear daughter," he moaned. "If only debt was my sole concern." He shuffled closer on his knees. His lips quivered as he spoke. "You must listen to Alvin. There are more than creditors after your father, dear one." He narrowed his eyes and slid a glance at the window near the ceiling then turned to glance up the staircase. He slowly faced her again. His hot breath heated her cheek as he whispered, "Murderers, Josephine. I am being chased by murderers—or I will be if you do not do as Alvin says. I've done terrible wrong. Only you can save me, Daughter." He blanched, as if he sat with her ghost and not her flesh.

A chill crawled along Josephine's neck and across her shoulders. Her throat squeezed tight with the same fear that encased her father's face.

"What trouble are you—" The door above creaked open, and light flooded the stairway. Dr. Chadwick's heavy plod started down the stairs. Josephine lunged forward, trying to grasp her father's hands, but she only sank to the mattress. Her body was too weak.

Her father scrambled to his feet. He leaned over and kissed her forehead. A sob caught in his throat, and she looked up at him. "Daughter, do as the doctor says."

"Please, return to me, Father!" she cried with shaking shoulders.

"I do not know that I can—" He hung his head. "The shame— it's—it's too much." He turned and heaved his lame foot across the floor, pushing past the doctor and up the stairs without another look at his daughter.

"Your supper is ready, Josephine." The doctor placed a tray on her table. He narrowed his eyes upon her. "I am anxious for you to get well. There is much to do."

"What is there to do, Dr. Chadwick?"

"Wait for Alvin. He will tell you." The doctor spoke as he climbed up the stairs. "No need to worry now. Your only concern is to heal." The door slammed shut, and once again, Josephine was left alone.

What trouble had found her father while she'd suffered on her deathbed? And why must she answer to Alvin, a robber of the dead?

The wind whipped against the window, howling through the seams. Braham stepped back from the dark glass and turned to the bed.

"Remember their songs?" The thin old man reached out his

13

hand. "I can almost hear them still."

Braham took his hand in a firm grasp, trying to appear unmoved. Yet, he did remember. Old spirituals moaned like phantoms in Braham Taylor's soul—the low notes in strange harmony with the wind. He dismissed the temptation to recall their meaning, their reasons for being sung, and instead swiped the old man's forehead with a damp cloth. Braham's knuckle brushed along his uncle's leathery skin. Its golden brown was evidence of summers spent in Georgia heat while keeping a keen eye on cotton tufts of fortune. Yet, here in Gloughton, Massachusetts, while the sun might not offer the same intensity as down south, life had shone just as bright.

Perhaps too much.

Was heaven's envy stirred up on this late spring evening? Reaching claws out like a thief?

"There, dear boy. No more tending to me." Uncle Bates let out a long, rattled cough.

"Sir, I will until—" Braham clenched his teeth, trying to calm himself amid the emotion that twined around his throat.

"Just sit by me until then." His uncle shuttered his eyes. "Do you remember the first time we met?"

"I do." Braham flipped his coattails up and sat back on the stool. "Father had negotiated his contract with you. I did not understand fully, but you had given me the best bread and butter I'd ever tasted." He allowed himself to smile at the memory. However, he did not admit the fear encased in that memory to his uncle. Not now, not after all that happened. Besides, he was a small child then. And he had endured a journey by sea that would haunt him for all his growing-up days. The stench lingered in his mind, and some nights he woke up still, sweat drenching the pillow he mistook for the stilled chest of his mother.

"Your father was a good man. A hard worker. The best. I would have offered him a permanent position once he'd finished his indenture."

Braham just held his tongue, knowing that his uncle's words might be his last. What right did Braham have to redirect this final conversation?

He winced at the man's coughing fit and looked away, spying the painting of Terryhold Plantation. Uncle Bates's niece by marriage had sat on the edge of the garden every day, perched behind an easel, while Braham and his father walked from the servants' quarters to the fields. The woman would paint, a slave girl would fan her, and the condensation on the glass jug of lemonade would tempt Braham to quench his thirst without permission.

The bedroom door swung open. Gerald Bates stepped inside as if bursting through some unseen shield. Perhaps a shield of peace? The air thickened with animosity at Braham's first glance of the master's son.

"I will take it from here," Gerald grumbled to Braham as he flung his hat atop the bureau.

Braham rose. While Mr. Bates Sr. was consistent in reminding Braham of his own hardworking father, his son was persistent in setting straight Braham's place—not as an embraced cousin, but an orphaned nuisance.

"Wait." His uncle's shaky hand hovered in the air between the men. A beacon of reconciliation? Hardly. Braham scoffed at the thought. More like an obstacle to battle that would soon fall away and leave Braham at the mercy of the new factory owner. "I would like to discuss my will with both of you present—"

"Father—" Gerald stepped forward enough that his father's hand pressed against his chest.

"Gerald, my time is near."

"You've worked hard, Father." Gerald spoke through tightly knit lips, as if he tried to withhold his words from Braham. Of course he tried. "And, I will be sure your affairs are taken care of by the finest of men."

Uncle Bates dragged his head across the feathered pillow to look squarely at his son. "You, my boy, will care for Terryhold. We have spoken of this before. And I have decided who will replace me at the factory." His heavy-lidded eyes found Braham. "Braham, you will run the factory now."

The steam from Gerald's reddened neck was almost visible. "You have appointed our places in life without asking our opinions, Father."

Braham's shoulders were firm with pride, but his step near such an adversary as Gerald was unsteady. "Uncle, are you sure I am fit for the position—"

Gerald slammed a hand on the polished wood frame of the bed. "You are not! Father, this boy has only worked with his hands, not his brain." Boy? Braham was twenty-one years old. A man, the same as Gerald. Yet one of them a gentleman, the other, a tyrant. "And there is nothing left for me in Georgia once you—"

A cough erupted from the elderly man's blue lips. Braham twisted his knuckles in the palm of his hand that was planted against his lower back. He did his best to hide his offense behind his concern for Mr. Bates. "Sir?" He knelt by the bedside, offering a glass of water. He stared at the weak mouth and the bead of liquid slipping down his chin, but he felt Gerald's heated stare.

Uncle Bates settled back on the pillow. "You have acres upon acres of land in Georgia. You have a firm foundation from the work of three generations. Gerald, you have a life in Georgia."

"What if I don't want it?" he seethed, but it did not appear that Mr. Bates heard it.

The man breathed hard and noisily but managed to say, "I have a trust in place. My greatest friend, Mr. Williams, will be sure the terms are followed." He turned to his son. "Gerald, continue to advise Braham in the business, and you will be rewarded each year." He reached a shaky hand toward Braham. "Dear boy, you will report all factory dealings to Gerald. The both of you will be quite a pair. I shall smile from heaven knowing my two establishments are well cared for."

Braham was overwhelmed by this confidence from his beloved guardian. "Thank you, sir. I shall do my best." This man was the closest living thing he had to a father. The only man who had gained Braham's trust after all he'd witnessed throughout his young life. And now it seemed Braham had gained Uncle Bates's trust as well. "I'll not let you down. Gloughton Mill shall prosper even more than you can imagine." He dared a look at Gerald. The man leaned his forehead on his clenched fist. "Gerald, we will make an effort to—"

A sudden jerk of his uncle's frail body gained both men's attention.

"Father?" Gerald leaned forward.

Uncle Bates's hand squeezed Braham's and then grew limp. His eyes glassed over, sending a shudder down Braham's spine. He had seen the eclipse of death before. He remembered the hollowed-out loneliness of being left by those he loved.

"You are my family." The dying man gasped for air. "Both of you."

"We are," Braham agreed as a tear dropped from his lash, trailing salt along the edge of his lip. Braham caught Gerald's stormy glare. "We will try and manage well."

A silence deafened the room at the interlude between the two cousins. Something had stilled besides the clock's pendulum on the wall.

Uncle Bates's body emptied of life.

Braham covered the man's eyes with his fingers and whispered, "Peace be with you, sir."

Gerald stood and bent over to kiss his father's forehead. "Good-bye, Father." But the flash in Gerald's eyes was not one of grief. It was no doubt the heat of anger that Braham had even been invited into the family quarters, let alone given a secure position over the Bates cotton mill endeavor. No, a man like Gerald would not make much of a business partner at all. Not with Braham's meager roots. While it had been a pleasure to live up to Uncle Bates's expectations all this time, Braham would never reach such heights as to meet Gerald's expectations. It was impossible.

Gerald turned from the bedside. "I shall call for the doctor to be sure." He hesitated at the door. "Do not bother to attend the will hearing. That is for blood relations only."

"But—"

Gerald disappeared into the hall.

The man was like an overgrown child, insisting on his way even if it was unreasonable. His father had been Braham's legal guardian since the summer Braham's father had passed away. There'd be no negotiating anything written by his guardian, especially with Mr. Williams as executor. He was another friend who was considered as important as family.

Braham sank down in the armchair by the window and waited for the doctor to arrive. All the while, he tried to convince himself that Gerald was so torn between his desires and duty not because of selfish entitlement, but because of a loyalty to his father that he could not snuff out.

Braham was certain it might be difficult for Gerald to plant his feet down south—after his frequent trips north, having attended school at Harvard. He despised Terryhold, yet he received such wealth and privilege because of the plantation's profit.

For Braham, north, south, east, or west did not matter at all. He was entrusted with a business—by the man he loved most. There was nothing that would stop him from running the factory to the utmost satisfaction of his late master. No, Braham Taylor was now reaping the fruits of all he'd endured, and he would give every ounce of himself to the mill.

Imagining that heaven-sent smile promised by the old man? Ah, even in his grief, the thought nearly brought a grin to Braham's face.

He knew that he was the man for the job. Gerald's snubs would not rattle his confidence.

If Braham had inherited anything from his own father, it was perseverance. Even if it meant persevering beneath the turned-up nose of his partner—that was nothing compared to the honor bestowed upon him today as Gloughton Mill's newest manager.

Chapter Two

The factory rose above with row upon row of sharp-edged bricks. Thick mortar promised strength against a loud drumming from within the building. Nothing like the worn and withered home of her father. Yet, his tender way was more secure than a thousand strong towers.

Bile swirled around Josie's stomach. "Are you certain Father knew this was the plan?" Her father's fear haunted her these past three weeks. He never returned to her. She had healed alone.

"Aye. Your father is a desperate man. This is a sure way..." Alvin fiddled with the brim of his hat.

"But the factory will provide me with good pay. Why do I have to...have to..." Josie winced.

"Help me?" Alvin raised an eyebrow. "Dr. Chadwick is counting on your replacement. That's how I kept you alive."

"But, Father...I cannot imagine him agreeing to this."

"I told you, your father is a desperate man." Alvin slid the floppy hat from above his ruddy face. "Providence was at hand that day I found you."

Josie gave him a sideways glance. "I doubt that. There's no hand of God in this scheme."

"Who said anything about God's hand, Josephi—I mean, Josie Clay." He chuckled. Only the slight tilt of his brow signaled his former kindness when he worked her father's farm.

"Do you feel no guilt in dragging us into your schemes? My father has only been good to you."

"I am doing this for him," Alvin muttered with none of his recent wit.

Josie halted midstep, her dress swishing against her ankles. She spun and faced him with her back to the stairs rising to the factory door. "What is his trouble, Alvin? He mentioned murderers. His fear was none that I had seen in him before."

The man diverted his gaze, staring off toward the back of the courtyard. "You would have been killed," he hissed, avoiding her question. The softness dwindled as quickly as it had graced his gruff face. "I bargained for your life with that mad Dr. Chadwick."

"Why? So I can be part of this horrendous scheme? You only stopped him because you need me to be your—" Josie pressed her hand on her woolen-covered waist. She swallowed hard, and her eyes fluttered closed. "Your spy," she whispered.

"You ask why, Miss Josie?" Alvin leaned in. Spittle clung to his lip. "I saved you for the sake of your father—men worse than Dr. Chadwick wait for him to pay up."

"How much debt has he acquired in such a short amount of time?" Sudden tears bobbled in her eyes, blurring the ugly man before her. She would go to the authorities as soon as she could. Even if she would also be convicted, she must stop this horrible plan. "Was he better off in debtors' prison?" She began to weep against her will. She wanted to remain strong, but this was all too much.

"Please don't cry." Alvin twisted his hat in his hands and began to pace back and forth. "You know I care about your father. He's like—like my own father to me."

"And then you turned away from all that is good. You are the prodigal"—Josie tried to refrain the sneer that formed in the thick of her throat—"who never returned."

"He doesn't owe money, Josephine."

"What?"

"He owes bodies."

She stepped back. "My. . .father?"

"You are replacing him at the graveside. You will be the signal, and you will return the grave to its original state after I've taken the body. Just as your father tried to do in New York while you were ill." He sucked in air from his teeth. "Until he was seen."

"My father works with you?" Blackness swallowed the edges of the courtyard where they stood.

"Not anymore." He spat on the paved ground. "Can't be trusted. But I cannot do this alone. Not after the past couple of jobs. I cannot work alone."

"Are the authorities after my father?" She considered the reason for her father's countenance last they met. Josie wrapped her arms around her waist. A weakness invaded her every limb and hollowed out her gut.

What wickedness had found the two remaining Claytons!

"Nay, unless he goes to New York once more. But your father's carelessness has angered the head resurrectionist."

"Don't call him that." He'd used that word on their journey here. Josie's spirit had recoiled then, and it did now. The word *resurrection* was sacred to some. Alvin's new attribution to it only darkened its brightness. Bodies stolen from graves? There was no resurrection in that. Just despicable crime. How could her father do this? Terror frenzied in Josie's heart. "Did Father know what Dr. Chadwick intended for me?"

"No, not at all. He truly thought you were dead and buried." Alvin squared his stance and locked her in an intense stare. "Understand this now— We'll supply Dr. Chadwick with his replacement, but we have much more to do. The deal I made with Dr. Chadwick was not just for the ridiculous doctor, but for your father's life." His eyes simmered. "Those men are ruthless. Your father ruined the network's chances in New York. Boston has already been too dangerous, what with the legal ramifications. If he doesn't make up for the loss, then I fear the worst. I fear murder."

Josie wagged her head, pressing her fingers on her temples. Her father's very life was in danger. His betrayal to all the goodness he'd instilled in her growing years wrapped its way around her heart like a vine of thorns. She had spent this past month in the cave-like cellar, breaking fever upon fever and shoveling in the dusty air—and he'd visited her but once.

"He didn't want to tell me himself," she muttered, thinking on that last encounter. Was it not just fear but shame that shook him in those moments?

Yet now, they were all guilty. She had recovered, only to heap guilt on herself as well.

Alvin slid his hand around her arm, but she shook him off. He hesitated then spoke. "For now, realize that we are saviors in a way." Josie glared at him. A tipped grin folded the skin on his cheek. "I am yours, and you are your father's, yes?" he quipped.

A caged sob shook Josie's shoulders.

Alvin's delight faded. He stepped back with a bent head, cramming his hat atop a fading hairline. "Look, your work at the mill will be honest, yet fruitful for our cause. Word has it that it's fatal work for some. I'm counting on that." He grimaced then sighed. "And when the time comes, this work shall only be a blink of your life—the life you would never have if it weren't for my loyalty to your father and your father's devotion to his land."

Josie ground her teeth, begging God for mercy toward the vengeful heart thumping in her chest. She was imprisoned by the dirty hands of this savior. Yet, she should not think on the injustice of it any longer. There would be nothing but disaster if she exposed this scheme to anyone. Her father's life was at stake.

She turned to the stairs and did not look back until she stood before the large wooden door. Alvin had retreated across the courtyard and leaned against the large trunk of an old elm tree. The gnarling branches seemed to twist and bunch against persistent new growth. Life was only precious to some.

Josie pulled at a rope to ring the bell then knocked hard on the broad door, releasing some tension through her slamming knuckles. Just as she raised her fist a third time, the door squealed open. An older woman wearing a plain dress without pattern or pleat cast a cool gaze over spectacles resting near the point of her nose. "May I help you?"

Josie fumbled with the advertisement in her cloak pocket and handed it to the woman. "I am Josie Clay. I would like to work here at the mill."

The woman searched her with glassy eyes, pressing her hand beneath her high-waisted bodice. "We are always looking for help, just as the ad suggests. But our beds are limited. Do you need boarding?"

Josie nodded, wishing she could retire to her own bed. Yet it was thirty miles away.

The chugging of machinery distracted Josie from her angst. She managed to peer inside the building. It was like the dark mouth of a hungry giant with a grumbling belly.

"Come inside." The woman widened the door.

Josie's uneasy first impression of the place had her hesitate at first.

"Come on, then." The woman waved her in. "Let us wait for Miss Jamison, the boardinghouse matron. She'll know better what we have available. I am Miss Clyde, Mr. Taylor's secretary." The corner of her mouth puckered as if she had tasted a bitter herb.

Josie followed her along a wide hallway with gleaming floors and whitewashed walls. A steady whir and series of thuds vibrated throughout the place.

Miss Clyde held open a door of sparkling glass. "Hurry now. The ladies will crowd the hallway any minute. 'Tis dinnertime. If you are hired, you will receive three meals a day. Work is from daybreak to dusk, five days a week. Half a day on Saturday. Sundays are off, but you are expected to attend church. There are several educational opportunities available as well."

"Educational?"

"Yes. The girls are not just working for factory life, but for future opportunities as wives and mothers. We expect each of them to become capable of entering society with dignity and civility." She pushed her spectacles up to the bridge of her nose. "Do you have any education?"

"I can read and write. My mother kept me in school until she grew ill—about four years ago." Mother hardly let Josie skip school to help on the farm, no matter the circumstance that might arise or the garden that cried for attention. Yet, while Mother sat for hours reading as her body withered away, Josie escaped the sorrow with hands covered in dirt, her nose sniffing pungent thyme and rosemary and her pen jotting down characteristics of plants and mixtures. Just like Mother had taught her. Her inherited passion for healing herbs made her transition from student to employee of the town's only physician a smooth one.

Miss Clyde craned her neck toward the end of the hall once more then closed the door. "Wait there." She offered a bench beneath a window that looked out into the hallway before she disappeared through a narrow corridor.

The noise from beyond the walls died away. A sudden silence startled Josie. She peeked through the window, careful not to smudge the glass with her nose. From the far end of the hallway, a flash of blues, golds, and pinks mingled with navy, browns, and grays as women tied colorful bonnets on their heads and bumbled along the shiny floor. Bright faces drew closer, and then they passed by on their way outside. How happy they seemed, and how lovely they dressed. Even though Josie's gown was a light blue, she was cloaked in the grim dealings of a persuasive doctor and the shady task of bargaining with bodies.

Lord, forgive me.

A couple of ladies caught her eye and flashed genuine smiles. Thirty or forty women passed by within a few seconds, pouring out into the amber daylight.

If only her father hadn't gotten involved with dangerous men. She would have gone to the authorities as soon as she'd accepted a position at Gloughton Mill. What would it be like to work the honest life as a factory girl only, without the choking attachment to Dr. Chadwick and Alvin Green? She jerked away from the window and warded off a fit of tears.

Had she looked upon the face of the next girl she'd offer to

Dr. Chadwick as her own replacement?

Braham ran his hand over the desk. The same scrawny boy who scrambled in and out of the cotton bales down south was now supervisor of one hundred women and men, producing fine cloth from the cotton he once picked. Even one month after his uncle had passed, he could hardly believe his good fortune.

Sorrow tiptoed beneath his starched white shirt, and he sighed. The past factory accidents dampened his joy. He had been careful to investigate each piece of equipment and replace anything that was worn. His chest tightened as he suppressed the uncertainty that dug deeper than the grave of his benefactor. He must live up to the trust bestowed on him.

The large glass window across from his desk framed the quiet factory floor. Power looms rested, crates of raw cotton dotted about, and the freshly folded cloth was stacked like treasure beneath the bow of an explorer's ship. Another good day's work was accomplished, and he had overseen it without an incident.

A knock turned him from the window. He cleared his throat. "Come in."

Miss Clyde appeared, her stance as rigid as usual. The woman never softened, even when she announced the fate of Mr. Bates to his household. She was a predictable asset to Braham's operation, but an unnerving likeness to the other statues transposed along Braham's life line—especially Mr. Bates Jr., who, fortunately, was in Georgia once again.

"Mr. Taylor, do you have time to meet with a Miss Josie Clay in regard to a position? I have spoken with the matron of the boardinghouse, and it seems that we do have one bed left."

A figure blurred just beyond Miss Clyde's pointed shoulder. He squinted to make out the slight woman pacing back and forth in the waiting area. "Very well. I will talk with her." He passed by his secretary.

Her sharp shoulders pricked up. "Sir, do you not want to meet with her here, as is custom?" Miss Clyde waved to his desk.

"My supper is waiting for me, and I am sure this will not take long." He had been a good judge of character all his life. Unfortunately, the skill had been practiced in the discernment of evil more than good—like the cruel slave master down south. Braham had been leery of him that first day he and his father had arrived at the plantation. While Father spoke with Gerald Bates Sr. about indentured servitude, the slave master had kicked at the boys in the rows and would soon do the same to Braham.

Braham could also distinguish what type of women worked here. There were those who worked hard for the good of the mill and their families' added income, and there were those who were only here to get away from their suppressive parents, caring little about their work. They spent their breaks gossiping, trying to decide if Braham's allegiance was only to the factory, or if he was open to a possible courtship. He had never before had the authority to reprimand them, but he would now, if the opportunity arose. Braham did not want any of that foolishness. Not when he had been given such a great responsibility. His fortune was not in marriage prospects but in the accomplishment of serving his master's legacy well.

He approached the small room lined with benches. The tall window gleamed with the crimson light of day, framing the woman before him in a sinister glow. Only her gold locks beneath a scalloped bonnet suggested innocence beyond the fiery glare that consumed her outline.

"Good evening, Miss Clay." He stepped aside, agitated that he could not make out her features with such a devilish flame surrounding her. He swallowed, his Adam's apple hard against his cravat.

"Good evening, sir. I am inquiring about a position." Her round face and bright blue eyes were not devilish at all but full of question. "I found this advertisement and was wondering if there might be room for me?" She handed him the paper. Her small gloved hands seemed to tremble as he took it. He looked at her again. A crease sliced between her eyebrows. Fearfully carved, or a sign of eager-ness? Her gaze skittered to the window.

He tucked his chin back to his neck. "Where are you from?"

"A small village west of here." She bowed her head. "I've just arrived to Gloughton. I do hope to find a means to help my—" Her long lashes dipped, and the crease grew deeper in her ivory skin. She licked her lips and said quickly, "—my father." Her timidity was not appealing for a man looking to hire a strong woman for long hours and dependable work.

"Many women come here to help out their families—whether it be to send wages home or to simply relieve their parents of one less mouth to feed." He paced toward the window that looked out upon the courtyard between the factory and the boardinghouse. A man leaned against the old elm, folding a piece of paper. His face was shaded by a large brimmed hat, but the wash of light revealed he stared in Braham's direction. When Braham drew closer to the window, the man disappeared behind the tree.

"Are you with that man?" Braham looked at Miss Clay.

Her eyes grew wide. Sapphire bobbles searched his face. She gave a quick nod then turned away. "Please, sir. It is necessary that I find a place. He waits to be sure—"

"The matron does have strict rules about male callers, you should know—"

She whipped her head around. "Oh, I do not intend for any-thing of the sort." The pinks of the day painted her face in a fury of color. She drew close, determination stiffening her brow. "He promises to only come and take my wages to my father."

"He's your father's servant?"

Her nose scrunched, and she pressed her lips together. "No. He. . .he was my father's farmhand." She walked to the window. "If I could arrange for anyone else to come each fortnight to check on me, I would. The man is repulsive." She faced Braham. "Please, sir, I am desperate to work—desperate to escape his company even for a handful of days."

Braham looked back out to the courtyard. The man was nowhere to be seen. He breathed in deeply, trying to push aside his unsolicited interest in this stranger and her predicament. He would consider her a little longer. She seemed stuck in the clutches of unwanted authority. Something he knew all too well.

"Miss Clay, we work long, hard hours. You will be responsible to maintain a certain pace at the machines, making sure that not one thing delays our production. Many women find the task tedious the first week, but they discover a rhythm and manage their duty well." Spinning on his heel, he tucked his hands in his waistcoat pockets. He puffed his chest a bit, just like he'd seen his uncle do with new hires. "Do you think you will be able to stand for hours on end without tiring?"

Miss Clay lifted her chin, her profile sharply outlined in front of him. A slender nose, not too small, not too large, a rounded chin, and lashes longer than any he had seen were only fixtures upon a serious canvas that had lost all anxiety. Perhaps his serious tone had displaced her worry.

"Sir, I have worked long hard hours on the farm and in assisting with my village's recent fever outbreaks. Operating machinery will be a welcome endeavor. I have endured caring for livestock and cleaning up death. Working for your factory would be a delightful change." She then tilted her face toward him, gave a curt smile, and stared.

His mouth went dry. A tremble seized his chest, foreign and unwelcomed. He took in a jagged breath and stared back at her, searching beyond the light that washed her face and trying to determine his next words. Her initial weak-natured posture now fled as quickly as the dying rays of sun, and she stood there, nearly daring him to hire her. He did not like it one bit.

She must have noticed his hesitation, because her smile vanished, giving way to an eager expression tainted pink in the strange light. "Please, sir, I am confident in my ability. But also, my father needs me. Since my mother's death he has not been the same. There is little for him beyond his property." She snaked a handkerchief from beneath her cuff and balled it up in her hand. "I fear the worst if he's not allowed to keep it."

A strike of the clock in the corridor gave sound to the pierce in Braham's heart. His mother was Father's joy. She lit every bit of his face when she'd appear from below the ship's deck. And every night, he'd kiss her brow before they dozed to sleep. Braham was only ten when he'd seen his mother last. In a way, it was also the last time he'd seen the father he'd once known.

"You shall have two weeks of work before you are paid. During that time, you will be evaluated on your capabilities." He walked past her and motioned for Miss Clyde to come from her desk along the corridor. "Miss Clyde, please make arrangements for Miss Clay at the boardinghouse. Show her to aisle four on the main floor first thing in the morning." He refused to look back at the woman and went straight to his office to gather his hat and gloves. He was famished. Certainly, his need for food had everything to do with his pulse's reaction to the newest employee. Only her mention of bold work ethic lured Braham to hire her.

At least, that's what he convinced himself of on his way from the mill to the rolling hills just beyond Gloughton.

Chapter Three

Relief coursed through Josie's frame as she followed Miss Clyde to the boardinghouse. The echo of their heels on the bricked courtyard accompanied the call of a mourning dove. As they neared the porch of another red-bricked building, smaller than the factory yet more vast than any shop in Ainsley, Alvin's wagon disappeared along a bridge behind a promenade of trees.

Good riddance.

She would try to manage her thoughts and forget him until he showed up next. Mr. Taylor was already suspecting him of nefarious intentions as far as she could tell. Of course, she hadn't managed her emotions very well at all. But, unlike her struggle to keep control of the fear that skimmed her heart, Mr. Taylor was controlled and mindful. She would be under a tight watch. That was enough motivation to be at her best. And while she was not anywhere close to being her best—with her growling stomach, sore bottom from the treacherous wagon ride, and an aching jaw from biting back angry words the entire journey—after a night's rest she would put every ounce of effort into her position and refrain from growing close to one soul in this place.

She tightened her grip on the bag that carried her black veil and ebony gown and glanced around for the mourning dove, the appropriate serenade for this procession to her dual purpose. She followed Miss Clyde inside.

"Supper has already been served. We shall go to the kitchen and see what Cook has left," Miss Clyde said as she hung her cloak up in the small square foyer. In the room's center, a staircase took several turns upward. A lamp on the wall lit up only the bottom few stairs. Josie imagined there were at least four floors above them. "Come on then, hang up your cloak. You are not the only one who missed a meal." Miss Clyde did not speak with contention, but Josie felt the stab of guilt knowing her late arrival had indeed caused Miss Clyde's delay.

"Forgive me," she muttered, taking her cloak off, then untying her bonnet.

"Leave your things here. We will come back for them after we eat." Miss Clyde disappeared in a hallway, and Josie followed. After a half flight of stairs down, they came to a large kitchen. The fire smoked, and a small maid stood at a propped-open door fanning the smoke out into a silvery dusk.

Miss Clyde whispered to a stout woman with a mass of peppered hair piled high behind a cap. The woman raised an eyebrow and examined Josie then pushed Miss Clyde aside and came up to her.

"Well hello, dear. I am Fran Parker." She tilted her head and continued, "Miss Clyde said you arrived at the dinner bell. I'd say you must be famished."

Josie nodded.

Fran dashed a look at Miss Clyde, who was no longer by her side. The rigid woman served herself a bowl of steaming soup while the maid began to chatter away. Miss Clyde hardly acknowledged her attempt at conversation, sitting down with her back to everyone in the kitchen.

Fran spoke from the corner of her mouth, "Come on, get your-self some food. And don't mind the woman." She directed her eyes at Miss Clyde. "I believe she might be made of stone more than flesh." A warm chuckle shook her shoulders as she picked up the ladle and a bowl. Josie took a seat across from Miss Clyde, who only looked down at her soup and slurped.

"Here you go, dear." Fran placed the bowl in front of Josie then bustled across the room. "That's enough, Abigail. You'll kill all my garden plants as hard as you're whipping that smoke out." The cook rushed to the door. "A little smoke never hurt anyone, and we aren't near the cotton. Nothing's going to catch aflame."

Josie kept her eye on the bit of shrubbery visible until the door blocked her view. She could hardly resist a garden. Perhaps she would find her way to the kitchen garden during her stay here. Her heart leapt. She ate more heartily than she had before. If there was one thing that could erase her sorrows, even for a day, it was using the earth, not to bury and dig up again, but to feed the life of a flower or herb.

"Mrs. Parker?" she inquired after finishing her soup.

"Dear, call me Fran."

"Fran, would you ever need help in your garden?"

Before the woman could answer, Miss Clyde snapped, "You will be busy with work."

"But after, when I have time off perhaps?" She avoided Miss Clyde's glare and kept her eyes on the considering cook.

"We hold education in high regard, Miss Clay," Miss Clyde explained. "Reading, sewing, and attending church services would serve you better than getting dirt beneath your nails in a kitchen garden."

"I see." Josie sank back.

When Miss Clyde excused herself and gestured for her to follow, Josie pushed aside her empty bowl and left the kitchen.

Fran called out, "If you have any advice on herbs, I'd be glad to hear it. . .when you aren't busy, of course."

A warm gush filled Josie, but she did not respond. Miss Clyde worked closely with Mr. Taylor. Josie must not bring negative attention to herself even if the anticipation of a garden in need was more satisfying than a full stomach.

Miss Clyde led her up the stairs to the second floor. They emerged into a large common room with two fireplaces surrounded by armchairs. Tables with four chairs each stretched across the entire length of the room. There were a few groups of women reading by the firelight, and a couple of ladies sat at tables with glowing lamps and ink and paper. Archways opened up to a hall with a long stretch of doors—no doubt, bedrooms. Miss Clyde knocked on the first door. Several heads turned their way. The door opened, and a woman with rosy cheeks and bright green eyes appeared. Her expression dulled at the sight of Miss Clyde.

"I've brought the new mill girl, Josie Clay."

"Ah!" The lady's face lit up again, and she barreled out the door. She gleamed at Josie and took her by the elbow, ushering her to the closest fireplace. "I've got it from here, Miss Clyde. I am sure your sister is wondering where you are at." The lady turned to Josie and rolled her eyes. Miss Clyde only stuck her nose up and disappeared down the stairs.

Josie noticed the stares and whispers of other women nearby, just like she'd received at home when the villagers scoffed at her interest in medicine and ailments. She caught some wary looks too, similar to those from wives and sisters of the male patients she would help. If these women only knew their wariness was justified.

"Now, Josie, is it?"

"It is." Josie swallowed past the lump in her throat. "And you are?"

The woman tossed her dark head back and giggled. "Oh, goodness. How rude of me. I am Fawna Jamison, the matron here." She held out her hand. Josie shook it. "I also help in the mill's carding room. Tell me, what made you come to Gloughton? We have women of all sorts. But I'd like to figure out which room to put you in. You know, there are four to a room, forty girls in all. Each dormitory has its own personality, really."

"Miss Clyde spoke little about the arrangements." She did not know any of it. "I—I would like to work for wages. My father's in need of help for his land." The excuse was a good one—laced with enough truth that it tumbled from Josie's tongue without hesitation.

"What kind of land?" Fawna's eyes flashed with interest, as if Josie offered a bit of gossip that she could not resist.

"A farm, west of here. I am here to send money back to him."

"I see." Fawna studied her. Josie squirmed, paying attention to the leaping flames in the fireplace. "What else?"

"What else?" Josie arched her brow, biting the inside of her cheek.

"Look, every one of these ladies has a story—a reason beyond the money—that brought them here. What is yours? You are too lovely to not have a match waiting for your hand. What else brought you here, Josie—?"

"Clay. Josie Clay," she blurted, her pulse racing at Miss Jamison's persistence. "Ma'am, I have little to care about besides my father." If the woman knew her story, she'd never believe her. Josie was certain she had the most horrific story in the room. The matron put a thoughtful finger to her chin then began to stoke the fire.

Josie paid closer attention to the others now. Gawking ones, spying ones, chittering ones. So be it. They should never invite her in.

"Don't mind them." Fawna waved her hand. "New blood is always welcomed, cautiously so. One more bed to fill, one more pocket too."

"Miss Jamison—"

"Call me Fawna."

"Fawna, I really just want to earn money for my father. There's nothing else." Her throat ached. "Please, just put me in a room with quiet women." The only way to keep her secrets inside would be to still her tongue and avoid any knots to complicate her story. The quieter, the better. Nobody would then question her when she'd have to dress in mourning for a complete stranger, for they would know nothing of her acquaintances on either side of these walls. "I am not much for talking. I only want to work."

Fawna's face blanched at her request. "You can imagine that I would not know how to be such a thing as quiet." She burst into laughter. Wiping her eyes, she continued, "I think the third floor would suit you better. Those women are mostly into their books and discussing philosophical things." She leaned in and quirked the corner of her mouth, saying, "A waste of good air, if you ask me." Then she straightened up with an apologetic tilt of her forehead. "However, if you prefer that kind of passing of the time, then it should be just fine for you."

"That sounds wonderful." Anything that would take the

attention away from her. Books and philosophy were enough of an escape for now.

She followed Fawna to a staircase. Beyond the banister, a tall narrow window framed the indigo night blotting out sunlight and the large factory across the way. She could only make out a faint reflection of the room behind her. Alvin's words played in her head, an unwanted voice but a hopeful declaration—this will be a blink of life.

Oh, how she prayed that would be true.

A thick cloud of dust hovered on the top of the hill just outside the Bates estate. Braham squinted. Surely the doctor hadn't come by again this week. No, it was an old work wagon. His pulse slowed to a normal pace. When the dust broke apart at the crest of the hill, he spotted the driver donning a familiar hat with a limp brim. Was it the man who'd accompanied Miss Clay? Her sour opinion of the man rattled Braham's nerves. When Braham arrived at the entrance, the gate was unlatched and swinging back and forth in the early evening. He looked up at the hill again, but the man had disappeared. Braham nudged his horse to a gallop through the gate and turned down the winding lane past the apple orchard.

The sweet scent of apple blossoms mixed with the promise of rain. His usual trot from the town to the countryside was one of peace and reflection, sometimes recovering from a tense encounter with Gerald. But right now, he forgot to take a breath, knowing that that man who seemed an unwelcome companion for Josie Clay may have paid a visit to his small piece of the world—a place where his only treasure rested day in and day out. He led his horse to the stable and then jogged beneath the covered porch of the smart, square home.

"Good evening, Mr. Taylor." The maid, Minnie, greeted Braham at the door. Although this was just the guesthouse of the larger Bates estate, he had resided here since he was a boy placed in the care of Mr. Bates's spinster sister. The privilege to live in such comfort was never forgotten in Braham's prayers.

"Any visitors recently?"

"Not that I know of, sir. Cook had me in the back garden though." Minnie gave a quick curtsy and disappeared through the dining room.

Braham entered the parlor where his aunt sat in her usual spot by the fire. "Good evening, Aunt Myrtle." He kissed her forehead.

She patted his hand. "I worried about you, boy." Aunt Myrtle cleared her throat then peered up over her glasses. "It is nearly an hour past quitting time." She placed her needlepoint in the basket on the hearth.

Braham bent over and offered his elbow. "Forgive me?"

She smirked, hooked her frail hand in the crook of his arm, and carefully stood. "Not another accident?" His aunt's voice hitched. Her lace-capped head of silver only reached his shoulder.

"No, no, of course not." Braham's jaw tightened. "I have taken great care in minding the equipment since the last one." He shuddered to think about it still. The woman's injury led to an untimely death. Gerald was livid and, of course, blamed Braham's poor management. Braham began checking the equipment more often, even stealing away on Sundays.

"Well then, what has you out this late?"

"I hired a new girl this evening. She showed up unexpectedly, having no other place to go."

"My, what an inconvenient time." Aunt Myrtle craned her neck toward the window on the other side of Braham. "'Tis almost dark. What would she have done if you turned her away?"

A shiver threatened to erupt along Braham's spine. The sinister onlooker came to mind. "I do not know. The man who brought her seemed less like a friend to her and more like a spy." He hesitated. There was no need to alarm Aunt Myrtle, but he needed to know. "Did anyone call this evening?"

She shook her head with an absent look in her eyes. "No, nobody that I know of. Might ask Minnie."

But Minnie had said she was in the garden. Did the stranger

visit the main house? Braham would go ask the servants first thing in the morning. It was rare to have visitors, especially with the main house only occupied by the butler, a groundskeeper, and a maid or two while Gerald was away. Miss Clay's man may have needed something as simple as a meal, or he may have lost his way and needed help. Braham was a careful fellow though, and he would not allow any disturbance go unexplored. Not now, when life had finally become his own.

Tonight, he must suppress his uneasiness. Aunt Myrtle would soon suspect it, no matter how distracted she was with her long gaze into the fire's flame.

She shook her head and sighed as Braham guided her toward the door. "Seems to me that girl will need some sense along with those wages." She gave him a stern glance.

"What?"

"That girl. Showing up at this time of night and making company with a shady fella? Seems to me she's the one you should watch, Mr. Taylor." She raised an eyebrow like she used to when she'd question young Braham's delay to supper after a day of climbing trees in the orchard.

Braham smiled back. If his aunt had been beside him at the mill, Josie Clay may have been more scrutinized. What would a girl so fragile, yet capable, do under a full-blooded Bates interrogation? He must remember that he also was tough, able to prove himself beyond his unbecoming roots. He must convince himself that he made no mistake hiring Miss Clay.

Braham led Aunt Myrtle to the dining room and helped her sit at the head of their simply dressed table lit by a silver candelabra. Taking his seat at her right, he shrugged off the last of his concern. Braham tucked his napkin in his lap, and when he looked up, he caught Aunt Myrtle's gleam.

"Do you remember when I taught you your table manners?" She grinned. "I was thrilled that my brother gave me purpose. You gave me purpose." Her eyes glistened in the candlelight. "Now, I just wait to follow—" A sob was caught by her shaking hand, but tears streaked her cheeks.

"Do not speak such things." Braham gritted his teeth. His throat burned with the truth of the lady's words. He had promised himself to ignore the inevitable. So much had changed. He'd not think of one more assault to his worn-out heart. "My dear aunt, you still have great purpose. I need you now more than ever."

Her weeping turned to a chuckle. "Why would you, a grown man now, need an old spinster around here?"

He dug his elbow on the table, clutched at her hand, and pressed toward her with the most determined brow he could muster. "You are my only friend." He'd not allow his eyes to water. He kept his brow furrowed and his jaw tight. "I'll not consider that God would take away my only friend. Much has been taken already."

The woman gave a sad smile. "Do not worry. No need to dwell on the inevitable any more tonight. My only ailment is my hunger." Her smile grew wide, and she quirked her eyebrow in jest.

Braham's laugh fell from his lips, and he sank back in his chair. "I am hungry too." Minnie hurried in with a platter. They prayed over the meal and began to dine.

"My nephew will arrive next week," Aunt Myrtle said. "He has news that he wants to share." She slid the bit of chicken carefully off her fork with her teeth. The scrape did not irritate Braham nearly as much as the announcement of Mr. Bates Jr.'s arrival.

"Interesting," he replied.

"I do believe it's an engagement announcement." She snickered.

"Engagement? Why would he come here and not just write it in a letter?"

"Do you not recall his latest fascination?" Aunt Myrtle wiped the corners of her mouth. "Elaine, the daughter of the owner of Bramswell Plantation. Not much to look at, but I think it is wise that he secure his connection down south and gain more cotton for Gloughton. Should keep morale high among the mill workers, don't you think?"

"Morale is high regardless of the absent Mr. Bates," Braham couldn't help but mumble.

"There, there, Mr. Taylor. He is your boss, after all." She clicked her tongue. "But, I will admit, you have much to do with the happiness cultivated among the employees. If not for your kind leadership, then for your handsome presence." She reached over and patted his cheek, a flush of jest crawling along her laugh lines.

"Enough, Aunt." He shook his head, trying to absorb her light spirits. All he could consider, though, was the storm cloud coming up from Georgia and the defense he must place around his position and authority. Especially with the past two accidents only a few short weeks ago.

One thing was good, however. If Gerald was occupying the main house, any trouble by strange men poking about the place would be his to deal with. And if Braham remembered anything at all from his time down south, Gerald Bates was possessive of his belongings and would not put up with one ounce of mischief.

Chapter Four

J osie wondered if she had slept at all. Every time she'd closed her eyes, the faces of unnamed women flashed in her mind then faded away to reveal a waiting Dr. Chadwick. Finally, an anxious wave surged through her body, and she sat up quickly in her bed. Three other women slept soundly—well, one was hardly a woman, probably no older than thirteen. Little Liesl shared Josie's bed, while the other two shared one. They had been kind enough, introducing themselves politely as they paused their reading of the *Boston Daily Times*. Sally and Sarah were sisters, and the youngest, Liesl, was a German immigrant who was sent from Boston by her uncle to make money for her sickly grandparents.

"I am a doffer," she had said with an accent that ended in the back of her throat. Josie looked over at the sisters, who were probably the same age as herself, and shrugged her shoulders.

Sally, with ebony hair and big brown eyes, explained. "She takes off the full bobbins and replaces them with empty ones." She pressed her shoulders back. "It's a pity, because she's more capable than that. Only gets two dollars a week. And much of her time is spent sitting in the corner with her journal and knitting basket."

Liesl looked away from Sally's lips, and a delayed understanding bloomed on her flushed face. She gave a sheepish smile. "I would rather not do much else. Not after all the accidents."

"Accidents?" Josie swallowed hard.

The sisters passed a look between themselves. "Just a few. Ever since Mr. Bates Sr. passed away. Some blame it on Mr. Taylor. But really, it seems the women are not careful enough." Sarah pushed her glasses up.

"Oh, I see." Josie grimaced.

"Just be careful," Sally chimed in with a playful grin. If only she knew that Josie was not concerned with her own safety but more with the severity of the next accident. Every breath hung on the morbid hope of death. Josie's spirit convulsed from deep within, begging for mercy on what she'd have to do to appease Chadwick and save her father. An ache grew from behind her eyes. She began to unpack her things, keeping to herself the rest of the evening.

Liesl was also quiet the rest of the night—changing into her nightgown, kneeling for her prayers, then slipping into the bed after blowing out a candle on her nightstand. A sniffle here and there made Josie wonder if little Liesl cried herself to sleep.

Now, soft snores rattled beside her, and the chilled air convinced Josie to snuggle deeper into her blanket. The accommodations were nicer than she expected. Cleaner than even her own bedroom. No matter how cozy Josie was though, her mind remained awake, and finally she decided to ready for her first day at the mill.

The house stirred as bell chimes serenaded Josie down the steps. She peered out the window to see what tower held the bell. She saw only darkness. It was early yet. Earlier than she had ever risen on the farm. Her lamp flickered as it swung from her hand. She passed by the common room on the second floor. Singsong voices carried from the bedrooms, and a few women sat and prayed beside the fireplace. The scraping of pans and a squealing door met her ears at the last step. She found her way to the kitchen.

"Good morning, Mrs. Parker—I mean, Fran." Josie approached the woman working at the kitchen table.

"Ah, good morning, Josie. You'll not get your breakfast till after your first shift, but it shall be a fine one—I decided to make my famous yeast rolls." She turned to the shelves along a stone wall and pulled down a small crock. "Did you sleep well?"

"Not quite," Josie muttered. The woman quirked an eyebrow at her. "A new place, I suppose." Josie escaped her inquiring look and walked to the open back door. A cool breeze scented with thyme and mint and dew-seeped soil met her cheeks. "What time must we be at the mill?"

"Half past five. Early for some, but my favorite time of day," Fran said. "I keep that door open even in the rain. Nothing better than the sound *and* smell of rain."

"I agree." Josie passed through the threshold, holding her lamp up as she admired the mounding rows of herbs and vegetables. She brushed her fingertips along the soft lamb's ears that lined a patchwork of thyme, parsley, and sage. Several of the plants were overgrown with weeds, and the roses along the stone wall had leaves eaten through by aphids. This garden was begging for Josie's hand. But Miss Clyde's warning settled in the front of her mind, and Josie forced herself to return to the kitchen. Although life in the garden was more enticing, she must ready herself to mill life, transforming the dead cotton bolls of last year's crop.

Josie put on her cloak in front of the parlor's fire. As she tied her bonnet beneath her chin, the foyer behind her filled with women hurrying out the front door. Josie was the first one ready, but now she was the last to leave as she followed the crowd across the vast courtyard to the mill.

Miss Clyde waited at the top of the stoop with arms crossed while women filed past her. Before Josie slipped by, Miss Clyde caught the door. "Come, I shall show you your station."

She led Josie past the office and down the long hallway. The women quickly hung up their cloaks and bonnets on hooks along the wall and then disappeared behind two double doors. Josie hung up her things and followed Miss Clyde into a large, voluminous room. Several women entered into side doors, while others filled the aisles of this main room. Thick pipes stood like columns and joined up with others that sprawled along the ceiling. Barrels and straps and wheels neatly marked each row with a purpose that Josie did not understand exactly. But she assumed they had something to do with the overwhelming noise from yesterday. Now, the only sound was the shuffle of women finding their places in rows of looms. The machines were like stout dressing tables that would work to provide their own cloths. Each machine held up a wooden bin filled with bobbins.

An overseer met Miss Clyde and Josie and directed Josie to the last row of the room. On the far wall, a broad square window show-cased an office. Mr. Taylor stood behind a desk lit up by a bright lamp. He made a quick signal with his hand.

A man from behind her called out, "Aye!"

A loud rush filled her ears. The machines came to life, marching in a rhythm not far from Josie's racing heart. The ruckus of knocking parts and spinning spindles vibrated through her body, as if she were not just a woman in the mill but a part of the machinery. The overseer explained to her the parts of the machine she was to manage. It was powered by steam, chomping down on the cotton with its lathes' steady blows. Josie was certain that she was, indeed, a part of a whole. She looked about her. The other women locked into place at their own looms, and little Liesl settled in at the end of one row with a basket of empty bobbins. Her eyes were red with sleep.

Every woman paid careful attention to their tasks. Only a slight mumble of talking could be heard between the pounding machinery. Whenever Josie looked around though, it seemed nobody was talking at all. Soon, a fine snow of cotton bits lingered in the air. She was in a sort of storm, one where the thunder banged from the machines, and the particles in the air floated without chill or wind.

Liesl crept along the rows, her movement the most human of anything else in Josie's view. At thirteen, Josie had been secure in her mother's care, not shouldering the weight of providing money for ill family members. Thinking on the past—her mother buried, and Josie herself having escaped the grave—she was reminded of her true purpose in this place. She shivered, as if she were in a very real storm or a very cold tomb. No matter if she played the part of a mill girl, she could not ignore the tangled thread of deceit that wrapped around her soul as tightly as the cotton on the bobbins.

After a couple of hours of work, an overseer shouted, "Break!" The factory exhaled its life. The cut-off water stopped the steam, and all machines froze to sleep. Josie stepped into the line of women marching through the settling bits of cotton, brushing themselves off when they entered the hallway.

"I am famished," her roommate Sally said as she tied her bonnet under her chin. She walked briskly ahead while Josie continued to put on her cloak. Sally called over her shoulder, "You'd better hurry. We only have thirty minutes for breakfast."

Once again, Josie was left behind by the mass of ladies and hurried to catch up, running through the door before it closed shut.

"Miss Clay!" Mr. Taylor called out to her just as the door clicked behind her. She froze on the top step of the stoop. Sally waved her forward, the distance growing between them. With a growl, Josie's stomach insisted she follow Sally. But her sense spun her around to wait on her boss. Mr. Taylor opened the door. He stood in the threshold, his sleeves rolled up and his hair tousled as if he'd been on the floor working even harder than she had.

"Yes, sir?"

"I—I wanted to see how your first shift went." He stepped from the shade of the building into the weak daylight. The sun was still sleepy, its far-off rays offering a colorless brightness. Mr. Taylor was handsome, his eyes glistening even without the sun, and his tight jaw released with a slight grin. Josie looked over her shoulder as the chatter of women disappeared. Only one woman, with a face framed in auburn curls and her arm held in a sling across her waist, remained at the boardinghouse door. She nodded in their direction then closed the door shut.

Josie turned back around.

"If they trouble you, you may tell them that we had to firm up the terms of your contract." He passed her with one long stride and rested his hand on the metal handrail. "That one in particular will be sure to ask you why you were alone with me."

Josie looked at the door and tilted her head. "That one?"

"Miss Jennings. She is our factory investigator, it seems." His nostrils flared a bit as he kept his attention across the courtyard.

"Is there something that needs investigating?" Her veins frenzied with the secrets that were hidden.

He turned to her. Now it seemed he was investigating her with the same scrutiny from yesterday. His brow tilted up beneath soft brown curls, and his sable eyes simmered with consideration. He leaned toward her and said, "Forgive my play on words. I only meant that Miss Jennings is a. . .a snoop?" He pressed his lips together, clamping down on a growing smile.

Josie could not refrain from grinning. "Ah, I see."

His demeanor lightened her mood, and a quiet laugh escaped her lips.

"Miss Clay, where did you say you traveled from yesterday?" Mr. Taylor shoved his hands in his pockets and rocked back on his heels.

Her stomach growled as if in warning. "A village, thirty miles west." She fiddled with the ragged edge of her glove. "As I showed you yesterday, I found the ad and needed work."

He hooked his hand on the back of his neck. "No need to justify your actions. It. . .it is good to know how far our ads reach. That is all." He gave her a bland smile, one that did not affect his eyes, and pulled his shoulders back. "You better go break your fast. There is a long day of work ahead."

She curtsied, relief and hunger carrying her off the stoop and across the courtyard. As she approached the boardinghouse entrance, she looked back at the factory. Mr. Taylor lingered on the steps, offering a hesitant wave and a face washed bright in the newborn sunshine.

Braham stood at his office window, observing the ladies dashing in after their quick breakfast. The golden hair of Josie Clay snagged his attention, but only for a brief moment. Audra Jennings's stare warned him better.

"That new gal is quite a beauty." Tom clapped his back. "And it seems that there are some who might feel threatened."

Braham turned to his head overseer. "You know the gals nearly as well as I do."

"Better. You get to stay in this office now. I get to canvass the rows, listening in on their gossiping." He gave a sly grin. "Your name comes up more often than is proper."

"Ah, you hear above the looms? Supernatural, friend."

"The frequency of your name is just as thunderous."

A motion from the window distracted Braham. Buck Walters, the overseer of the east side of the floor, dashed across the aisle toward Josie, who was hunched over another girl two rows away from her usual station.

"Something's gone wrong," Braham muttered. He snatched his waistcoat from the hook and followed Tom to the floor. All heads were turned their way. Buck flung his arms here and there, probably demanding the women return to work. His shouts carried above the drumming machines as the two men approached, yet another voice carried higher than his. When they passed the center pipe that marked the room in two halves, Braham was taken aback at the sight.

Josie Clay stood with her hands on her hips, her face aflame and her hair lighter than ever with a soft sprinkling of cotton bits clinging to her curls. "I beg you, sir, this woman needs help. She cannot wait until the noon meal."

"What's going on, Buck?" Braham stepped forward, but he kept his eye on the new mill girl. A permanent position for Miss Clay was looking less probable at the moment. She was demanding, hot with temper. Nothing he could stand for much longer. Not after all the anger he'd seen in the past.

"That girl there's been sitting on the floor, her head in her hand, forcing another to carry on her job." Buck pointed to the woman hidden by the protection of Miss Clay's long skirt. "Then I saw that one"—he sneered at Miss Clay—"leave her station in the care of another and come tend to her. Sir, we can't have people running about the place, heaping their duties on others."

Miss Clay took an immediate step closer to Braham, her sapphire eyes round and pleading. "Mr. Taylor, if you please, I can explain."

He read her lips more than hearing their sound. Every piece of machinery drowned out this confrontation. Braham motioned for Miss Clay to go to the hallway, and then he flicked his head at Buck to follow. They tromped off past the girl on the floor. She was pale, with sweat beads covering her forehead.

Braham turned to Tom. "Take her to my office." Tom gingerly took the arm of the woman and escorted her across the room. Several workers gave curious glances at the almost limp lady against the side of the large overseer.

Braham stepped into the cool hallway and shut the door on the thick air and drowning noise. He was not sure if the tension between his overseer and his employee was any less aggravating than straining to hear over the drumming lathes.

Miss Clay stood with her arms crossed, peering into the glass door of his office, while Buck sat on a wooden bench with his fists pressed on his thighs. His eyebrows were set along one long ridge, shading a glare in Miss Clay's direction.

"Miss Clay, if you would please explain yourself," Braham said.

She dragged herself away from the door and approached him in an almost ornery way—more self-assured than she'd shown him over the past twenty-four hours. Usually, it took a month or so for a woman to be comfortable here—at least thirty winks to adjust to the long work and strict lifestyle of the boardinghouse. The mill girls rarely showed their strengths—or weaknesses—until they'd completely acclimated. This woman only heightened Braham's skepticism.

"Mr. Taylor, I was trying to tend to that woman. I saw her faint, and nobody noticed." She gave a side glance to Buck. "Or if they did, they hardly cared." A slight uncertainty flashed in her eyes, as if she doubted what she had declared.

Buck sprang to his feet. "You never leave your station, at any cost. That is unacceptable."

Miss Clay dug a fist into her hip. "So, would you have the lady just lay on the factory floor until quitting time?"

Braham stepped between them. "Miss Clay, I understand your concern for the woman, but next time, you bring it to the overseer. It is not your duty—"

"Braham!" Tom called from the office.

Braham signaled for Miss Clay and Buck to stay put with a raised finger. He headed into his office. "What is it?"

Tom crouched beside the woman draped in a chair. "She fainted for good reason. Look—" He gently lifted her arm. "She must have gotten caught on the equipment." The underside of her forearm was drenched in blood. The wound was a nasty one.

Braham looked away, trying to keep from being sick. Memories of Terryhold invaded his mind. Bile crept up his throat as he thought about his slave friend, Jeremiah, who'd endured a beating with lashes on every inch of his small back.

"I—I will call for a doctor," he mumbled, feeling as though he might faint also. Miss Clay and Buck stood at the door. Miss Clay hurried away while Buck just stared.

Braham demanded, "Buck, go check this girl's station for any blood."

The overseer skulked back and disappeared. He'd not gotten the justice he'd probably hoped for. Miss Clay was still off task, and yet Buck was ordered about.

Where had Miss Clay gone, anyway? Braham stormed down the hallway and found her hunched over a washbasin in the water closet.

"Miss Clay—"

"Sir, I know what to do. The wound must be cleaned." She hardly looked at him when she dashed past, running with a damp towel dripping on the floor. She stopped where the ladies kept their belongings. She shoved her hand into a cloak pocket and pulled out a small bottle then continued toward his office.

Her determination was intriguing, but irritating too. She acted as if she were her own supervisor, annoying Braham more than it should. "What are you—"

Miss Clay called over her shoulder, "Come on. I've worked with the sick these many months." She flung open the hallway door to his office and disappeared.

Braham followed, his jaw tight and his fists balled. How could this woman make him feel so foolish?

"There, there, my dear." Miss Clay's tone was an angelic bell compared to the clanging machines beyond the walls. The injured girl cradled her arm. "May I see it?" she asked gently. The woman allowed her to tend to the wound. Miss Clay's brow was cinched in concentration as she tapped the wound with the towel. She spoke as she worked. "What is your name?"

"Amelia."

"Amelia, I have just the ointment for you. Your arm shall heal quite nicely."

Tom tossed a questioning look to Braham. He knew what he might be thinking. The apothecary or region's physician should be called on. This new factory girl should get back to work. A practical assumption, but by her surprising confidence, Miss Clay had taken away all of Braham's practicalities.

Miss Clay opened the bottle she'd retrieved from her cloak. An aroma of lemon and flowers filled the room. "This is a mixture of several herbs that will stop infection," she explained with a smile. She held it beneath the patient's nose. The distraught girl nodded. Carefully, Miss Clay administered the ointment to the clean wound. "Mr. Taylor, do you have a fresh cloth for Amelia?"

Tom shifted his weight, throwing Braham another baffled look. Braham straightened his spine and suggested, "Perhaps we should call on Miss Young? She's the apothecary and town midwife. She's helped our women before—"

Miss Clay rose and raised an eyebrow. "Perhaps. But the time would be wasted, sir. I am certain if I can dress the wound now, she might even be able to continue her work." She then glanced down at Amelia. "After a short rest, of course. The lavender mixture will soothe her, almost immediately."

Her reasoning was valid, as if she understood the priority of efficiency around here. Braham had assumed Amelia would be done for the day. Miss Clay seemed not only to care about the health of this woman, but she also kept in mind the need of duty to the factory. Admirable, and yet, a startling sense of what was expected.

A strange creature, this Miss Clay.

Braham's role as manager of the place sank a little this hour. Josie Clay, however, was rising on a platform of stubborn compassion with a work ethic to admire.

Josie's exhilaration dulled as she settled back to her station. She tried to focus on cotton spinning from thread to cloth but could only consider the fuss she'd just made. Every once in a while, she would catch Amelia's eye, and the woman would nod and smile. Josie refrained from groaning. She had vowed to remain a stranger in this place. But all eyes were upon her today. Her quick response upon seeing Amelia crumpling to the ground scared her more than affirmed her now, hours later. What had she done? Factory physician was not her job. Her purpose was quite the opposite. Just as Dr. Chadwick used to leave Josie as sole provider for the next patient, surrendering his help when he was consumed with his experimentation, Josie must also relinquish her assistance to heal here in Gloughton. She was bound to spying, not healing.

But she could not deny the brimming satisfaction at the return of color to Amelia's cheeks and the ease of pain in her eyes. Could Josie truly plug up all her passion during this grim season? How might her unrestrained reaction to heal defy her duty to supply Chadwick and her father's enemies?

Even if she had not helped, at least Amelia would not have perished from such a wound. Josie convinced herself of that.

Oh, the shame of such a thought!

As Josie took care with the whirring machines around her, she prayed forgiveness that, for the first time in her life, she despised her God-given gift.

A tap on her shoulder spun Josie from her work and her tense thoughts. Little Liesl held her basket of bobbins on her hip, the opposite hip completely hidden by the much-too-large dress that hung from the girl's tiny frame.

"Is anything the matter?" Josie spoke loudly then leaned her ear in the girl's direction while returning her attention to her work in case that overseer was watching.

The girl rummaged through the empty bobbins in her basket and pulled out a bottle. Not the bottle of her ointment for wounds. Josie had certainly returned it to her cloak pocket. No, this was another one. This was her mixture that she would leave for the grave robbers to ward off disease. Heat rushed through her. The machines slowed. After an eventful morning, the noon break had crept upon them. She glanced about as if her secret spilled forth from the palm of the little German girl.

Quickly, she snatched it, shoved it in her pocket, and snapped, "Where did you find this?"

Liesl's eyes grew wide. "I—I am sorry, Miss Josie." She spoke with a slight accent. "It is so pretty—the dark green glass—and it smells lovely too. It was by our bed. Reminds me of my *oma*." She shook her head and stepped back. "I did not know it was yours until I saw you with Miss Amelia. Forgive me, miss." Liesl spun around, almost as fast as the bobbin on the loom, and disappeared down the row. She was timid, like Father's calf during its first steps away from its mother. If Liesl knew that the fragrant bottle was a shield for body snatchers as they desecrated a possibly diseased grave—then perhaps the girl would appeal not in wonder but in accusation. The fact that her belongings were so easily incriminating was too much to consider in this public place. Every emotion threatened to show itself upon her face.

Josie withdrew from the other women as they crossed the court-yard and filed in the boardinghouse. She ate her lunch with Fran in the kitchen and was the first to return and fix her attention on her work.

The rest of her first day was uneventful. Josie's shoulders ached, and her feet were swollen from standing for nearly fourteen hours straight. After supper, she followed Sally and Sarah to their room, imagining worming her way between the cool sheets, her head sinking in the feather pillow, and dozing off to a place where her mind would no longer dwell between guilt and worry. But as she passed the common area of the second floor, a flurry of women rushed up to her. Amelia stood at the front of the crowd.

"Miss Clay, I do want to thank you for your help today," she said, her cheeks flushed. "I am certain I would have lost a day's wages if it weren't for you."

Three other women nodded. One with frizzed hair said, "Were you reprimanded at all? Nobody has ever raised a voice to Mr. Walters."

Josie shook her head. "I should not have. I am trained to aid the wounded and sick. I acted on impulse."

"You are trained?" A lanky woman with spectacles threaded her arm through Josie's and led the gaggle to the closest sitting area. "Trained how?"

A knot tightened in Josie's stomach. She did not want to be known here. Not when she would be the betrayer at the graveside of one or more of these women. But they waited for her answer, their stares intent and her mind too fuzzy to supply an excuse to not talk.

"My mother was an herbalist," she offered. "She taught me remedies from the moment I could walk." Life under Dr. Chadwick needed no mention—let her remain the girl she was in the more innocent past.

The woman reached out her hand. "I am Molly O'Leary." Her dark ringlets fell forward. A ribbon was tied around her wrist, no doubt the ribbon that held her hair back during today's work. Her coloring was the same as the matron's, but Josie was certain Molly towered over most of the women here. Josie shook hands with her. "May we interview you for our newsletter?"

"Newsletter?"

Molly smiled brightly at the women who huddled with her. "Yes, we are starting up a newsletter. We've got a lot of talent in these girls. Some come from poor families and others from families who demand their sons receive an education using their wages. We might not have the status to go off to prestigious schools and find glorious apprenticeships, but we are hard workers with the most important thing of all—" A deeply carved dimple graced her cheek as her emerald eyes flashed. "Freedom."

"Oh, I see." Josie let out a small laugh. "When do you have time for such a thing? I am exhausted." The women's faces were bright and eager, as if the day were just starting out, not ending.

"It is her first day, girls," Amelia reminded them with a gentle smile. "Perhaps we should talk more tomorrow?" She patted Josie's arm. "Do not worry, you shall get half a day on Saturday, and of course a day of rest on the Sabbath."

Molly gave Amelia a sharp look through her spectacles. "I was excited to see someone with a spine among us." Josie squirmed. She was not someone to admire. If they only knew how she would misuse courage. "Usually spine comes with an intellect, and we value such things around here." Molly tapped her temple and crossed her arms. "Why not have a newsletter with substance?"

The air thickened with silence, and once again, all eyes were on Josie. She cleared her throat. "So, you have a newsletter to put your intellect to good use?"

A ripple of laughter filled the crowd. "Yes, yes. That's it!"

"Good for you." She wiped her brow with the back of her hand. "I cannot interview tonight. Amelia is correct. I am exhausted and would just like to sleep."

"Very well, we'll wait until Friday," Molly said.

A flurry of chatter went through the crowd while Molly whispered in one gal's ear. Josie opened her mouth to object, closed it, then finally found her voice. "I. . .I do not think an interview—"

Molly interrupted. "Oh, you will be fine by Friday evening. Do not worry. The work will become mundane enough that you will enjoy evenings of conversation." She leaned in and spoke low. "Second floor is so much more entertaining. We know everything about anything in town. Including available suitors and all the insights of a socialite without the fuss of stuffy parents breathing down our necks." She tweaked the corner of her lip. A flash of mischief brightened her green eyes.

"I have no interest in suitors." Josie sighed. But the opportunity to find out more about the folk in Gloughton caught her attention and she continued, "Insights, though. That's always exciting, isn't it?" She gave a thin laugh to encourage the interest this gal had shown her, an interest that might deflect the use of mill girls for a scheme and find true strangers for the robbers. Would that make this wait easier? She could only hope.

Josie climbed the stairs after a brief farewell to all who gathered and watched through the rails along the staircase. The women retired to their rooms. Josie's stomach soured as she turned from the landing. Night had fallen outside. This second day of hiding her purpose had proven a touch productive and gave her hope that she might not know any of Dr. Chadwick's victims on this side of death. Like the calm of a patient's relief once the ointment began to work, the plan was taking its root. The initial pain became numb at the opportunity to learn about the social comings and goings of Gloughton—the names and news of those who could fulfill her ransom, and her father's.

Chapter Five

Even after Josie's long hours, sleep was still scarce. The slumbering room became a wide empty stage for her mind to prance about and pluck any peace within her. Dr. Chadwick was a hungry vulture waiting for her replacement, yet Father's debt to the grave robbers seemed more pressing. The moon shone through the thin curtains, forbidding her eyes to stay closed for very long. Josie sat beside the window, shivering in her nightdress as she began letter after letter to the doctor, begging him to forget her and release her from the debt of…a body. Her script was as shaky as her confidence in the plea to change Dr. Chadwick's heart though. She tore the pages in tiny pieces and stuffed them into her drawer.

Each night, sleep escaped her once the room darkened and the soft sleeping breaths arose from the others. Josie would pace the floor until the creaking boards seemed to stir her roommates. Then she'd crawl into bed and weep into her feathered pillow, careful to not shake too violently with Liesl sleeping so close to her. Pity flooded her at the thought of Father's surprised face being seen assisting such gruesome work—work that shamed him enough to keep hidden from his only beloved daughter. How frightened he must have been that eve in New York, and how foolish his being caught made him seem in front of Alvin and every other man. She balled her fists. What a wretched creature she was to pity the man whom she'd exchanged all her goodness for. Even if he was her father.

When the small wall clock struck four hollow chimes, she was easily aroused from a fitful doze. Josie crept downstairs before the rest of the house awoke and stole away to the garden. The old ritual of spending her morning hours among plant life had been lost during her own illness, presumed death, then sudden resurrection. Her garden at home had been a footstool for prayer and praise. She met God there before she fell ill. After these miserable nights though, she did not sneak to the garden to cast herself before a God who she'd presumed hardly recognized her now. No, she hurried to the boardinghouse garden to find the only sure relief, temporal as it was, among the scents, textures, and memory of a less complicated time.

On Friday evening, Josie lit the lamp hanging from the stand and sat on the bench half-invaded with ivy. Even if she'd managed to engage in little conversation these past days, that Molly O'Leary was adamant about this interview. Josie prepared herself to think on nothing but her knowledge of plant materials.

Fran scuttled along the flagstone path, her apron brushing against the long spindles of purple salvia flowers. "Miss Clay, how was your first week?" She knelt beside the bench, snipping some thyme from its sprawling bed and plopping the tufts in her apron pockets.

"'Twas tiresome. But the work is reasonable, and I expect the pay will be good."

"I have not heard much complaining from the ladies these few years that the mill has been open—" Her lips parted as if she would say more. Perhaps about the accidents? She gave Josie a sideways glance, probably deciding it best not to scare the newest mill girl. A fruitless endeavor, Josie thought. Laughing nervously, Fran continued, "Most enjoy their freedom from home, so I'd say they don't have time to dwell on negativity." She dropped her shears in her pocket. The evening bells from a nearby church began to chime, and Fran smiled up at the fading colors of twilight. "Only one half day of work and then a day of rest. Have you been through town?"

"I have not." Josie plucked some rosemary leaves and rolled them between her fingertips. The spicy sweet fragrance filled the night air. "I have been anxious to see beyond the walls of the factory though."

"Ah, well you can follow the girls on the Sabbath. They are expected to attend worship. Gloughton boasts three churches." She turned back toward the kitchen. "I am of the reformed religion."

"I attended the same back home."

"We can walk together, if you'd like?" She stopped at the door.

"Of course, there are plenty of girls who go as well."

"I should like to walk with you—"

Molly came up from behind Fran and shoved past her then bolted to the garden gate.

Josie bounced a look between Molly, who was propped up on her toes with her hands wrapped around the wrought iron spires, and Fran, who huffed and scowled in the woman's direction.

"Is anything the matter?" Josie asked.

"Shh." Molly waved her hand as if shooing a fly. Josie crept up behind her to see what had her in such a frantic state. A soft spring breeze spilled from beyond the walls carrying the soothing sounds of dancing leaves and chirping crickets. Only Molly's curious behavior gave the surrounding softness a sharp edge.

"What is she doing?" Molly whispered. Josie peered over the gate also. The figure of a woman disappeared down the steep bank to the canal, just beyond the bridge.

Molly spun around, nearly knocking Josie back into an elderberry shrub. "She's gone." Her eyes flashed. "As always."

"Wh–who is she?" Josie brushed off the back of her skirt and sidestepped her way to the bench.

Molly sat right next to her and leaned in. Mischief flashed in her eyes. "That's Audra Jennings. She's more spy than factory girl. At least, that's what the rumor is. Always last to dinner and first to work. She's hurt her arm, but won't let anyone know how. Every Friday evening she slips out after dinner."

"Has anyone asked why?"

Molly snickered. "I'm a reporter, aren't I?" She winked. "Audra has a good excuse—saying she's off to see her sister who works at the Bates estate. But—" Her black curls slid across her shoulder as she glanced at the gate. She whipped around, her nose only inches from Josie. "Most wonder if she's trying to snag the attention of Mr. Taylor. Supposedly, they were brought up here together."

"Brought up here?"

"From the south." Molly pulled out some parchment and ink

from the satchel at her side. "'Twas a long time ago. But many women have seen the two in heated conversations. Cannot tell who's pursuing who, nor who is refusing." She giggled. "I've been watching her. Even have a story snippet in our newsletter." She ruffled through her papers and pulled one out from the middle of the stack. She handed it to Josie. "Here."

Mistress Mystery Sighting:
She skims the grounds of Gloughton Mill,
slips in and out like cotton dust.
Give us a clue, miss, if you will,
as to what you wish to hide from us.

Josie scrunched her nose. "If you know who she is, then how is it a mystery?" Although the thought of another woman stealing away some suspicion was just fine by Josie.

"Ah, that is partly in jest. She loves the game of it. Often brags about her knitted heartstrings with the Bates men."

Josie thrummed her fingers on her knees. "Or perhaps she just wants attention. Most snoops do."

Molly burst into a hearty laugh. "My! For someone who has been here only a week, you have pegged Audra Jennings with the appropriate title."

"It was the word that Mr. Taylor used, I believe."

Molly arched an eyebrow, now seemingly more intrigued by Josie than the subject of her jingle. Josie cleared her throat and looked down at the top paper on Molly's stack. A pretty drawing of a woman in black graced the side column of the jingle. An empty square below was titled "A Healing Angel among the Girls." Josie glanced up at Molly. Her white teeth gleamed in the soft glow of the lamp hanging across the path.

"That's where your interview will go." She tucked the sheet with the verse back in her stack again.

"Angel?"

"Of course. Amelia coined it, actually." Molly set her inkpot by her feet and poised her quill above a blank page. "I will write it out here, then transcribe it neatly in that box. You shall provide a different kind of conversation around here. An honorable, less suspicious object." She winked.

Josie gave a tight smile. Her shoulders slumped, but not enough that Molly might wonder. Before the interview began, Josie said a quick prayer of forgiveness for the deceptive mask of an angel that she seemed to wear.

That Audra Jennings was no doubt more innocent than the spying Josie Clay.

Sunday morning carried a cheerful buzz about the boardinghouse. Nobody had made a sound at the usual early waking hour—at least, Josie had slept through any noise, stirring when the sunshine kissed her eyelids. She'd finally found rest. Her body was desperate for it, or willing, since Sunday held no possibility of a factory accident. Her roommates all woke up at the same time, and they readied for church with an extra ounce of sleep than on a regular work morning.

Josie followed the sisters and Liesl downstairs. The second floor's bedroom doors were propped open as girls chatted in the hallway while braiding their hair. A small group of women stood in a huddle in the common room practicing a hymn.

"We are lucky to have our peace upstairs, are we not?" Sally whispered as they rounded the banister to the final flight of stairs.

Sarah and Liesl both said, "Oh yes," simultaneously.

Josie nodded, trying to push away the wonder of what it might be like to be a girl on the second floor. She'd shied away from Ainsley's social events. The girls gossiped, and her parents had needed her. Now, the thought of her allegiance to this insidious scheme pierced her well-rested mind with a sliver of resentment—even for her father.

They broke their fast in the bright dining room. The serving girl, Abigail, had traded her black frock for a lovely mauve dress, protected from the crumbs and splashes by an apron. As each table of six filled in, the room buzzed with conversation. When the meal was over, Josie stayed back, waiting for Fran at the small nook outside the kitchen.

Audra Jennings approached her as she put on her bonnet without tying the ribbons. Her sling was hidden behind the folds of her cloak. "I trust that your first week went well?" She spoke in a cool tone. "Or at least, uneventful, after the scene you caused."

"It was a good week." Josie offered her hand for a shake. "I am Josie Clay. And you are Audra Jennings."

The woman smacked her lips together. "Of course. You've been informed, I see." She only considered Josie's outstretched hand with a glance then turned her nose up and away. "I have been here the longest of this lot, so it's no wonder they talk. Braham and I are cut from the same cloth, if you will." She laughed with a fiery glint in her hazel eyes.

Josie raised her eyebrows at the woman's familiar use of the manager's first name. "I hear you are both from the south."

"*We* are. Escaped the heat and much hardship. Has grown both of us strong and capable." Audra spun on her heel, looking over her shoulder. "You have much to learn, Miss Clay. And if I were you, I'd be more careful on the factory floor. It seems to me Mr. Taylor is keeping watch on you only because of a lack of trust."

"Have you spoken to him about it?" A small thread of fear sewed into her spirit. There was no doubt that Josie's time at the factory was in a fragile balance. One more snag—like her overwhelming need to help Amelia—would ruin everything.

Audra just shrugged. "I know him well. Better than any other woman." She smiled and disappeared around the corner.

"Do not listen to her." Fran appeared at the bottom of the kitchen steps. "Everyone knows she has an eye on something well out of reach."

"I am not concerned by her. Not when what she says contradicts what I've been told." Josie rolled her eyes. "Or who has told me so."

Fran bounded up the stairs and hooked arms with Josie, guiding her out the front door. "And who is that?"

"Why, the man who Audra thinks she knows so well." Josie laughed. "He warned me about her on my first day."

Fran chuckled. "She's not as mysterious as she might like to seem, is she?"

"Not at all." Josie *did* take the woman seriously though. Audra's words were a sobering warning to stay on task at work. And she'd also sparked Josie's curiosity about Braham Taylor.

What had he escaped down south, and could Josie grow just as strong from the hardship she'd left behind?

"Aunt Myrtle, our neighbor will take you to the church." Braham kissed her cheek. "I will join you shortly."

"What is this, Braham?" Aunt Myrtle leaned forward as he leapt down from the carriage and headed toward the factory gate. "You will not work on the Sabbath!"

"Of course not," he said. "I just have to check on the office door. I worry that I did not lock up last night."

"Very well." She was resigned. "Do not be long."

"Yes, Aunt." Braham gave her a wink and then jogged along the canal that flowed into the back of the mill. He prayed for forgiveness for his fib. But he could not share the truth of his errand. It might only frighten his aunt. That man who was with Josie Clay had lurked about last night, and when Braham called out to him, he disappeared into the wood north of town. Braham's excuse was only partially untrue though. He did want to check on the security of the place. He also hoped to confront Miss Clay, whose arrival had brought about this uncertainty since her very first day.

As Braham crossed the bridge to the factory courtyard, he spied Audra strutting toward town. He ducked behind the old elm tree. Braham did not want to be trapped by her flirtations or, worse, insistence that he accompany her to church. She breezed past, her nose up in the air and her flaming hair as crimson as a fox.

He cupped his hand over his mouth to suppress a chuckle at his childish hiding.

The woman was sly. He'd never trusted her. Ever since he'd seen her mocking and stealing from Terryhold's youngest kitchen help, he chose to stay clear of Minnie's older sister. When Braham warned his uncle after he placed Audra as bobbin girl their first year in the factory, the wise man insisted that the journey north was good for leaving things of the past behind them. A motto Braham had found attractive for himself.

He stepped out from his hiding when Audra turned the corner. Another figure snagged his attention. Miss Clay crossed the courtyard accompanied by the boardinghouse cook. His pulse raced at the sight of her. Braham must be more anxious about her acquaintance than he thought. When her eyes met his, his pulse quickened all the more. She appeared cheerful on her first day off. Her blue eyes shone bright, and her ruby lips tilted in a soft grin.

Braham took in a breath of the crisp morning air and diverted his gaze to the ruddy complexion of Fran Parker. "Good morning, ladies."

"Good morning, sir," Miss Clay replied.

The cook cocked her head. "Are you to work this fine Sunday, Mr. Taylor? I would think your aunt would not be happy with you."

"You are right, dear woman." Braham chuckled. "Of course, you know her nearly as well as I do."

The cook informed Miss Clay, "I was once the cook at the Bates estate. Miss Myrtle and I became rather close. But then Mr. Bates insisted I take on the boardinghouse when the factory was built." She pursed her lips. "Or rather, when that Audra Jennings needed watching over."

Braham tried earnestly to keep his gaze between their two bonnets, avoiding the pretty mill girl beneath the periwinkle brim. From the corner of his eye, he caught the cook's crooked smile. "You were one of the first overseers, weren't you, sir?"

"I was." He grinned wide. "Seventeen and ready to work."

"Yes, and today you are more eager than you should be on a Sunday, I suspect," Miss Parker said, wagging her finger.

"No, not to work. In fact, I do wish to speak with Miss Clay." His voice cracked, and he shifted his weight. Miss Clay's lips circled into an O. Heat crawled up his neck.

Before any other word passed between them, her father's man appeared in the back of the courtyard. Unexpected appearances were this ruffian's specialty. Braham knew better than to judge a creature by his tattered clothes and ugly sneers, but Miss Clay had mentioned her own aversion to him too.

"That man is here again." He nodded in his direction, and both women turned. The man fiddled with a satchel, his face darkened by the large-brimmed hat.

Miss Clay's face drained of color. "Oh, if you will excuse me, I shall see what he wants." She detached herself from the cook's arm and hurried away from them, calling from over her shoulder, "Please save me a seat at church, Fran. I shan't be long."

"I would like to speak to you, Miss Clay," Braham shouted after her, a defense marching along his shoulders as his whole body tensed.

She swiveled around to face him, holding her bonnet to her head. "Perhaps after church, sir?" She glanced quickly at the man on the other side of her then back at Braham. "I fear he has word about my. . .my father." Her chest heaved with labored breath, and she appeared to wait for his approval.

He gave a curt nod. She turned and ran the rest of the way.

"My, she seems more nervous than a trapped deer," Fran mumbled as Braham offered his arm.

"Yes, she does." And he did not like it, nor his reaction to the new employee who was as much of a stranger as that man. Yet, she seemed terrified—a look that flung Braham to earlier times he wished to forget. "I do wonder why that man keeps hanging about. I spied him last evening, and now he arrives today."

"Who is he?"

"Miss Clay mentioned that he works for her father."

"Perhaps her father is ill," Fran suggested. "I do hope that is not so. She is a kind girl. Gives me company in the kitchen garden."

"The garden?"

"Yes, you have not visited in some time, Mr. Taylor." She narrowed her eyes.

"Much has happened, hasn't it?" Braham tilted his head to the tall factory, the red brick washed in sunlight. He would not worry about the office now. "How are my vegetables?"

"They are well cared for." Fran patted his arm.

"Good."

They strode across the courtyard and turned to town. Fran went on about her recent crop of carrots, while Braham tried to enjoy the stroll. However, his mind was back with Miss Clay facing that man. Braham prayed her father was not ill, nor that the man had some nefarious intent for the woman. There was a story here not being mentioned. One that held more than the care of a daughter for her father or a man escorting a woman to a career. Something lay beneath it all. He had seen the unraveling of secrets before. His father had hidden his need to leave Ireland, trying to forget among the cotton rows of the Bateses' Georgian plantation.

"Miss Fran, I will wait here to be sure Miss Clay knows her way to church."

The cook stared at him. "Very well. See you there, Mr. Taylor." Did she wink as she turned to cross the bridge?

Braham leaned on the rail, trying to shove aside his thoughts. He craned his neck to see if Miss Clay was in any harm, but the low branches of the elm hid his view.

The same fear he'd grappled with as a child shone clearly in the eyes of the new mill girl when that man appeared. A dormant protection woke up in Braham with great force. He gripped the rails, refraining from storming into their meeting and demanding an explanation.

What was this factory to Josie Clay? Truly a place to work? Or a place to escape?

Chapter Six

Alvin waited for her along the thick wooded edge of the court-yard, opposite the entrance into the village of Gloughton.

"What is it, Alvin?" Josie's heart raced. Would this plan begin tonight?

He rubbed his stubbled chin and squinted over her shoulder. She followed his gaze to Mr. Taylor and the cook turning down to the bridge. Mr. Taylor looked back at them. Josie wished she was the one on his arm going to church—not standing here with this crooked creature.

"Is my father with you?" She looked around, but she could not even find Alvin's cart. "How is he?"

"Your father is seeing things." Alvin finally spoke. "Forget debtors' prison, I fear he's going insane."

She pinned him with a desperate stare. "What does he see, Alvin?"

"Shadows that he swears are men." Alvin rubbed his jaw. "I assured him that we have time, and they won't be after him...yet."

"Are you certain?"

Alvin shrugged his shoulder—an unsettling answer. Josie's insides were crumbling in anguish.

He shoveled air in through his nostrils. "Your father is worrisome. His nerves are giving him fits of anxiety now. He carries his rifle everywhere he goes." Alvin wiped his brow.

The same black fog that eclipsed her consciousness on Dr. Chadwick's table began to invade her from both sides. "He must not understand completely—"

"He's as desperate as you were to escape the knife, Josephine, although you were saved from your demise within minutes." His lips twitched as if to smile with pride. Josie's lips curled in bitterness.

"Your father's troubles are far from being over." Alvin folded his lips together then let out a sigh. "That's why I am here. We must be diligent." He leaned close. "Do you remember the old blacksmith who was in his last days in Ainsley?"

She swallowed hard and nodded. It had been a tough week with Mr. Brown. He was in much pain, and once again, Josie was left without the doctor's help while he dissected the dead.

"Did you give him something to ease the pain? Perhaps quicken his eternal sleep?"

Her mouth fell open. "Oh Alvin! I would never induce death. He was given a tea of Bee Balm to help calm him." She lowered her voice. "He died on his own." She let those last words stab at the air between them. She wished they would pierce his conscience too.

"We do what we must to survive." Alvin clutched at her arm, and even though she wanted to squirm away she was thankful to be held in place instead of collapsing from a fainting spell. "I have found one who does not have much longer on this earth. If we could help her along—"

"You know the first person we will—" She could barely speak. "We will take?"

"I do." He looked off in the distance. "I have been—er— scouting out the surroundings. Who knows when the factory will offer up its next victim." He patted the bag at his hip. "These here mushrooms are a good excuse when my lurking about is questioned by nearby farmers and townsmen. They are in season now—" He pulled one out, a large brown one with rust-colored edges. "Remember? Your mother's favorite."

He did not have to say it. Josie knew her mother a thousand times better than he did. She could almost taste Mother's gravy on her tongue.

"In my hunting for these, I have also found the oldest living person here. Rumor is, she is suffering from an incurable illness."

Josie's heart began to thrum. The nostalgic taste turned bitter, and she could nearly smell the sickness of Mother's last days. She whimpered, and Alvin gripped her tighter.

"Be strong, Josie Clay. If there's any woman who is strong, it is you, I'd say." For a second, she saw the hard worker of her father's farm—before he sold his soul to the closest bidder of fortune and grit.

"Yours is the least incriminating duty," he mumbled. "You'll be safe from any accusation—as long as you play your part well." He tapped her nose with the same dirty finger that stole from the earth. Alvin made every penny from robbing and spying. His hands, no matter how much he might scrub them, were covered in the muck of graveyard soil and the blood of someone's deceased family member.

Both remaining Claytons had been infected with such defilement, no matter how Alvin tried to lessen their participation.

Josie took a step back, shifting her eyes across the courtyard. "I must go. The factory expects its workers to attend church." She was relieved to have an excuse to leave this man. Yet part of her did not feel satisfied. Would she ever feel satisfied without communicating with her father? Josie tried to soften her voice. "Please, have my father write to me. I'll have my first wages in a week's time. Please bring a letter when you come."

Alvin gave a slight nod. "Go to church, Josephine. I'll check on your father." He began to walk away, adjusting the satchel from his shoulder to across his chest. "If only you could fix up these mushrooms for our dinner." He rubbed his jaw. "One day, perhaps." He disappeared into the wooded area.

Hot tears pooled in Josie's eyes. The resentment that had sprouted for her father now withered, turning back into pity for the man—and herself, truth be told. Mother would be ashamed to know the unlawful acts they were tied to.

Josie strode across the courtyard. When she turned the corner to the bridge, she slowed her pace. Mr. Taylor was at the bridge's railing, his broad shoulders set back and his attention on the canal waters below. She swiped at the moisture in her eyes and approached him. He noticed her when she was only a few steps away.

"Hello, Miss Clay." He wrung his hands. "I—I wanted to be sure that you did not need my assistance—" His eyes were eager as they glanced behind her. "I am concerned about that man—" His Adam's apple bobbed above his cravat. "I am concerned about you, Miss Clay."

"Oh?" Josie's throat tightened. "I am in no harm, if that's what you mean."

"That fellow does not appear a trustworthy sort. I have seen him near my home."

"He hunts mushrooms," Josie blurted.

"Mushrooms?" Mr. Taylor tilted his chin.

"Yes, he even showed me his satchel filled with them." She gave him a weak smile. "They are in season." He looked down at his pocket watch. She scrunched her nose. Alvin better not be up to anything else but mushroom hunting and eavesdropping.

Mr. Taylor tucked his watch in his pocket and rocked back on his heels. "That is not what I expected, but it is a relief, for sure." He looked up and down the bridge and then held out his arm. "May I escort you to church?"

She nodded, slipping her fingers onto his woolen jacket. It carried the fresh scent of a warm blanket soaking up the sun. She wanted to lean into him and absorb the comfort that Braham Taylor offered this day.

As they walked across the neatly lined boards of the bridge, a gap offered an occasional glimpse of the shimmering waters below. Josie released the last bit of air she'd held on to so tightly. All thoughts of Alvin and crime slipped away as she reveled in the fact that this man had waited for her, was escorting her to church, and for now, considered her nothing less than a mill girl.

After they left the bridge, the wrought iron fence of the Gloughton cemetery rose next to them. Crooked tombstones and stoic crucifixes were guarded with lilac shrubs, just like her own mother's grave. Her mood darkened. She shivered at the thought of the heaping dirt upon her own life-filled grave. How long had she sat as worm's food? What care did Alvin take when he first thought she was dead? He had been gentle with the work horses on Father's farm. She'd often admired him for it. That was until he showed up with the first corpse for Dr. Chadwick, revealing the grim work he'd traded for a full pocket. To think that Father had hired such a man.

Mr. Taylor glanced down at her, and she realized the tight grip she had on his arm.

"Forgive me." She forced a smile. "I do not care for cemeteries."

"Nobody does." He chuckled softly then placed his hand on hers. "Do not worry. Look, we can almost see the steps of the church."

They passed a tavern and a tailor's, each with dark windows beneath their signs. A narrow church with a towering bell tower arose beyond a blacksmith's yard. At the top of the church's steps, an elderly woman gripped the rail. She was dressed in white and wore a pretty hat piled with lacy frills tied beneath her chin in a purple ribbon.

Mr. Taylor quickened his pace. "Ah, there is my aunt." He pulled his arm away from Josie and hurried to the bottom step.

"Braham, dear. You had me worried," the woman called in a shrill voice.

Mr. Taylor offered Josie his hand and led her up the steps. "Aunt Myrtle, this is the newest girl at Gloughton Mill, Josie Clay."

Josie quickly dipped into a curtsy. "Good morning, ma'am."

"Good morning." The woman clutched at Mr. Taylor's arm. "My nephew told me of your rather tardy arrival that first day. I trust that you have adjusted to the work now?" Her cold stare was nothing like her nephew's kindness. Josie was taken aback, scrambling to answer. But the woman did not wait for her and instead pulled Mr. Taylor away and led him to the door. As he reached to open it, the woman swayed from side to side then let out a cry and crumpled backward. Josie caught her by the elbows just before she fell to the floor.

"Aunt Myrtle!" Braham released the door, dropping to his knees beside the woman.

She moaned and wagged her head back and forth, her eyes shuttered behind cinched lids. "Get me home, Braham. Get me hooome," she groaned.

"Miss Clay, will you carefully sit her up?"

Miss Clay leaned forward so Aunt Myrtle settled against Braham's chest. His heart raced beneath her frail shoulders resting against him. "Please, will you get our driver? He should be in the last row—Jim Barlow."

Miss Clay disappeared inside the church.

"There, there, Aunt." He slipped his arm around her waist and carefully brought her to standing. "We shall get you home."

He should have never made her wait for him. His suspicions about that man had gotten the best of him and caused his aunt unneeded anxiety.

He gathered up the fragile lady into his arms—her head against his shoulder, and her legs hanging over his other arm—then he carefully descended the steps.

The driver hurried down the steps and ran to get the carriage. When the carriage arrived, the driver helped Braham situate her inside.

Miss Clay waited at the bottom step. "Sir, can you direct me to the nearest physician?" She blocked the bright sunshine with her gloved hand. "I can be sure to send for one to tend to your aunt."

"You are very thoughtful, Miss Clay." He pointed down Main to the first intersection. "There's a small cottage at the bend along Mosgrove Way. Call on Miss Young. She will not be at church today as the Hendersons have just given birth to their fourth child in the early hours this morning. But she will want to be wakened for news of my aunt." Miss Clay nodded and hurried down the street.

Braham slipped inside the carriage. The scent of old leather and his aunt's lavender fragrance engulfed him as he settled beside her. She leaned against the wall, dabbing her forehead with a lace handkerchief. Her skin was much older than he'd noticed before, the carves and folds appeared jaundiced.

Braham's teeth gripped so tight his jaw began to ache. When they began to move forward, Aunt Myrtle pushed back against the cushion and closed her eyes. As they turned onto the old country lane, dust began to cloud the small space.

"I am sorry that I caused you to worry, Aunt." Braham spoke low, the guilt twisting his throat. He'd promised himself to care for this woman just as she had cared for him when he was a boy—just as much as he cared to run the mill as successfully as his uncle.

"Oh dear," she exclaimed before coughing into her handkerchief. "My, my, this dust." She lifted her head and leaned toward him. "This has nothing to do with you, son." Her light eyes sparkled with moisture. Only the slight tip of her brow suggested that they pooled from emotion and not because of the gritty air.

Aunt Myrtle pressed her lips together in thought. After a pause, she said, "Do you recall the spring when you were fishing at the back of the property, and I was trapped in my room with a terrible cold?"

"I recall you sending Minnie down with a coat. And I refused it." He could almost hear his aunt's holler across the treetops: *"You wear that coat this instant, Master Braham. Or else you'll go to bed with no dinner."*

Aunt Myrtle patted his knee. "I was in a tizzy over a slight breeze only because of its effect on my chest and throat." She gave a wistful smile. "I knew what I was facing, so I wanted to protect you."

"You are a good guardian." He smiled.

"Today, I did not worry about you going to the factory or sitting in church. If you thought my spell was because of some worry you caused me, that isn't so." She settled her back into the seat again. Her profile, with the slight hooked nose and thin rosy lips was near-identical to her brother's. A sad flutter disturbed Braham's steady breath.

"Braham, I cannot protect you from what ails me. There is no coat for the sadness I'll bring. No hot tea and warm blanket for its chill." She licked her lips and shook her head. "No, there's nothing to be done. But I want you by my side as I suffer through it."

"Suffer—" He leaned forward. "What do you mean, Aunt Myrtle? You fainted. It is not uncommon, especially when I caused you to worry about my errand."

"You are not listening, boy. I was outside because the spell was coming on. I am ill, Braham. And it will be the death of me." Her stare was dry, no emotion or tears. "I am dying."

When Josie arrived at the small gate in front of an overgrown garden, she was curious who this Miss Young might be and wondered if Mr. Taylor was foolish to not inform a physician about his aunt's incident.

The gate squealed open, and Josie waded through overgrown grass. A shutter hung on one hinge in front of a dingy window that flanked the low entrance to the cottage. Josie jumped when the door flung open.

A young woman stood in a traveling coat and bonnet. She glanced at Josie then pushed her nose up to the sky as she called over her shoulder, "You have a visitor, Daisy." She stepped from the dark house and squinted. "My, it's as bright as a Georgia day out here." She continued down the path, passing by Josie as if she weren't there. "Excuse me, I must get back to the house." Her polite words did not change her aloof look or tone of voice. A citrus scent followed her. Perhaps lemon balm? Josie had often administered it to a patient's sour belly.

A small lady with bright eyes stared at her from the doorstep. "You must be new around here. I've not seen you before." She stuck a hand on her hip and swiped away a chestnut-brown strand from her forehead. Even though she stood in the shadow, her face gleamed white.

"I am new. To Gloughton. My name is Josie Clay—" She took care walking down the uneven path. "Are you Miss Young?"

"Call me Daisy." She sighed, opening the door wider. "Josie Clay, I have spent most of the past twelve hours tending to a baby who made her way to this world upside down. Praise God that both mother and child live and breathe. But I am exhausted. Come in and let me get off my feet."

"It is just that—" Josie tried to explain her urgent errand, but Daisy disappeared into the house. For such a petite woman, she was authoritative. She couldn't have been much older than Josie, yet Josie felt young and timid compared to Daisy.

Josie entered a large rectangular room and closed the door behind her. A long table with benches on either side sat in the middle, and a bookshelf lined one entire wall at the far end of the room. A doorway beside the bookshelf spilled with light. Perhaps a well-lit kitchen? Savory smells of garlic, onions, and boiled meat watered Josie's mouth.

Miss Young reclined on a cushioned window seat with her bare feet propped up on a pillow. "Come sit." She waved her hand at the table. "I know your name and nothing else." Daisy shoved herself up on her elbow.

"Mr. Taylor sent me." Josie clasped her hands together, only inching toward the table, not sitting. "He said you would care to know that his aunt fainted before church today. They are on their way home."

"Fainted?" The woman's countenance changed like a cold wick lit with fire. She sat up quickly. "Oh dear." She sprang to her feet and rushed to the door, slipping on boots and grabbing a cloak from a hook. "I do hope Aunt Myrtle has told Braham by now." She shook her head. "This secrecy has gone on too long." She ran into the other room. Clanking and clattering caused a ruckus followed by a slosh and splatter of something hitting the floor. "Rats," Josie heard Daisy mutter.

Josie followed her. The room was indeed a kitchen, and Daisy was putting the fire out. "Excuse me, are you a relative?"

"Relative?" Daisy put the iron down and began to tie her cloak as she walked toward the front of the house. "Not related. But I've known the Bates family since I was a young girl. My best friend is that Minnie who just left. She's Aunt Myrtle's maid. I've called her aunt just the same as Mr. Taylor. My mother and Myrtle were near sisters." She crossed herself. "My first lesson on distilling herbs was when Mother tended to Aunt Myrtle after her arrival to Gloughton."

"Your mother was an apothecary?"

"Yes, and so was my father. He died when I was an infant. I'm the only one left and the only apothecary in Gloughton." Daisy flung open the door and motioned for Josie to follow. "Come on. Minnie was just picking up Aunt Myrtle's tonic. I've been treating her these many weeks—" Daisy hesitated; her mouth remained open. But she closed it, pressing her lips together. She shut the door with such force that the shutter slapped against the window. She took a key from her cloak pocket and locked the door. "I never do lock this door. But I've come home lately to it ajar."

"Well, that's alarming." Josie looked about. "Was anything disturbed inside?"

"No. There are some rascals down the way who stir up mischief. I don't want them getting ahold of my calomel. That will give them—"

"Terrible vomiting."

"Ah, you know your remedies, I see."

"I used to help my own mother." She'd not mention Dr. Chadwick. "She was an herbalist and taught me much about healing."

"Interesting." Daisy stared at Josie, her bright eyes filled with intrigue. "You and I are not so different, it seems. We both have mothers who taught us. Is your mother a working apothecary?"

"No, she died two years ago."

"As did mine." She narrowed her eyes. "Very interesting, indeed."

They left through the gate just as church bells began to chime the hour. Daisy threaded her arm through Josie's. "Tell me, how do you know the Bates?"

"I only know Mr. Taylor, really. I work at the mill."

"Ah, you helped with that wounded woman, didn't you?"

"Why, yes, how did you know?"

"Audra told us about it. She's Minnie's sister." Daisy pulled them down to a dirt path where a cart and horse waited. "If it weren't for your occupation as a mill girl, I'm afraid you would be my competition." She yanked herself up on the bench.

"I will return—" Josie began to turn back to the lane.

"Come along." Daisy waved her to join her. "Perhaps we could work together? Aunt Myrtle means very much to me. She truly is like an aunt—or even more, a mother. Two educated opinions would be reassuring—or at least, undeniable."

"Has she had this problem before?"

"Before? I don't know. But it's only a symptom of something worse. She has a tumor." She hung her head and sighed. "Besides, her age is against her—she's the oldest woman in town."

Josie gripped at the cart's edge. The town's *oldest* woman?

Her insides lurched as if she'd taken the calomel.

This Aunt Myrtle, beloved by her nephew and Daisy, was to be the very body she'd signal for Alvin to steal away.

Chapter Seven

Braham stood at the window, rubbing the thin curtain between his fingers. Every corner of the property flung him back to when he was a boy—fully dependent on the love of his father's master turned guardian, and fully trusting in the woman who now lay resting on the bed behind him. He could imagine himself, scrawny legs and wild hair, walking down the road that curved around the house and past the orchard.

Wheels whined from below. Daisy sat atop her cart with Miss Clay beside her. Never before had a mill girl come out to the Bates estate. He had little desire to maintain a professional countenance when he wrestled with his childish emotions. Even so, he buttoned his waistcoat and straightened his cravat.

He left the window and approached the bed then clasped his hands over Aunt Myrtle's. "Daisy has arrived. She'll know what will be best."

"I've taken the tonic already." She kept her eyes closed. "Minnie brought it."

"Yes, but perhaps there is something else that can be done. You know Daisy, she does not always use drink and food." She was a good apothecary, he'd give her that. Although it was difficult to speak well of her. Nearly every place on this land that reminded him of his childhood was no doubt shared with Daisy. They had become good friends, just like their guardians had. But as they grew, Daisy became more attached to Gerald. The first days of the factory's opening were miserable. Braham had worked long and hard only to spend his few short hours off chaperoning Daisy and Gerald. When Gerald returned down south after his visits, Braham was relieved and kept to himself, while Daisy, who'd absorbed much of Gerald's animosity toward the ward of his father, sat at home writing letter upon letter to the man who would eventually break her heart.

Gerald did little to hide his snobbery when he began to attend balls down south and then later when he would travel north to Boston for society gatherings. Once he became well connected in the city, Daisy was nothing but a village apothecary's daughter.

Minnie tapped at the ajar door and stepped inside, announcing the women's arrival.

Daisy sailed to the bedside, acknowledging Braham with only a nod and a smirk. The poison of Gerald's distaste for him would remain potent at every interaction with her. She cooed, "Aunt Myrtle, you look beautiful."

He peered at the door and waited for Miss Clay. Yet she did not come. He decided he would rather play the part of employer and go find her than sit in Daisy's disdainful company.

Braham descended the stairs, spotting Miss Clay admiring the view out the parlor window. "Welcome to my home." He cleared his throat.

She spun around, her hand pressing a handkerchief to her mouth. Her sapphire eyes were red rimmed, and her cheeks were flushed. "Oh, thank you, Mr. Taylor. How does your aunt fare?" Tucking the handkerchief in her cloak pocket, she rushed toward him, an earnest concern flashing across her own grieved face.

"She is better," he mumbled, moved by her display. She mirrored the emotions he had tamped down at Aunt Myrtle's bedside. His heartbeat was so strong that it no doubt caused the air to shimmer around them. Or was his vision wobbling because of her beauty, even in her sorrow?

His breath caught in his throat.

An escaped tear slid along her jaw, and without thinking, he caught it with his finger. Miss Clay's lips parted, and his pulse thrummed in double time. He let out his trapped air, disturbing a gold strand from her forehead.

He realized just how close he stood to her and stepped back.

"Excuse me." He whipped his hand behind his waist, the tear still lingering on his fingertip.

Miss Clay lowered her chin. "I apologize for my unbecoming state. It is difficult to hear of such illness as your aunt's—" Her brow folded deeply in thought. "I—I am reminded of my mother's own struggle."

"Your mother?"

"Yes." She breathed in deeply and lifted her face. "My mother was ill for many months. I do not wish that on anyone." She drew close and put her hand on his arm. "I do not wish that on those who love the patient most." Her smile did not reach her eyes, but her words sounded sincere. "Mr. Taylor, I am so sorry." Even though she spoke a considerate kindness, there was something that slowed the pace of his overactive pulse, causing him to step back once more.

The woman was desperate with her apology, as if she herself had caused the misfortune—as if she needed him to believe her words for more than just comfort to him, but some kind of peace for herself.

Josie returned to the boardinghouse, spent from the tense afternoon at Mr. Taylor's home. After their desperate interaction in the parlor, his cook insisted Josie dine with them. Minnie, who had nearly ignored her on the path to Miss Young's, served them. She was just as aloof in the dining room as a servant as she was as an errand runner for Myrtle Bates's tonic.

Now, Josie hung up her bonnet and cloak on one of the empty hooks and decided to retreat to the garden before dinner was served. She had no desire to take up interviews with the newsletter gals or pretend to focus on books and papers with her roommates.

She craved anonymity. She longed to hide, even from herself. The anguish pressed outward from deep within. Would she explode from the pressure? Only if she could crawl out of her very being would she find freedom at last. Her spirit recoiled. Who had she become?

Fran stood over a pot with her back to the kitchen. Josie tiptoed across the stone floor and slipped out the open door without being noticed. She felt like a child, but even if in foolish tiptoeing, there was also some joy in her childishness. How she wished she were a child once more, wrapped in the arms of her mother, protected from the pitfalls of this world.

The sun bled red from beyond the garden walls, tingeing the sky in a subtle pink. Sparrows hopped along the stone, and a robin flew to its nest in the towering elm just beyond the building.

Josie ran her fingers over large rhubarb leaves, remembering her mother's warning, "Only the stalks, Josephine. We never use the leaves except to stop the weeds." Mother would lay out the leaves across fresh-tilled soil, protecting the bed from pesky weeds.

But to eat the leaves? That could kill you.

Josie dragged herself to the bench. Just like the rhubarb, she was also made of two parts. One—thankful and hopeful, knowing goodness would follow her if she remained faithful. But the other— part of a dangerous plot, twining its way around all the goodness, hiding her with its broad reach like the poisonous leaves of the rhubarb plant.

What horror to know that the man who had entrusted her to work in his mill, and whose money she would take, would grieve the next victim of Dr. Chadwick's twisted exploration by the very signal from Josie's hand?

She looked down at her tense fists and unfurled her fingers. There were no dirt stains as there had always been at home. When was the last time she'd felt the earth beneath her nails?

Falling to her knees, Josie began to part the canopies of plants, begging relief for her pristine fingertips. The weeds hid behind the rosy stalks then paraded around the cabbages that mounded further down the bed. Daggers of weeds invaded the fragrant marjoram and delectable thyme in the kitchen herb plot. Every plant had its purpose in Fran's dishes, and the weeds tried to force their death. Pluck, pluck, pluck. The cool soil clumps fell apart from the exposed tangle of roots. Josie tossed them onto the flagstone path by her knees. The sharp edges of the stones dug through her skirt and stabbed at her kneecaps, but she continued, feeling the urgency to lose her thoughts among the beds.

Josie would much rather be useful with her grubby fingers and sweating hairline than disturbing the earth for more frightful reasons. This was where she belonged. Among the life that smelled of a wholesome dinner and a helpful remedy. The treasures of life were here among the greens, pinks, browns, and purples. And the yellows. Such beauty in the yellow center of chamomile flowers—like a swollen light held up by the pure white petals. Josie plucked the pretty daisylike flower and twirled it about.

The sound of a whip spliced the air, disturbing her small dose of peace. A horse whinnied just beyond the garden wall. The back gate flew open and a woman burst inside, slamming it shut. Covered from head to foot in a long dark cloak, she leaned up against the gate like she had escaped something dreadful.

Josie sprang to her feet. As she drew close, the intruder removed her hood, revealing her face. Audra Jennings held no frown, but cheeks taut with an exhilarated smile and narrowed catlike eyes that Josie would hardly forget.

"Is anything the matter?" Josie cleared her throat as she rounded the center patch of leafy plants surrounding a birdbath.

Audra tilted her head back against the gate and loosened the tied ribbons around her neck. "The matter?" She shook her head, nibbling her lip as if she pondered a delicious secret. Perhaps she did.

"I see." Josie stepped back. *Dear weeds, I'd much rather spend my time with you than with that woman.* She found her pile of gnarled roots scattering the path beneath the rosemary shrub. Once more, she took to her knees and continued her chore. Yet all grew dim as Audra stood above her, her bruised boot tapping on the stone beside Josie.

"What do you know of me?" Audra hunched over farther,

darkening even the brightest flower.

"I know nothing." Josie continued to nudge aside the fuzzy lamb's ears without pressing too forcefully. "You appear to be well enough tonight. So, nothing is the matter, is it?"

"Right." Audra stood to her full height and cradled her wounded arm. "Although, if anyone should be questioned, I'd say it's the newest mill girl. She's found herself all over town, and it's only been a week."

Josie stared up at her.

"You've been seen on the arm of Mr. Taylor, so I've been told."

"He offered to show me to church."

She threw her head back and laughed. "Ah, yes, but to dine at his home also?" She strode away, heading to the kitchen door. "He is quite the catch. But somewhat of a bore, in my opinion." She stopped short of the doorstep, running her fingers along some creeping ivy. "Just mind where you tread, Miss Clay. There are webs in Gloughton that you do not want to be caught in."

As Audra slipped into the warm glow of the kitchen, Josie diverted her eyes down to the soil. What did that woman know about webs? Although she had seemed like a spying spider during the short time of Josie's stay here. If the woman knew anything at all, she'd know that it was Josie who was watching for her prey. The newest mill girl was the creeping spider, having just dined with her first victim a few short hours before.

Josie could not focus on weeding anymore. Anxiety stayed close, as if Audra had sprinkled it about as she passed by. Josie collected some lavender, marjoram, and spearmint to dry for quick remedies. When she passed through the kitchen, she greeted Fran quickly then tried to calm herself enough for the busy dining room.

Little Liesl found her at the washbasin, and together they sat at an empty table. The girl laid a volume on the table between their place settings. "Have you read William Shakespeare, Miss Josie?" she asked.

"My, that is quite a complicated English work you read, young

Liesl." Josie covered the leather binding with her hand. "My mother read it to me as a child. We'd act the scenes for Father on wintry mornings." She sat back against her chair and drew her hand to her lap.

Before slipping into the brighter corners of her mind, the aroma of the herbs in her apron pocket nudged her to the present moment. She gave a slight smile to Liesl, who then reached over and plunged a serving fork into the roasted chicken and leeks at the center of the round table. Josie served herself and, after a short prayer, began to eat. With every forkful to her mouth, the scent grew stronger. Perhaps the pungent smell of her garden work lingered on her hands even after a good washing? Her pulse made an erratic thrust in her chest, and she slid her eyes to the book.

What, will these hands ne'er be clean?

The tragedy spoke from the closed covers, not as Lady Macbeth, but in Josephine's own voice. Even if she had a future beyond this season as Alvin tried to convince her, would she wear the stains on her memory? Would she ever be able to wipe them away?

No prayer could erase the memory, she feared, no washing could make her clean.

Chapter Eight

Nearly all the apple trees along the main drive had bloomed, their pale petals washed by moonlight against the dark sky. The evening air was crisp, a soothing remedy for Braham's worn-out emotions as he walked to the main house. He caught a glimpse of the first stars of the night. If only he could reach up and pull away that dark canvas.

Lord, not too soon.

How cowardly a man was he, unable to handle the inevitable. His aunt was the oldest woman in town. He knew the time would come, but he wasn't expecting the flood of memories with Aunt Myrtle to throw him even further back. If he closed his eyes too long, he would sway with the rocking of a ship and cover his ears to the sounds of moaning and screaming and whips snapping against backs. Braham clutched at the fence that led up to the house, grounding himself to his reality.

The lit windows of the main house flickered up on the hill. The butler and maids must still be awake. He ran his hands through his hair. He did not care to speak to anyone. At least he'd not have to stumble through a dark house to find the family Bible his aunt had requested. Braham entered through the side entrance. He had never been comfortable entering through the front door like a guest or resident. Even though the late Mr. Bates had treated him as a son, Gerald would have none of it. He'd often reminded his father of his rightful inheritance and the true status of Braham, an orphan of an indentured servant. Mr. Bates would only hold his tongue. He'd not try to defend his own treatment of Braham. So, while Mr. Bates treated Braham with the utmost kindness, there was a line drawn and pointed out time and again. Whenever Braham entered this house, he assumed the customs of an employee, not a family member at all.

He ducked beneath the low ceiling of the hallway between the kitchen and pantry, the soft murmur of the servants at dinner in the kitchen mingling with the clink of utensils and dishes. He would try to make it through the house without being noticed. He pushed through the door to the dining room but froze in the threshold. Candlelight filtered through tobacco smoke hovering above the well-laid dining table.

Gerald Bates sat at one end, his riding boot slung up unmannerly on the table's corner. His elbow was propped beside a crystal canister of whiskey, and he held a cigar between his fingertips. Beside him, a man with a full silver beard stared at Braham. His eyes were large and round above a goblet at his lips.

"You have a visitor, it seems," the man spoke behind the gold rim.

Gerald dropped his leg with a loud stomp and glared at Braham. "Don't tell me you've taken the house as well?"

Braham bowed his head. "Pardon me." He ground his teeth at the spoiled heir's words.

"What are you doing here, Braham?" Gerald tapped off the ashes gathering at the tip of his cigar then sucked on it with a chest-heaving drag.

"I have come for the family Bible—" The glint in Gerald's eye promised challenge. Braham should have said *your* family Bible and avoided any ammunition thrown to this man's advantage. Yet he had been a legal ward of Gerald's father. "*Your* aunt requests it." Inwardly, Braham winced.

"Ah, I see." Gerald slid a more cordial look to his visitor, who tipped back his drink and set it down with a heavy fist.

Braham tugged at his coat lapel and cleared his throat. "I suggest you visit Aunt Myrtle at your earliest convenience. She is not well."

Gerald held his stare, no emotion on his face. His mustache was perfectly combed and his eyebrows trimmed. He was always groomed in a way that made him appear more statue than man.

Gerald gave a quick nod then broke his rigid stance and leaned toward his guest. "Mr. Bellingham, you have the honor of a premature introduction to the factory's manager."

The man, Mr. Bellingham, pushed back in his chair. The chair's burdened slats moaned. "Ah, let us talk shop tomorrow. For now, come have a drink." He reached for the canister, but Gerald was quick to slide it away from the guest.

"Sir, we shan't have much to talk about with Mr. Taylor. He is only on the labor side of things. Business matters are not his concern." Mr. Bellingham cocked an eyebrow. Gerald began to laugh through a long exhale of smoke. "We shall discuss more later. Go on then, Braham. Find that Bible for the old woman." Smoke continued to pour out his nostrils.

Braham was happy to leave the polluted room. He had descended from the sweetness of Aunt Myrtle's cottage to the brusque belly of Gerald's dealings. There was nothing more that Braham wanted than to excuse himself from this place.

He entered the dim parlor and reached for a lantern on the tidy desk. He struck a match and lit the wick, praying that he would find the Bible quickly and escape any more engagements with Gerald. Yet, as he began searching the shelves and tables and drawers, a foreboding overwhelmed his spirit. The lit dining room over his shoulder held a palpable darkness that not even the yellow glow of this lantern could chase away.

Miss Clyde had made a sharp announcement at the end of dinner that an important colleague of the owner, Mr. Bates Jr., would be given a tour of the factory promptly after their break for the morning meal. Every woman took great care to ready for the day. There were whispers among the women, prayers spoken with pleas of uneventful work, free of accidents. The workroom had harbored so much danger over the past weeks, and all were concerned about this tour to be given.

While Josie and Liesl left the dining room, Audra's sharp voice blurted among the whispering ladies. "It would serve that Bates right for having such carelessness with his northern exploits, I'd say."

Molly sneered with her arms crossed. "Oh Audra, you're just sore that he moved your family here from the swamps of Georgia." A few tinkles of laughter skipped about the crowd.

"Swamps?" Audra smacked her lips and rolled her eyes. "My, for such a reporter as you are, Molly O'Leary, you'd think you would know your geography better. There are no swamps on a cotton plantation." She emerged from the ladies and continued, "Only pests." She slipped out of sight as Liesl and Josie hurried to retrieve their cloaks and bonnets.

"I do not care for that woman," Liesl said while she tied a bow beneath her chin. "She did not like my friend who perished." The young girl dropped her laces and began to cry.

"There, there," Josie said, nudging her out of the way as Audra barreled out of the room, shoving past them. The cross woman only gave Josie a flick of her fiery hair, snatched her things from a hook, and left.

"Come along, Liesl. Let us go to the garden and collect some peppermint to put in our pockets. It is a pleasant scent and will keep you on your toes as you work." Josie tweaked the girl's cheek gently. A prayer tumbled unexpectedly from her heart—*Lord, keep this child safe.*

Liesl smiled. Josie repeated the prayer again with more fervor.

They greeted Fran as they passed through the kitchen, plucked a few leaves of the spicy herb, and tucked them into their apron pockets. Instead of going back through the kitchen, Josie and Liesl slipped out the garden gate. Josie did not feel comfortable with the conversations in the boardinghouse. She bore her own secrets. One day she might be the center of that chatter. She prayed that would not be so.

"Look!" Liesl drew close to Josie's side. "It is Mr. Bates himself." Beneath the row of trees that lined the factory's canal, a man stepped down from a carriage. He was tall and lean, wearing a top hat and a bright white cravat. His hands were folded at the small of his back as he waited at the side of the carriage. Another man, rounder and shorter, tumbled out. He blew his nose loudly in a handkerchief then tucked his disheveled mane beneath a crooked hat.

"Is this who we are to impress?" Josie pursed her lips and gave Liesl a playful wag of her brow. The girl giggled.

"Hallo," the tall man shouted in their direction, waving broadly.

"Oh no. We've been caught," Liesl cried, gripping Josie's hand tightly.

"Caught?" Josie swallowed hard. "We've done nothing wrong."

The man waited for them as they approached. "Ah, two strays, it seems." Mr. Bates Jr. was handsome. His teeth gleamed beneath a manicured mustache, and his dark lashes framed sparkling eyes.

"Pardon me, sir." Josie bowed her head and curtsied. "We were just in the garden, since it is not yet starting time."

He stared at her. She was not sure if it was a look of interest or irritation. "No, there is nothing wrong with that." He turned to the shorter man. "You see, Mr. Bellingham, the women are given the most wonderful chances to thrive, even beyond the factory floor. We have gardens, libraries, and even a small printing press amidst our ladies." He chuckled.

Josie was just as surprised as Mr. Bellingham appeared to be. She'd seen a small kitchen garden and shelves lined with books, and knew of a few women who'd written a newsletter together. But the mill boardinghouse was not hardly as grand as Mr. Bates described it.

"Our pristine record of factory success is matched in the life-styles given to these farm girls and women of high ambition." He tugged at his collar and addressed Josie. "Would you be so kind as to allow Mr. Bellingham to escort you inside, Miss—"

"Miss Clay." Josie barely spoke around the lump in her throat. Mr. Bellingham's eyes were unlit beads above a hungry smile. He held out his arm to her.

"Oh no!" Liesl exclaimed. "Please, Miss Clay, take me back inside. I forgot my bobbin basket." She tugged at Josie's sleeve.

"I apologize, sirs." Josie willingly stepped away. "I will help little Liesl, if you do not mind. We have only a few moments till the water resumes."

The men appeared dazed but nodded in dismissal. She and Liesl hurried back to the garden gate. When they were safely inside the walls, Josie leaned into the girl and breathed, "Thank you."

"You are welcome, miss," Liesl replied. "But you know as well as I do that my bobbin basket stays in the factory."

Josie stepped aside, brushing up against a large juniper shrub. "I do. And why did you fib?"

"I did not like the look that man gave you."

"Neither did I." She was grateful for Liesl's quick thinking, praying for the girl a third time. Walking into work on the arm of that man would stir up plenty of questions. Josie had drawn enough attention to herself tending to Amelia. She'd not run the risk of a soiled reputation too.

"And besides, it wasn't just me who fibbed." Liesl strolled down the garden path. "That Mr. Bates hardly spoke the truth. We've had three women hurt in accidents, one dead." She loosened her bonnet tie. "Pristine? What does that mean?"

"Clean, unspoiled." Josie followed her. The girl's mention of death nagged at Josie's light mood.

Liesl twirled around with her finger to her chin, appearing to be in deep contemplation. "I suppose Mr. Taylor has tried to make it clean."

"I suppose." Josie brushed past her and stepped into the warm kitchen.

"Liesl, do you think Mr. Taylor is a good manager?"

"Oh yes." She snuck a roll from Fran's pan while the cook rustled about in the cupboard. "He's kind. Tries his best. But a woman *did* die under his watch."

Josie clung to the banister going up to the foyer. "That is unfortunate."

"Accidents are bound to happen," Fran called out from behind some tins. "Mr. Taylor is as good as they come."

"I have little reason to think otherwise," Josie assured the cook before they left the kitchen, and then she assured herself also. Josie said a prayer for Mr. Taylor. She hoped that such a good-natured fellow was not at fault for the terrible accidents that had occurred—and would occur.

Braham clenched his teeth, determined to finish up his morning inspection. Ever since the last woman perished, he made sure he would never let it happen again. He could still recall the metal in her chest and the violent red seeping through her shirt. Gerald had been furious to learn of the incident. The words in his letter to Braham nearly burst into flame on the parchment.

Braham had often wondered if there was some stipulation that might take away his position of managing the factory. Each accident chipped away at his confidence. Now, the man who might have the power to destroy Braham's future waited just outside the doors.

After carefully examining the last section—Josie Clay's section—he headed to his office. Miss Clay had invaded his thoughts more often than he'd care to admit, especially after the kindness she showed his aunt at dinner. Even Miss Young was impressed by the knowledgeable Miss Clay. She'd offered her to assist in conjuring remedies when her factory contract was up.

Braham was more impressed, however, that Josie announced her loyalty to stay on longer than a year, the minimum expectation.

Now, as his boots struck the floor with long strides amid the softer, quicker patters of women filtering past him, he smiled equally at each one. But above all else, he anticipated Josie Clay's warm greeting this morning.

These thoughts would not do at all.

His breath hitched, and he grimaced. All his musings fled at the sight of Gerald and Bellingham entering among the last of the women, their top hats towering above the sea of bonnets. Braham turned into the waiting room and headed to his office.

He stopped at Miss Clyde's desk. "Please do not send Mr. Bates in until the looms have started."

"Very well. But Mr. Bates's directions will be followed over yours," she barked as she arranged items on her desk, a typical tone when Mr. Bates arrived. Miss Clyde had an obvious allegiance to him.

Braham entered his office and stood in front of the glass. The women took their places along the aisles. Miss Clay helped the bobbin girl with her basket. They patted their pockets and smiled at each other with a look of secrecy. The corners of Braham's mouth twitched. He wasn't sure if he should be concerned or if he had witnessed an obvious friendship growing between the two. He chose to accept the latter as the bobbin girl had hardly smiled the entire six months she was here. Miss Clay might have mysteries about her, but her bright spirit was difficult to deny.

The door swung open just as the rush of water roared through the pipes above. Bates and Bellingham burst into the room.

"Braham, I see you have chosen your watch over hospitality for our guest?" Gerald tossed his hat atop Braham's desk.

"Ah, forgive me." Braham ignored Gerald. He extended a hand to Mr. Bellingham. "Welcome to Gloughton Mill, sir."

"Good morning, Mr. Taylor." The near-limp hand of the guest reminded Braham of the good master Gerald Bates Sr.'s wisdom: *"Grip strongly with enthusiasm. There is nothing more appealing than a man with a solid handshake."*

Mr. Bellingham was not appealing at all—in personality nor in strength. The pale fellow pushed his chin into the folds of his neck as he examined the corners and ceilings and walls. He then peered out the window, his hot breath fogging up the glass while the machines began to work. "It seems the view is rather distracting," he grunted. "I can see why accidents so easily occur." He turned an arched brow to Braham.

"Distracting, sir? I beg to differ. This is the best view of the main room. My overseers keep a keen watch over the machinery—"

"Machinery? Ah, there seems more than machinery to keep their attention." A devilish grin crept onto Bellingham's face. He exchanged looks with Bates then they both burst into laughter. Gerald sprang from the desk and slapped Braham on the back. The sting was less painful, though, than the displeasure of being part of some callous joke. He suspected what they meant. And it was improper. Downright crude.

"Don't mind my manager here, old man," Gerald jested. "We are often perplexed as to how to scrub off the green behind his ears." Another mutual roar of chuckles filled the office.

Braham's anger simmered. "There is a difference between misunderstanding due to naivete and choosing to ignore someone's humor for propriety's sake."

Gerald's grin melted into a contemptuous glare. Bellingham only cleared his throat and looked down at his belly—his shoes were no doubt hidden from his view.

Braham continued, "Now to business." He stepped to the chair behind his desk and pulled it out with a sharp screech. "What exactly would you like to see first, Mr. Bellingham? We can start in the carding room, if you'd like?"

Gerald's stare cooled. "Yes, let us start there. Mr. Bellingham is a keen investor for many establishments." He snatched his hat from the desk. "He has had his eye on Gloughton since my father became less involved in the business side of our factory."

"Investor?" Braham pushed his chair back under the desk. "Mr. Bates, you seem to provide adequately for our mill." Braham gave a genuine smile, for he knew it was true. "Do we plan an expansion?"

The two men passed a look, a secret look, but less innocent than that of Miss Clay and the bobbin girl. Gerald hooked his thumbs in his coat pockets. "I'd consider it more of a transaction than expansion."

Braham's stomach jolted. "Do you mean to sell the factory?"

Gerald avoided eye contact and pulled the door open. "It is my right, Braham."

A flood of relief should wash over Braham at the thought of cutting his ties to this man once and for all. But with Mr. Bellingham promising little in the way of a worthy owner for the late Mr. Bates's family-owned mill, only disquiet howled through Braham's mind. He dared not ask the questions that pulsed at his temples and begged to be spoken.

Could Bellingham continue the good work that Mr. Bates had started, and what was in store for Braham's position at the factory?

Chapter Nine

Josie was the last woman to retrieve her bonnet and cloak that evening. She'd purposely waited for Mr. Bates and Mr. Bellingham to leave before her. Her skin was afire with humiliation. Had she imagined the oaf's hand trailing along her back as they passed her station today? Another shiver coursed through her veins at the thought of it.

She dragged her feet across the room and into the hallway, plucking the bits of cotton from her apron at a careful rate. Anything to procrastinate and keep away from the attention of those men. The last few women stepped into the orange daylight just as Josie tied her bonnet. The slamming main door echoed down the hallway. The racket of looms and shouts of overseers were only lingering shadows in her ears. Nothing could be heard besides her own breath. Her heels clicked on the polished floor. Had she waited so long as to raise suspicions about her delay? At least she'd noticed Miss Clyde leave with the other workers.

Josie passed by the waiting room window, which was filled with the same strange sunlight when she'd arrived in Gloughton. Her stomach knotted. Distant footsteps sounded behind her. She spun around, a chill spreading up her spine. The creak of a door crept along the silence. Mr. Taylor appeared just outside his office side door. He did not see her but kept his head down as he thrust a key into the door to the rest of the factory. He disappeared inside the room of settled cotton bits and sleeping cogs.

Hurrying, Josie pulled open the main door and escaped interrupting Mr. Taylor at this hour. She was tempted to accuse that unbecoming Bellingham of not keeping his hands to himself. However, a woman was not expected to complain about such things.

The courtyard was barren in the onset of dusk. Shadows were

dark and ominous at either end of the vast expanse of brick-paved ground, especially beneath the large elm tree where Alvin had left her that first day. A shift beneath the tree's canopy tricked her eyes. Was someone there? Another movement affirmed there was. She raced across the courtyard to the door of the boardinghouse. As she fiddled with the doorknob, the voices of a man and woman carried from beneath the tree, now only a few yards from where she stood.

"You never said you were coming." The woman's voice was agitated but disguised in a whisper.

"I come and go when I please. You know that." There was a low growl beneath the soft voice.

"I was not ready—I have not had a chance—"

"You've done enough. It won't be long now—"

"But what about him? I—I don't know how to tell him. It will break his heart."

"No, the man has no heart."

Josie barreled inside, unease shaking her frame. She could not bear to eavesdrop on some sort of lovers' dealing. Who was the woman, and whose heart might she break? Josie hung up her bonnet and cloak then descended the steps to the kitchen and escaped to the garden. The conversation needled her more and more. She hurried down the flagstone path and looked through the gate's iron rods. Still as can be, she strained her ear. The tree was just over the wall. There were no longer voices. The clop of horse's hooves grew louder and a wagon appeared with Mr. Taylor at the reins. Josie had just left him at the mill. He was not caught up in secret meetings beneath the elm. And he was not the heartless man those two whispered about. Braham was anything but heartless. As his carriage crawled away, Josie welcomed the warm gush of nearby memories. His kindness, his gentlemanly hospitality, and his willingness to hire her.

She leaned forward, pressing her face against the gate. His wagon crossed the bridge then passed by the cemetery's lilacs that no doubt filled his nose with a pleasant farewell to a hard day's work. While she imagined herself also enjoying the sweet fragrance beside the handsome manager, he looked over his shoulder and caught her staring. She gasped and pulled away. Heat raided her cheeks, and her hand flew to her mouth.

Mr. Taylor slowed his horse and raised a gloved hand to the brim of his top hat. His wide smile sent a flurry of wings flapping within Josie's frame. All she could do was offer a weak wave of her hand. He wagged his head, his shoulders shaking with a laugh. Mr. Taylor snapped the reins and disappeared into the village.

Josie twirled on her toes and fell back against the garden wall. She rolled her eyes at her carelessness, but she could not refrain from smiling. What was it about that man that caught her feelings and released them in a current within her?

She bit her lip. She knew what it was. It was his goodness. The same goodness she'd seen in the love between her mother and father; the same goodness she'd witness when loved ones would care so tenderly for their sick. 'Twas the same goodness she craved for her own life. If only he knew how closely knit he would be with deceit by her hand. Had he invited friend or enemy to dine with him on Sunday evening?

Oh, how Josie so wanted to be the friend and not the foe.

She kept to herself at dinner, struggling between wishing this wait for death was over and fighting the shame of desiring such a thing. Her roommates climbed up the stairs ahead of her, little Liesl bouncing ahead, occasionally looking back at her. The child's eagerness would not move her any faster. Josie peered out the windows that looked down upon the factory courtyard. Night was a black cloak covering the looming mill. A yellow glow seemed to sit upon the top step of the factory stoop. Josie hesitated at the top stair.

Who was there? Surely Mr. Taylor had not returned at this hour?

Fear laced the back of her neck. She prayed that Alvin was not waiting for her. The hoot of an owl seemed to scare away the light. It vanished as if it had never existed. Perhaps the person with the light had gone inside the factory walls. She continued to watch, waiting for the office windows to brighten. But only her reflection stared back at her now. Was the glow a reflection as well? She hurried up to the third floor.

After a frustrating day, Braham's anger had cooled at the sight of Miss Clay blushing through the garden gate. The rest of the way home, he allowed himself the distraction of thinking on her pretty face while he admired the setting sun. But as he went about the usual routine of caring for his horse and visiting with his aunt, his troubled stomach had stopped him from eating much. He retired early while his aunt snoozed by the fire. Braham tried to recall the interaction with Miss Clay once more, hoping to will away his nerves, yet the woman's sweet bashfulness and the setting sun were not strong enough to keep his mind from its darkening spiral.

After locking up the factory for the evening, he had passed Audra in an intimate conversation with Gerald. Back and forth they went, those two. An unlikely attraction—one that seemed to head nowhere but gossip. Gerald was too proud to court a woman of her meager status. And Audra? She was not one who'd do well with any kind of promise, matrimonially speaking. Just the other night Braham had seen her disappear across town on the arm of a stranger.

Most frustrating of all, Audra obviously pulled Gerald north with her flirtations. Would his visits become more frequent? When Gerald was away, Braham was firmly grounded in his purpose to do well for his late master. But Gerald was a spying hawk when he visited. His claws were just inches away from all that was good in Braham's life. Today was no different, except maybe Gerald's talon had finally snagged Braham by the neck.

How could a loyal son sell all that his father had worked for? Would Braham really have to answer to that man Bellingham?

Braham tossed and turned all night, finally throwing back the bedsheets with the first sound of a mourning dove. An alarming thought pried his eyes open and refused to let them close again. If an accident occurred now, while Gerald was here negotiating a sale, he'd have every right to nullify his father's last wishes and kick Braham out. The suspicion of such a possibility was materializing more and more. He'd watched Gerald inspect the belts and wheels.

"The accident rate is like nothing my father witnessed, for sure," he had divulged beneath his growl when Mr. Bellingham browsed the records.

Braham dressed quickly and crept through the dark house, hesitating when the clock struck four chimes. Nearly an hour before he usually left. He lit a candle and wrote a quick note to his aunt so she'd not worry about his early disappearance, then set off to Gloughton.

The moist air cooled his nose and filled his lungs with a chilled gust. Whatever sleep he'd struggled to summon fell away. There was something about this dark hour—on the brink of a new day and the final slumber of an old one—that invigorated Braham to accomplish much. As a young boy, he often woke to the soft hum of his father's best friend, Howie, smoking his pipe around the dying embers in the slaves' quarters. If Howie noticed Braham awake, he'd pull on his pipe, put a large finger to his plump lips, and then whisper, "Ain't quite done with yesterday, son; go back to sleep." Braham would close his eyes but wonder what yesterday was waiting for. How he'd wish that some of those yesterdays would stop creeping into his todays, especially when he'd long for his mother—and later on, his father.

While the horse trotted down the narrow main street, Braham swiped at his eyes with dew-laden gloves. He gave a quiet signal to the horse to speed up at the bridge to the mill. Yet when he came to the other side, a golden light bounced off the stone wall beyond the gate to the boardinghouse garden. He pulled his wagon to the side of the wall and tied his horse to a post. Maybe Fran would have something to settle his stomach. He'd often found her recipes better than his own cook's. Braham fiddled with the gate and opened it carefully.

The fragrance of herbs and flowers was nearly medicinal itself, and he breathed deeply. As he stepped onto the small flagstone path, the tip of his boot knocked against something—or more accurately, someone. A person sprang up to standing.

"Oh sir!" Miss Clay exclaimed, rubbing the side of her leg. "I—I did not hear you approach."

Braham released the gate, which shut loudly against its frame. "Did I hurt you?" He leaned toward her, bouncing his attention from her leg to her wide eyes. "I am very sorry." He reached his hand to hers but then pulled it back.

She pressed her chin to her shoulder. Shaking her head, she said, "I am fine."

Braham shifted his weight. Miss Clay's hair was unpinned; cascading waves of gold rippled across one shoulder. Her face seemed kissed with recent sleep. A slight pink blush across one cheek marked where she may have slept against her hand. He'd never seen a woman so beautiful, so untarnished by the toil of the day. All that fragrant breath he'd borrowed had depleted from his lungs. He found it difficult to do anything but stare.

"I—I came here—" Why had he come? He diverted his gaze to the quiet garden. Above the walls, the black sky smudged into gray. "I—I need an elixir."

"An elixir?" She straightened and cocked her head.

"Um, yes. My stomach has been—" Uneasy? In knots? "Upset. I was on my way to inspect the machinery one last time, and I thought I'd have Fran—" Before he could explain further, Miss Clay ducked down among the plants and came up with a handful of herbs.

"Come inside. I can make you a tea I have often made for myself." She did not wait for him to follow her but swiveled around, leaving behind a scent of rose and mint. Braham wondered if the fragrance was from the garden or Miss Clay. He strode down the path and ducked beneath the low kitchen doorway.

Two candelabras sat upon the long table, casting an amber

sheen on the wooden surface. Miss Clay stood in front of a neat kitchen fire blazing beneath a hanging pot.

He unbuttoned his coat in the warm place and lowered onto the edge of the bench. All his nerves from before were shoved aside by the quiet anticipation of being alone with this woman. She'd pricked his curiosity. He had seen her help Amelia and tend to the little bobbin girl, but now he would receive her care. Even if he did not really know her at all, he could think of nowhere else he'd rather spend this slice between asleep and awake. Only when she sat across from him at the table, her round face alive and bright, was he fully assured that this was truth and not a dream.

Braham swallowed the earthy spiced liquid. It warmed his belly with a surprising calm. The woman across from him mirrored the calm in her peaceful state, unlike any other time he'd seen her. She drank her cup with relaxed shoulders. Although he sat in a meager boardinghouse kitchen, with an employee beneath his own position, the sense of home blanketed him now.

Was this the life his parents could have once dreamed of? Sitting in the quiet morning, sharing a hot drink at a comfortable kitchen table? How he'd wished their own ambitions hadn't fallen to the misfortune of hardship and disease.

"How does it taste?" Miss Clay spoke from the rim of her cup. "Does it help at all?"

"Yes, surprisingly so." He placed his drink down. "Where did you find this remedy? It does not taste the same as Fran's."

"My mother. She taught me much from our small garden."

"Your mother." The flame's reflection danced upon her nose and down along her dainty cheekbone. The reddened spot was not visible now. Braham lowered his gaze to the sage-colored liquid in his cup. "Do you miss her?"

Only the popping of the fire and the cooing of a dove outside could be heard. Miss Clay's brow furrowed. "Very much. She would never believe all that has changed." A grimace marred her lips, and her long lashes fluttered against her cheeks.

"My mother is also gone." Braham tapped his cup with his finger, while Miss Clay's slender fingers encircled her cup with white knuckles. "She passed away on my journey here as a young boy."

Miss Clay's hand slipped to the table. "Journey from where?"

"From Ireland. The ship was diseased. My father and I were fortunate to survive." He breathed in the scent of mint and earth and last night's baking. Yet the stench of virus and the smell of his mother's hair as he lay against her lifeless body were on the very edge of his senses. He twisted in his seat, the heel of his boot striking the floor as he forced himself into a different memory. "My father found work at a plantation in Georgia, and I found favor in the eyes of the late Mr. Bates, more as a son than a serving boy." He faced the fire. "He became my legal guardian after Father passed away." He slid a look at her from the corner of his eyes.

She tilted her head and asked, "Do you remember much of Ireland? Traveling from a country far away is hard to imagine. I've never been farther from my home than Gloughton."

Braham was thankful for her focus on the lesser tragedy of leaving his homeland behind. Although he could not speak as lightly as he'd like. Could he remember anything besides the impoverished life of begging on Dublin's streets or the rats who'd shared the same meals as he had most nights? "Too much has filled up my mind since then. Some good, much bad." He spoke through clenched teeth. "I only look forward, not behind." His nostrils flared. "Or at least I try."

She nodded. "Yes, that is a good perspective. I hope, one day, that I can rest assured and never look back." She pressed her lips together, eyeing her finger trailing along the rim of her mug. Silence sat between them again. She seemed to be lost in thought as she fiddled with her drink, while Braham found himself in the very present, wondering about the beauty across from him.

"What would Mother think of me now?" Miss Clay spoke low, more to herself than him. Braham opened his mouth to speak, but with a sudden movement she pushed back on the bench. "I must finish readying for the day." She stood, placed her mug in a wash-basin. Braham also stood. "Pardon me, sir." She dipped into a quick curtsy, refusing to look into his eyes, then swiveled around and headed toward the hallway. She hesitated. "Mr. Taylor?" She turned to face him. "Is it usual for someone to tend to the mill at night?"

"At night?"

"Yes. I thought I saw a light near the factory door when I stood at an upstairs window last night."

His stomach rejected all the peaceful effects of the tea. "Oh, really?"

She shook her head. "It must have been a reflection, now that I think about it. No light filled any factory windows after it disappeared. Good morning, sir." A faint smile tipped her lips, and she left him.

Braham approached the fire, placing his mug in the bin. The warmth of the blaze did little to heat an icy shiver crawling across his skin. He couldn't decide if the chill was because of Miss Clay's unsettling inquiry about the factory, or the simple fact that Josie Clay was no longer near.

Chapter Ten

Josie climbed the stairs with reluctance. She had not been so content in conversation since the days when she tended to her father by the warmth of their own kitchen fire. Mr. Taylor's attention left her with more than just comfort though. He'd drawn out a piece of her soul that she'd kept hidden for so long. His story—his loss—mirrored her own. Had she ever understood a man before? She could hardly understand her father. Especially now, when he was caught up in such schemes. But she'd hardly spoken with a man about anything more than her duties and instructions for healing. Mr. Taylor's countenance reflected all she had felt when Mother passed.

Josie must be more grieved than she imagined. Maybe lonely. In this place filled with women at every turn and overseers and operatives dotted about the factory? Yet Josie knew her loneliness eclipsed her peace because of the wall she had hidden behind these many weeks. She had not felt like herself at all until Braham Taylor sat with her this morning.

"Miss Josie!" Abigail ran up the stairs from behind her. "You have a visitor," she whispered breathlessly, her eyes wide with an intensity that could only be interpreted as warning.

Visitor? Was Mr. Taylor asking after her? Heat filled her cheeks. She followed the serving girl down the stairs, suddenly aware that her hair was down and bouncing along her shoulders. Her blush deepened. She had sat with Mr. Taylor all this time without realizing her appearance. She quickly tied her hair back with a ribbon as she descended. Yet, when she turned at the landing, she noticed the stout grave robber standing in the parlor below. Her hand fell, leaving a half-tied bow in her hair.

At the bottom stair, Abigail leaned in, whispering loudly, "You're not allowed male callers during the week."

"He's hardly a caller." Josie rushed past. "I will only be a moment."

Alvin did not look at her but surveyed the maid, who retreated to the kitchen. Josie took a rigid stance with her hands on her hips. How foolish for him to arrive here at this time.

Josie kept a watchful glance over her shoulder until the maid disappeared. She whipped around. "Do you have a letter from Father?"

"I do." He pulled a folded piece of parchment from his coat pocket. Josie snatched it and strode to the fire, leaning against the mantel as she read:

My Dear Josephine,

Please do not despise me, Daughter. I could not bear to tell you my involvement at Chadwick's. Forgive me for not return- ing to you. To face you and know what I've dragged you into—it has been my worst nightmare.

There is nothing I can do to change the past, but hear me now— Hurry, Josephine.

Has Alvin told you? Men creep about my place, warning me with cocked rifles if I do not supply them. And worse, Dr. Chadwick has found my sin out. He knows that I was seen in New York. The man who was once a friend during your mother's illness now threatens to turn me in if you do not hurry with a replacement.

What am I to do, my dear Josephine? All are against me.

My time is coming to an end—I am so ashamed.

I love you with all my heart,

Father

"No, no—" She lifted a desperate brow and cupped her hand over her mouth.

"What is it?" Alvin neared.

"The men, Dr. Chadwick, they. . ." She could hardly form words as her heart ached for the wretched man whom she loved more than any living person. Alvin slid the letter from her fingers. She was too forlorn to resist.

Alvin read beneath his breath. He groaned. "Blasted Chadwick!" He tossed the letter on the hearth.

Josie sank down beside the letter and slowly folded it up. She should burn it. Who might find her out with this evidence? But she could not let it go—not with her father's familiar script, and his heart, on the page. "How did Dr. Chadwick find out?"

Alvin sighed. "I told him. But he cannot call on the authorities, not with evidence stacked against him."

"What evidence?"

"I know every grave in Ainsley that sits empty." Alvin's nostrils flared. "An anonymous tip to any law enforcer who is willing to come all the way down here will incriminate the doctor, whose secret laboratory is covered in blood and bile." He placed a hand on Josie's shoulder. "I will remind the doctor of this as soon as I leave here. Do not worry."

Josie took in a jagged breath. Alvin's assurance was only a slight drop in her anxious sea. "But the others, the men with rifles. . . threatening my poor father?" Tears stung her eyes at the terror aflame in her childhood home.

"That is why I have come, Josephine." A flash of devilish anticipation crossed his eyes. "It is time."

"What—" Josie's mouth went dry. "Not Miss Bates?" All she could consider was Mr. Taylor. The poor man—

"Nay, not her." Alvin tucked his hat beneath his arm and rubbed his gloved hands together in front of the fire. "A man in town. Visits the tavern often. Found out last night that his heart gave out."

Josie wagged her head. "The poor soul."

"Do not worry—he had no family. Practically a hermit, so I've been told." Alvin gazed into the fire.

"He had breath, did he not? That is valuable, regardless." At the distant shuffling of women from above, she glanced to the stairs, terrified that she'd been so caught up in these matters to forget to keep a keen watch out for any witnesses.

"It is an intricate thing, Miss Clay." Alvin scratched his chin. The confident man was not so confident as to look in her eyes right now. "That is why I have decided to wait on supplying Chadwick."

"What?" Her remorse for a stranger fled, leaving behind fear of her almost murderer hollowing out her stomach. She leaned and whispered, "But he's already desperate enough to blackmail my father…" She squeezed her eyes shut, blocking out the grave robber who had relinquished her own body to the doctor. "What might he do to us?"

"I said I would stop him."

Josie swallowed hard. "Be swift, Alvin. And tell those other men to leave Father be." Had she unashamedly found necessity in her role as a grave robber's spy?

Her shattered world was grinding to dust.

Alvin gave a sharp nod then began toward the door. "The funeral is during your working hours. You'll come as soon as you are off."

"Wait!" Josie ran up to him, staying behind the door, not wanting to be seen with this man by any outsider. "How will I know what to do?"

"Do not worry." Alvin's emotionless face softened. "Help will be waiting for you beside the lilacs. Don't forget to wear black." He adjusted his hat and stepped into the courtyard. "Oh, and don't forget your ointment. We need it just in case disease is about. Be there at half past seven. That's when the gravedigger is set to arrive."

Alvin slipped away, and Josie slowly shut the door. She pressed her palm against it, choking back a sob. The clanging from the kitchen pierced her ears. Her heart skipped a beat, and she swallowed back tears.

Was Mr. Taylor still here? Had Abigail informed him about this unexpected visitor? Josie rushed to the kitchen. Her employer was gone.

Fran glowered at her as she tied her apron. "Abigail told me you had a male caller. That is not allowed at this time, you know."

"I know." Josie slumped her shoulders. "Was Mr. Taylor here?"

"Aye. He just slipped through the garden."

"Oh." Josie sighed. "Did he know about that man?"

Fran shook her head but pursed her lips. "Well, what did the man want? Abigail said you did not appear very happy to see him. Was it the same man from your father's farm last Sunday?"

Josie nodded. Her blood raced, and her eyes pricked with moisture.

"So?"

"There's been a death." She grazed her lip with her teeth. "I am to go pay my respects this evening."

The cook's sullen face softened. "I am sorry."

"So am I." Josie shook her head then headed back upstairs.

What gruesome schemes she was part of among these hardworking women, although she was relieved that she'd not mourn one of them tonight. And she was grateful that Miss Bates was alive.

Mr. Taylor had trusted her enough to share some of his story, yet he did not know that Josie Clay would be directing the hands of men captured by bloodlust, greed, and desperation. She refused to think that her father's greatest motivation was greed when he chose to help with the bodies. Desperation was a terrible temptress. However, she fought to rise above the devastation of Father's weaving her into this wicked plot.

Braham looked over his shoulder, wondering if someone followed him. Just moments ago, whispers traveled across the courtyard followed by the click of a door. He could barely see anything through the fog. As his eyes adjusted to the dim morning, he was certain that he was alone.

He approached the mill door, which was firmly shut and locked. There did not appear to be evidence of any kind of tampering. Miss Clay must be right—she'd seen a reflection only. Braham looked back again. The thick layer of fog hovered above the paved courtyard. Yet the lit windows of the boardinghouse gleamed in the mist. It was nearly starting time, and Braham had wasted his early arrival sitting in the kitchen.

He grinned. No, not a waste. Admittedly, his mood had shifted greatly, even if his conversation with Miss Clay took him to dark corners of his memory. The ease of her company, the solitude of sitting with someone who had no notions about him, filled him with a new sense of hope. Josie Clay might have some mystery behind her quiet mumblings to herself and her affiliation with that suspicious man who brought her here, but she donned a trustworthy spirit. Her innocence shone bright, like the lanterns through the fog.

He unlocked the door and grabbed the knob. His finger ran along a ridge on the smooth metal surface. Braham held up his lantern. "What's this?" He removed his glove with his teeth and picked away at a glob of wax with his fingernail. There was splattered wax all down the door. A couple of drops had hardened on the brick stoop.

"Mr. Taylor?" Miss Clyde's sharp tone cut into the cool air.

Braham spun around. His lantern swung from his hand, nearly knocking into the brick wall. "Whoa." He righted it carefully then stuffed his glove into his pocket. "You startled me, Miss Clyde."

The pointy woman raised a brow and looked him up and down. "You appeared to be in a strange train of thought." She stepped up to his level and examined the door. "What then?"

"What do you mean?"

"What was that train of thought?"

"Do you not see it?"

"See it?" She looked down her nose and continued to stare at the door.

"Here." Braham held the light at just the right angle to reveal the mess of wax.

She scrunched her nose as she squinted, then stood straight. "It appears to be wax, Mr. Taylor."

"Exactly."

"Well? What is the problem, sir?"

"Did you dare to bring a candle anywhere near this facility, Miss Clyde?" Braham hoped she would say yes. He could lightly reprimand her and shake his suspicion of tampering.

"Sir, if you remember, I have been part of this mill since the first day your guardian opened the place. I would never bring an open flame anywhere near this factory." She spat her words. "Besides, it doesn't appear that anyone entered the door. Those of us with keys know not to use candles." Her usual bitter countenance soured even more.

Only Miss Clyde, Braham, and Gerald had keys. And as much as he disliked Gerald, he knew the man would never take such a risk to the property. Especially not now, with his plan to profit by selling the place.

Braham cleared his throat and pushed the door open. "Of course. So then. Who has been about, not only with a candle near a mill of cotton, but with an unsteady hand to cause such a mess?"

"There is not much to steal, Mr. Taylor, and there has been no fire." Miss Clyde briskly entered the dark hallway and lit the gas lights. "Perhaps a beggar was out last night. You know, I've noticed that ruffian who accompanied Miss Clay lurking about."

Braham grimaced.

Miss Clyde continued, "However, you might want to hold another meeting with the girls to remind them of the rules."

Braham gritted his teeth then barreled down the hallway.

"Will you not go to your office first?"

"No. I must check on the equipment before the girls arrive."

"Why would you be concerned about that?" Miss Clyde called to him.

"It is what I do every day, Miss Clyde. We cannot afford another accident." He did not expect Gerald to give him a high recommendation to Bellingham, but Braham was concerned that he'd need to impress the prospective buyer in order to stay on at Gloughton Mill. The more Braham pined over this situation, the more certain he was that the terms of the trust would not hold up if the factory was sold. Would Gerald pass up his chance at his trust money to let go of the mill? Although he might no longer need it, depending on the sum Bellingham was willing to pay for the factory. Braham's throat tightened as he fumbled with the door to the factory rooms. His future was bleak, indeed.

He made his way between the rows of machines, checking each loom and pipe, each band and wheel. He came to Miss Clay's station, checked all the nearby machinery with care, and continued on. On his way back down the row, he stopped at Miss Clay's once more. Just to be certain.

All day, Braham kept a watchful eye on the women, wondering if any of them had attempted to enter the factory. He held a quick meeting at the first break, reminding them of the severity of using open flames and that if they ever needed to retrieve a forgotten item, they must wait until the next work morning.

Miss Clay caught his eye more than once as the day went on. Each time, she'd smile then return to her work. She could very well be considered under suspicion at this point—but he'd rather assume she only cared for his approval.

Just before the noonday meal, a screech went through the place. Braham immediately gave the signal for the water to be shut off. Exactly as he had planned after the last accident with Amelia. He rushed to the area where a group of women had huddled around. His overseers followed behind him. Miss Clay was in the very middle of the huddle.

"What is it?" He pushed through the crowd. The women moved out of his way. He towered over Miss Clay and an injured woman.

"Her fingers are mangled," Miss Clay said. The woman moaned, tears streaming down her reddened face. Braham tried to remain calm, but the fact that yet another accident had occurred, no matter his watchful eye, weighted his shoulders with grim defeat. He knelt down beside Miss Clay, who was wrapping the injured hand with her apron.

"May I tend to her?" she asked. Her voice did not carry the forcefulness it had when Amelia was hurt. This time, she was respectful and eager. Her sapphire gaze dried up any words that formed on his tongue. He merely nodded then helped both women out of the room.

"A shuttle flew from a loom and slammed against my hand," the woman moaned as they stepped into the hall. "I've been here two years. I have never been injured before."

"At least it was only your hand. Imagine if—" Miss Clay's face blanched, and she flung a gaze between Braham and the woman. She bit her lip and looked away.

She implied a more dangerous wound—or possible fatality. Braham swiveled on his heel to return to the woman's station. He barked orders at his overseer to hold off on powering up again. He inspected all around. The loom's wooden shuttle was clear across the aisle on the floor, split in two. He could not tell exactly why it had flown off, but he'd never seen a shuttle so destroyed.

Braham had not inspected close enough. Did he really need to though? The factory had only been open for a few years, and it was well run before his uncle had passed away. Either Braham was forsaking a vital task of managing the place, or his guardian had left him with machinery that needed more repair than use.

Reluctantly, Braham requested that Tom repair the loom before the power started up again.

"Quickly, Tom!"

Anxiety snaked around his chest as he spied Gerald and Mr. Bellingham standing at his office window.

Chapter Eleven

Miss Josie, are you very sad?" Liesl asked as she lay on their bed with her diary at her knees.

Josie nodded. She placed her hat on her head and adjusted the black veil that hung from the brim. She unfolded her shawl from the dresser beside the window. Her movements were reflected in the mirror above, but she could not look at herself as she readied for the funeral. She could hardly form a thought in her distressed mind. Liesl did not know that Josie's sadness was not in mourning but because she pitied herself. That man who now lay in a wooden box, waiting for the desecration by some unknown physician, was nobody she knew. Only an acquaintance of her father's farmhand. At least, that was the explanation she gave. A far-fetched assumption based on Alvin's mention of frequenting the same tavern as the deceased. Josie tried not to lie. Her life was as dark as this black veil she wore on her face. More than tears would be hidden this eve.

She did not linger very long in her room but hurried down the stairs, knowing that most women had retired for a night of reading, prayer, or conversation before their eyelids weighted with exhaustion after a long day's work. As she approached the second floor, the prattle of women was loud enough to allow the stairs' creaks to go unnoticed by the few who gathered at the hearths and tables.

When she finally stepped back out into the newborn night, barely dark at all, a loud sigh escaped her. Pulling her shawl tighter around her shoulders, she began toward the bridge. Its rails gleamed bright with the moonlight, as if it were some unearthly gateway summoning her footsteps. The elm loomed on her right, and just beyond the tree was the garden wall. The savory aroma of Fran's stew lingered in the night air. Clanking pots and pans disturbed the quiet, and as she passed, the kitchen glow bled through the garden

111

gate. How she'd rather be within the confines of the stone wall than trapped in the vise of grave robber threats.

Her footsteps quickened as she drew near to the bridge. She focused on the path ahead, begging for God's protection despite the unholy predicament. A movement snagged her attention. She could just see the tips of the lilac shrubs lining the graveyard. The chimes of the church signaled that she was prompt—it was half past seven.

The flowery scent met her nose, and she breathed in deeply, hoping for the glorious lilacs to comfort her nerves just as they had done when she'd visit her mother's plot at home. Yet the closest purple flowers suddenly jerked from her view as a dark figure emerged from along the fence line.

From behind a black veil, a voice whispered, "Here." And shoved some lilac flowers in Josie's hands. "Hold on to those. We'll arrive just as the minister leaves."

"The minister is there?"

The woman dressed in the same black garb as Josie stepped closer, handing her a handkerchief. "He often meets the graveyard attendant to give one final blessing over the coffin. If anyone asks, we knew him from the mill." She parted the hanging flowers and peered over the fence. "He used to be an operative—but couldn't keep himself sober enough."

Josie's stomach rolled at the thought that this woman might also work at the mill. No matter how much of a burden her secret had been in the face of her future possible victims, she'd rather bear it alone than share the awful predicament with any other woman. Her hope skittered away this night of her first grave robbing. Any inkling of relief that she might find once her father was safe would never be enough knowing that she was found out by another—even if they were accomplices alike.

Josephine Clayton would forever be tarnished.

Could she strike up the courage to ask who this woman was? Or perhaps Josie was unknown herself? Would they both be anonymous in this?

She was grateful for this dark garb after all.

A soft song rose from the gentle light of the funeral site. It was a melancholy hymn sung by a man and woman.

When the song ended, her fellow mourner knelt down beside a lantern tucked just beneath the shrubbery. She retrieved a candle from her pocket then threw it down. "This is too short." She dug into her other pocket and pulled out an unused candle, placing it inside the lantern.

"We shall light this when we enter the gate."

"But we will be noticed."

"Of course. We are mourning the loss of Harry Garnett." She snickered beneath her breath—a choppy laugh sending a chill down Josie's neck. "You unlatch the gate." She stepped aside, holding the lantern.

The minister and his companion were leaving through the gate closest to the village shops. Josie unlatched the side gate, pushed it open, and held it ajar while the woman slipped into the cemetery. "Here, light it." She motioned for Josie to take the box of matches in her cloak's pocket. Why could she not light it herself? Josie wondered if this was a test to see how much she would comply.

She had no choice in the matter. Trying to still her shaking hand, she struck a match and lit the candle.

"I think he sees us." The woman's voice now grazed above a whisper. It was tight, as if spoken behind clinched teeth.

"Who?"

"The minister—"

The minister entered the cemetery again, holding his own lantern. He called out, "I apologize, but the funeral is over."

"We could not leave the mill until now, sir," the woman called out breathlessly. "Please, do not hinder your leave, we shall say our prayers and be gone shortly."

"Ah, very well. I am sorry for your loss. God's peace on him." The minister tipped his wide-brimmed hat and backed out of the gate.

"Pray for us, sir," the woman sniffled. She then elbowed at

Josie and snapped, "Come on."

Agitation crept along Josie's nerves. This woman played a part, owning her act in a most unapologetic way. But something else about this woman irritated Josie. Perhaps it wasn't the woman but the fact that Alvin forced Josie into this charade with no instruction. He'd given Josie over to take orders from this stranger. So, maybe Alvin was the cause of Josie's irritation. He had been so many things to the Clayton family.

Josie wished she'd never met him.

A soft rhythmic thump met her ears, and she tried to see beyond the yellow glow that led them between headstones. They trampled the long grass springing up from the beds of final rest until they came upon a hunched man working a shovel. The shovel dug the earth, unapologetically also.

Thump of soil.

Stab of the shovel.

Thump of the next heap upon a wooden box.

Harry's wooden box.

"Poor Harry Garnett," the woman muttered.

"You missed the funeral." The man kept shoveling, hardly looking up at them.

The woman stepped closer, shining the light down into the hole. The box was completely covered. "You work fast, don't you?" Her honey tone coated each word as if she complimented a child.

"Aye." He heaved another pile of dirt, then his shovel hovered in midair. "Would you like a moment of quiet?" He shrugged his shoulders and spat out a piece of grass from the corner of his mouth. "I can stop if you'd like."

"No, no." She sniffled. "We do not mind, sir. It is peaceful. I can rest assured that his final resting place is well secured." Her head turned toward Josie. Perhaps she was smirking at the irony of her words? The sarcasm, the wicked lie.

"Good." The man declared then continued at a slightly quicker pace.

The woman set her lantern at the headstone, seemingly looking up and out toward the village as she did so. She must be positioning it for some sort of signal.

Thump.

Stab.

Thump.

Josie and her accomplice stood like statues watching the burying of Harry Garnett. The mysterious woman sniffled and cried, while a hopeless prayer poured from Josie's heart with her head bowed. The night darkened, and the yellow lantern outshone every shape and form. Even the hunched old man, who now patted the dirt with the back of his shovel, seemed only a shadow of life. The glow of the lamp consumed all of Josie's attention. No moon shone in the dark sky. The lantern was the only light.

"May God be with you, madams. All is done now." The man slung his shovel on his shoulder and tipped his hat. He stomped through the graveyard. His final farewell sounded in the loud slam of the cemetery gate.

They waited. Josie was not sure what was to happen next. Her unsteady breath warmed the air beneath her veil. Her skin crawled as silence widened between them. Life was far away, the distant murmur of the village carried on the breeze.

"There now, easy enough." The whisper came like a slithering snake into Josie's consciousness. "Only a moment longer. There was nothing unusual. No traps set."

"What traps?"

"Sometimes they'll lace the dirt with straw so it's more difficult for grave robbers to shovel. In Boston, they've even made cages to go on top of the dirt. Sawing through that creates quite a ruckus for the snatchers."

"Are they that desperate for a body?" Josie barely said. It was a thought more than a question.

"The price is right, and besides—" The woman pulled her shawl closer, a smart idea in this chilly night. "Imagine the discoveries that might be made."

Josie understood how important discoveries were—she'd longed for them when her mother was ill. Yet, she'd known no other doctor but Chadwick. And he was hardly someone to depend on for advancements in medicine. His wild face haunted Josie's mind, setting off an uncontrollable shiver throughout her body. The glint of the knife, the fog in her sickened head, the fear that iced her as if she were a corpse already.

Hollow church bells called her from the nightmarish memory. Eight o'clock. She would never listen to those wise notes the same again. They may as well be a banshee cry. That clock tower was a holy mourner standing tall at a distance, saddened beyond the death, but in the thick of thievery.

"We shall both kneel," the woman instructed.

"How will Alvin know it is safe?"

"We'll blow out the candle. He'll know that all is well." The woman began to kneel. "If we keep the candle lit past the hour, then he'll know something is off."

"Would he come?"

"No. Only if he sees the light snuffed out."

Josie joined her on her knees, the fresh earth cooling through her skirts. She reached out and pressed on the soil, once again praying God's mercy.

The woman leaned over and blew out the candle.

Every image was a smudge of charcoal against even blacker shadows. The woman's breath was steady. "Any moment now. . .we'll hear—" The gate moaned. All seemed still around them; no footsteps could be heard. Josie's stomach shook. She pressed the flowers to her nose, begging for some calm. But none came. She squeezed her arms around her frame, trying to warm up, but she was certain the chill came from the inside out.

"Do you have your ointment?"

"I do."

"Pass it to him." The woman sat back on her heels. "Now."

Josie looked around but could see nothing. She may as well have been stuck in the box below. "Where—where is he?"

A warm breath skimmed her ear. "I am right here." Alvin's sinister words lurched Josie forward and away. The lilacs tumbled on the fresh earth of the grave.

Both the woman and Alvin chuckled. Josie stood up and flung the ointment in Alvin's direction.

"Ow," he rasped. She could not see where it hit him, but she was satisfied that it had.

"How dare you, Alvin Green." Josie crossed her arms. He shuffled on the ground beneath her, probably looking for the ointment bottle.

The other woman stood with Josie. "You are as foolish as your father," she hissed.

Josie clenched her teeth. Her heart thudded against her chest, beating anger and sadness and heartache all at once.

"Enough." Alvin stood up and pushed past them. The aroma of cinnamon and cloves filled Josie's nostrils. He had used the ointment.

The crunch of a shovel plunging into the earth made Josie jump. It had begun.

"As soon as the body is lifted out, you will fill the hole and then place the lilacs atop the dirt. Good as new," the woman instructed.

"What will you do?" Josie's patience was thin, and she could not withhold the challenge in her voice.

"I will tell *you* what to do," the woman warned. "And I will wait for him at the gate to help."

Josie's lip began to quiver. All she could do was pray for God to be near. She bent down and gathered up the lilacs. What had Mother said these flowers symbolized?

A small whimper escaped Josie as she realized she had forgotten her mother's wisdom.

"Hush," the woman whispered.

They stood by Alvin, hearing more than seeing his work. Alvin dug at a faster pace than the gravedigger had. There was no rhythm to the dirt being dumped into a heap beside the grave. After several minutes passed, a blunt thud told her that he'd reached the box. What was next, how would he—? Josie strained to see through the dark into the silence. But it wasn't quiet for long. The sound of a saw scraping into wood signaled what Alvin was doing.

Oh Lord, let us not be found out. A selfish prayer, yet the only prayer that bubbled from her soul.

After some time, the moonlight offered a translucent view. Josie gripped her mouth with a clammy hand. Alvin pulled the body up by the head through a vertical hole in the dirt. The rigid corpse's bloodless skin caught the eerie moonlight, and Josie gasped. She could look no longer, turning away and weeping into her elbow.

Lord, forgive us.

"We'll be at the canal," Alvin whispered as he wrapped the body in a blanket. The woman had gone. "You must leave this grave like you first saw it then bring me the tool I left for you." Alvin trudged away with the body across his shoulders.

Once she could no longer hear him, Josie crumpled to the mound of dirt, crying and shaking.

Could she ever do this again? She prayed for deliverance from this night forward. She must be brave now though. Gasping in the crisp night air, she wiped her tears away.

With her gloved fingers and a small spade that Alvin left behind, Josie began to fill in Harry Garnett's empty grave.

Chapter Twelve

Braham stormed out of the tavern after sitting through an infuriating reprimand from Gerald while Mr. Bellingham guzzled his drink. There was no reasoning with Gerald. He would never take Braham's word that everything had been done to prevent accidents from occurring. The man would forever see Braham as the servant beneath him instead of a partner in keeping Gloughton Mill up and running.

Mr. Bellingham held a nasty sneer throughout the whole conversation then finally piped in, "I've got at least two good men who can take the burden from you, Mr. Taylor. They'd love nothing more than to tighten up shop around that factory."

Braham took that offer as a replacement for his position, not an addition to it. His heels stabbed the road with heavy thuds as he stomped to his horse. The blood pumped in his ears. He'd write his uncle's executor to outline the conditions of the trust, and then he'd try to convince Gerald to reconsider selling. If Aunt Myrtle was not so ill, he'd seek her advice. She would have a mighty opinion about her brother's mill leaving the family by Gerald's whim. But Braham could not risk upsetting her now.

He took in a long breath to cool his anger. A shadowy movement caught his attention down the road. Mist rolled onto the factory bridge, and a figure mingled within it. He rubbed his eyes and looked again. There was nothing. Perhaps his temper had gotten the best of him. He continued to his cart, but a miserable moan erupted from the mist. The dark movement from before once again appeared. He stumbled forward, trying to keep his gaze steady enough to make out whatever it was that made such an agonizing sound. But the mist swallowed up the figure again. His heart stilled. All was still. Silence was thick.

Just like the wax he'd found on the factory door, Braham suspected that mischief lay somewhere in the mist. He prayed that he was meant to find it out instead of turning the other way and calling on Constable James.

He rubbed his hands together, trying to warm up the chill spreading through his veins.

There! Another shadow. Yet, it was gone as quickly as it appeared. What moved along the bridge? Something strange was going on near his factory.

"Hello there," Braham forced out.

The squawk of a crow answered him. He looked up and around, but he presumed the bird was hidden by the trees towering over the cemetery to his right. Another moan from beyond the mist summoned him closer to the bridge. The railing appeared through the fog. He reached out to steady himself. Closer still. The board creaked as he stepped on the bridge. The mist broke apart, revealing a figure dressed in black standing at the very center of the bridge.

"Who is there?" Braham bellowed. He tightened his grip on the rail.

The figure turned, lifting up a black veil.

Pale, beautiful, wrought with fright.

"Miss Clay?" He dashed toward her. Her round eyes were rimmed red, and her cheeks were stained with tears. She was cloaked in black from head to toe; only a few golden curls fell around her face from beneath the veil piled atop her hat.

"Oh Mr. Taylor," she blurted in the same tone as the cries that coaxed him near. "I apologize that you are seeing me like this." She shook her head and pressed a handkerchief to her mouth. Her fingers trembled as she wiped her eyes.

"You are shivering." He quickly unbuttoned his coat and wrapped it around her shoulders. A mint and floral scent filled the air. He stayed close, wrapping his arm around her. "Come, I see the light from the kitchen over the wall. Let us warm you up."

"You mustn't—" Miss Clay tried to pull away. A splash came

from below. The woman stiffened in his arms. "Please, Mr. Taylor, you must go."

Braham's nostrils flared as he searched her widened eyes. He then rushed over to the rail and called out, "Who is there?" But the mist was thick. Rhythmic slaps of water grew faint.

He spun around. Miss Clay leaned against the opposite rail, sobbing into her handkerchief. His coat hung off one shoulder.

"Come, Miss Clay. You shall explain this oddity. But first, we must go inside." He led her across the bridge and through the garden. All the while she leaned into him, sniffling. Her frame shook with silent weeping, and his heart nearly splintered in his chest. When they entered the kitchen, Fran gawked in their direction, holding a shovel of ash over a dying fire.

"Do not put that out quite yet, dear Fran. Miss Clay is chilled to the bone." He gently guided her forward with his hand on her back. Fran set the shovel down with a clatter and rushed to retrieve a stool. Miss Clay sat, reaching her hands to the heat. Her crying had settled, but her body still shook.

"I was just going to bed. Been a long day." Fran worked about the counter beside the hearth. She poured some tea into a cup and handed it to Miss Clay. "My, my, dear girl. I've never heard of a funeral lasting this long into the night."

"The funeral ended several hours ago, Fran. I missed it. Only went to pray over—" Miss Clay's words were weary as she held the cup to her lips but did not sip. "I—I cannot say—" Her lips quivered, and streams of tears spilled down her face.

Braham said quickly, "Fran, I shall speak with Miss Clay. Please, do not worry. I shall put the fire out and lock up on my way home."

Fran nodded fervently. She tossed a worried look to Miss Clay. "You comfort her, sir." She patted his arm. "Such a sweet girl, she is. You are a good fellow for her." Her brow lowered with seriousness, yet the edges of her mouth wobbled with a smile. She bustled out of the kitchen. He should not even consider being a *good fellow* for anyone—not now, when so much was at stake. Although, he could not control the emotion swirling about at the sight of this distressed woman. Just as he could not control the careless accidents of his employees.

He pulled up a chair beside Miss Clay. "Please, tell me that you are not hurt."

"No, not at all." She breathed in deeply, cradling the cup in her lap. "Well, perhaps my heart hurts the most." She wagged her head and seemed to swallow back a sob. "'Tis my father."

Braham was tempted to gather her into his arms and comfort her properly. "Is he ill?"

She shook her head then looked at him for the first time since they sat down. Her lips were blood red, glistening in the warm light. "I found out that he is in much danger because of his business. . . mishaps."

"I see." Braham leaned his forearms on his knees. "Was his man in the boat?"

"Boat?" Josie stared hard at the fire. "Yes. He brought a boat here."

Relief filled Braham knowing that the mysterious meeting on the bridge seemed to stem from a family affair—nothing to do with his factory. This woman, though, was not relieved one bit. He refrained from reaching out his hand.

"Didn't Fran mention a funeral?" He spoke softly.

"Yes," she said as quiet as a leaf falling upon the forest floor. "I went to show my respects. The poor soul had no family." She grimaced then turned away.

"I am sorry for your loss, Miss Clay. It is never easy—"

"No, it is not," she nearly snapped. Her mouth fell open and she turned to face him quickly. "Oh Mr. Taylor, I am sorry for my tone." She placed her hand on his. Her slender fingers were tiny against his own. He could only stare, afraid she would feel the pulse her touch ignited. She pulled her hand away. Her brow cinched, and she once again paid attention to the fire. "You see, my tears, while partly shed for the fate of that man—" She shook her head. Her chest rose with another deep breath. "But also because my father's future is nearly as desolate. His man does not assure any good news."

She set her cup of tea on the hearth at her knees then untied her hat and placed it in her lap. Braham shifted his gaze from the loosely bound mass of curls cascading down her back to the dancing flames. He refrained from wondering at her beauty and instead pondered her words. He leaned back in his chair, having just sat in a business meeting with terrible fellows.

"Business is a tricky thing, especially when your heart is involved." Braham leaned near her, nudging her shoulder with his own. "Your father is blessed to have your kind watch over him."

If ever there was an embrace given by a look, it was now. The sapphire hold enraptured Braham in a trance, as if Miss Clay's very warmth soothed every chill from the night air without even a touch.

She smiled. "I thank you for that, Mr. Taylor. Although, I wonder if it's so kind as it is desperate?" Her eyes fluttered closed.

This woman was wrought with some unknown grief or disturbance. If only he could reach over and smudge it all away. If only his task going forward was to help Josie Clay through her father's business mishaps instead of being wrapped up in his own.

They sat in silence, Braham wishing he'd not thought about his own predicament. He would rather salvage some peace for Miss Clay. His woes seemed far too complicated for any more thought this evening.

He pushed his chair closer to her and pressed his shoulder to hers again. "I am here if you need any advice, Miss Clay."

She smiled once more. Her gaze skimmed his face as if she searched for advice without words. Her lips parted and she drew closer. With a tilt of her head she laid her cheek against his shoulder. Soft curls pressed along his jaw sending gooseflesh across his skin. His every breath was fragrant with the fragile yet bold Miss Josie Clay.

"I have lost my mother, and I fear I'll lose my father too," she whispered. "How could he have been so foolish?"

"There was a day when my own father's choice piled much shame on me," Braham muttered, uncertain he wanted to remember.

"What shame, Mr. Taylor?" She pressed her head closer to his neck. A perfect fit as he rested his cheek on her crown.

"A crime he committed at sea was found out by the foreman down south. Everyone who cared for Father was beaten." He winced at the memory. "Mr. Bates was away from the plantation and did not realize the way we were treated."

"How old were you?"

"Only twelve." He swallowed, trying to forget the smell of the salve Howie used to doctor the lashes. "I didn't have it nearly as bad as the slaves. But Father could only endure it once. The second time killed him."

Josie sat up, stealing away the warmth of her head on his shoulder. "That is terrible, Braham—" She widened her eyes, pressing her lips together in obvious embarrassment. He enjoyed hearing his first name for once. Especially from her. "Mr. Taylor, did justice come from such an awful—" She grimaced.

"The late Mr. Bates became my guardian. My father never saw justice for his beating, yet there was nothing better to come from my grief than finding favor with Mr. Bates." He hooked her chin with his forefinger. "I pray that the good to be found in your father's misfortune will be immeasurable for you."

She slid her fingers into his hand and pulled it to her cheek. "Thank you. I have no friend to confide in. But you have been one tonight." Braham had sworn to never grow close to a mill girl, but sitting here with Miss Clay—Josie—he wanted nothing less than to be her friend.

A slam of the back door forced her to jump up from her stool. Braham twisted about in his chair.

Audra Jennings stood there, her attire matching Josie's. Her face was nearly as ghostly as Josie's when Braham first spotted her on the bridge.

"What are you doing here, Mr. Taylor?" Audra's auburn locks

were released from her own ebony hat, and even though she addressed Braham, she stared only at the woman by his side.

Braham stood up, tugging at his lapels. "I found Miss Clay quite distraught tonight." He cleared his throat, embarrassment flooding him at Audra's obvious surprise. Of course the woman appeared shocked. She had caught them in an intimate moment, with their hands entwined together.

"Mr. Taylor, you should leave. 'Tis late." Josie's voice was soft but urgent.

"Yes, forgive me, Miss Clay, for—" Braham curled his fingers, but he regretted nothing except that Audra had interrupted them. He gave a quick bow. "I do wish you a good night's rest."

He took his hat from the hook by the door and mumbled a good night to Audra. Her surprise fell away to reveal a look of mischief. He did not trust that Audra Jennings. And by the horrified look on Josie's face, he feared that nothing good would come from being caught in a tender moment. Poor Josie.

As he left the boardinghouse grounds, the haze still hovered on the bridge like a whisper over the waters. He traipsed through the fog and finally came upon his horse. The murmur from the tavern was ever buzzing in the dark village street. The journey ahead seemed a long one. Home was often a destination to which he was eager to return to. But tonight, a tug held back his enthusiasm. He knew what it might be, and as hard as he might try to deny it, he surrendered to the truth.

He was not ready to leave Josie Clay behind.

He'd have stayed till dawn if he gave in to his senses. As he steered the horse down to the country path out of Gloughton, he wondered—would Josie have chosen to stay with him too?

Chapter Thirteen

I t's you," Josie exclaimed as soon as she was sure they were alone.

"Did you not know?" Audra marched across the floor and collapsed in the chair, no doubt still warm from Braham. She yanked off her hat and tossed it on the hearth, dangerously close to the flames. "Alvin surely told you."

"He did not." Josie sank down on her stool. "He tells me very little."

The fire popped during a few breaths of silence.

"Strange, he talks my ear off." She grimaced. "I was not planning on being a part of this any longer."

Could Audra and Josie be kindred spirits in this? Audra was nothing like Josie—with her fiery tongue and crass attitude toward most. And, by the way she acted in the graveyard tonight, Josie had taken her for a coldhearted player. Perhaps that wasn't so far from her impression of Audra Jennings in pure daylight. But now, maybe they were tied by mutual unwillingness.

"I don't want to be part of it either," Josie admitted.

"You must. I can do nothing with one arm, and your father cannot be trusted."

Josie's skin pricked. "What happened to your arm?"

"I stumbled on a job. Fell wrong."

"How long have you been. . .a mourner?"

"Long enough." Audra smiled as if she recalled a pleasant memory. "Alvin and your father were sent to New York shortly after my accident. Alvin was disappointed he'd not work with me, but that won't stop him from continuing"—her lips froze with hesitation, and then she pressed back in the chair with a lazy smile—"in the business. It's a contagion that clings close to the desires of the thieves. The excitement of slinking about at night, plunging their spades into moist soil, and stealing away the bags of bones for some sort of good, earthly use." She shook her head like a disapproving schoolteacher.

"I pray that heaven is pleased with the soul only." Josie was sure of it, having convinced herself each day at church. But there were suspicious folk who believed the body was part of the grand entrance into the other world. And for the very possibility that might be true, Josie's conscience twisted even more.

"I do not know about heaven, but you better not think on that. So much more ahead of you." She stood up and straightened the sling at her shoulder.

Josie crossed her arms at her waist then whispered, "I just want this to be over."

Audra placed a hand on Josie's shoulder. "Alvin is eager for it to be over too. Your doctor is withholding quite a sum from him because of you."

"Is that why he could not guarantee Dr. Chadwick's silence to the authorities?" A fresh wave of the same hysteria that overwhelmed Josie at the canal threatened to wash over her again.

But Braham was nowhere near to offer comfort.

Audra slid her hand away and crammed it in her pocket. "I do not know nor care how Alvin deals with mediocre doctors. I'd suspect he was in love with you to even consider losing that much money from the doctor."

Josie twisted in her seat. "What? He's much older than I am. He—he did it out of decency. I was nearly killed—"

"You are getting worked up over nothing. I am sure that Alvin is committed to one woman only." She stared at the shiny pot hanging above the mantel, primping her hair in the disfigured reflection. "And, truth be told, you Claytons came just in time. I wanted nothing more to do with this part of the business."

She snatched up her hat and crossed over to the hallway. "Thank you, Josie—or is it Josephine?" Her eyebrow cocked above a devilish face. "You've given me a chance to move on to more intriguing obligations." She spun on her heel and left the room.

Josie sprang from her seat, desperate that Audra not say a word to any other gal, but she had disappeared around the corner. Josie slunk back to the hearth, not wanting to speak of it beyond the confines of this solitary room. She poured the ash atop the flame, smothering any light in the cold kitchen.

What a difference mere minutes could make with a change of company. Josie had nearly buckled with thanksgiving at her time with Braham. She was safe. Braham had endured much also. He offered a wide-open compassion—a lovely place to collapse into. If only Audra Jennings hadn't interrupted them.

As Josie dragged herself out of the kitchen, all the warmth of Braham's comfort was squelched as she recalled Audra's words. They were as suffocating as ash. Of all the women in Gloughton Mill, Audra Jennings was the last person Josie would have confided in. And now, Josie was taking not only her father's place but Audra's as well.

What would Braham think of Josie, knowing whose footsteps she would willingly follow?

Josie woke up to Liesl's wide hazel eyes watching her. "You were crying, Miss Josie."

"Oh." Josie sat up and touched her cheek. It was moist. A soft glimmer from the bedside candle softened the dark room. The sisters stirred in the bed next to them. "What time is it?"

"It's half past four. I was about to dress, and then I heard you cry."

"I must have been dreaming." Or everything she'd shoved in the secret corner of her mind had flooded her pillow as she slumbered. That was more likely it. She could not recall any dream, only the nightmare that she lived while awake.

Two uneventful days had passed since the funeral. There had been no accident at the mill, and the evenings were filled with interviewing for another newsletter article. Molly insisted on writing a piece about Josie's favorite herbs in the garden. She'd found a girl who would illustrate the plants for new summer gardens. Molly was hopeful that townsfolk might find it a useful guide. Josie was thrilled to lose herself in this type of work instead of waiting for news of death or worrying about her father.

As she splashed cold water on her face and braided her hair by the candlelight, she prayed for her father's well-being and for his enemies' hearts to change. A futile prayer, but all she could think to do. Today was payday. If only debt were Father's greatest concern.

Once the workday began, Josie pushed aside her thoughts and focused on her tasks. The bellows of the machinery thrumming through her frame and the swaths of newly spun cloth rushing across the loom were enough distractions. Occasionally, she'd glance over at the office window and spy Braham with hands on his hips, his face determined at overseeing the operation. No rude men filled up his time with tours or crude remarks this day. She was pleased to be under the noble protection of his sole watch.

Josie returned her attention to her work, near-satisfied with the exact place she stood at the very mill that rose around her and the gentleman's attention only a glance away. If Josephine Clayton could run away from all that strapped her to this unfortunate path, this one man might be her greatest memory of the place, and her biggest regret in leaving it behind.

Her heart pounded in succinct opposition to the thuds that trembled the floating cotton bits around her. When she looked back at Braham, his back was turned and he faced a very solemn Miss Clyde, who handed him his hat and coat. Braham looked over his shoulder and scanned the room through the glass, his sable eyes locking with Josie's gaze. His chin pushed up his lips into a deeply set frown. He gave her a short nod and then turned to leave.

His distress penetrated through Josie as if it were her own—as if she were still standing at the bridge, weeping over her wayward father. Her spirit deflated the same, and she was desperate to go to Braham. At that moment, the bell rang, indicating the breakfast break. Amid the sigh of quieting machines, Josie pushed her way toward the hallway. She found her bonnet and hurried toward the doors. Braham stepped out of the waiting room door ahead, pulling his coat on as he reached the large double doors to the courtyard.

Josie ran toward him. She caught the door just as it closed behind him. In the bright sunshine, she tied her bonnet about her chin and scrambled down the steps. Braham crossed the courtyard and climbed atop his wagon on the other side of the old elm tree.

"Mr. Taylor?" she called breathlessly, running after him.

Braham turned to her. His top hat cast a dark shadow in contrast to the beaming sun. "Miss Clay, you are the first one out this day." He gave her a smile that did not reach his eyes.

"I am concerned for you, sir." She caught her breath. "Is there anything I can help you with?"

He grimaced and looked away. "Come with me. We've only an hour."

The factory doors opened, and the rest of the workers began to pour out of the building. Josie quickly rounded the other side of the cart and climbed up with the help of Braham's extended hand. Before any curious eye could catch a glimpse at the newest mill girl riding off with the handsome manager, the cart scampered across the bridge.

After they passed through the village, Braham signaled to the horse to move faster. Josie gripped the edge of the cart with tight knuckles. She held her bonnet to her head as the warm breeze rushed at them. The hills were a vivid green, edged with rich emerald tree canopies. As they raced through the country, she glanced over at Braham occasionally. He never once looked back at her. His simmering gaze was fixed ahead.

The dreaded outcome of this sudden journey sat heavy on Josie's heart. There was one impending sorrow complicating her acquaintance with Mr. Braham Taylor. The dying aunt he so dearly treasured would provide, in all inevitability, another payment to Dr. Chadwick and the resurrectionists.

"Let us pray we are not too late." The words tumbled from

Braham's tight lips as they turned through an open gate.

"Too late? Is it that dire?" Josie bit the inside of her cheek as panic bloomed within her.

Braham maneuvered the cart down a lane lined with apple trees. The sickly sweet smell of rotten blossoms mixed in the breeze. "Miss Clyde said that Minnie went to the apothecary's home this morning. They asked I come as soon as I was able."

Josie began to pray that his aunt only needed comfort from her nephew at this hour. Against her own best interest, Josie also prayed that this was not the end.

"Perhaps you can help Miss Young with tending to my aunt? I would feel better having you by her side, Miss Clay."

"I am sure Miss Young will know more than I."

"She is not trustworthy. She lacks quick thinking when it comes to tending to the sick." He pushed the words out through his teeth as he pulled back on the reins, bringing the horse to a stop in front of the stable.

Trustworthy?

Josie batted her eyes closed, an uncertain wave crashing against her stomach. Why was she here? She wished that she had not come along but stayed among the flying cotton bits and mill girls. If only she were just a mill girl now. How much different her life might have turned out. Her affection for this man would be unashamed, and her conscience would be clear.

"Come, let us go inside." He swung his legs over the cart and jumped down, hurrying to Josie's side. She placed her hand in his and stepped down. Her chin was just below his shoulder as she stood across from him. His grip on her hand did not lessen. He faced her with his back turned to the house and his broad shoulders filling her view. The size of the space between them would be questionable to any onlooker. A leathery smell mixed with fresh cotton reminded her of his coat around her shoulders the other night.

Josie dared to look up at him. His soft brown eyes did not waver but drank in her gaze. His Adam's apple bobbed against his high collar, the hard swallow obvious even though she was bound to his stare. Her breath barely gathered in her chest. If she had time to consider the consequences of such a loss of air, she would have gasped aloud. But any slight movement threatened to end this trance. There was nothing she wanted more than another second trapped by his regard.

"Miss Clay, you have impressed me much—" he said. "I am confident in your ability. And your care." He lifted her hand to his mouth, pressing his lips softly on her ungloved skin. The warm touch sent a current all the way through her arm to her fluttering chest. The bloom of heat on her cheeks would not be contained.

She lowered her head and gave a meek curtsy. "I am here for you and your family, sir." Tears sprang behind her eyes. "It is the least I can do." Josie tamped down all her erupting sorrow.

Braham's brow furrowed, and he stepped aside. She released all her trapped air.

With a wave of his arm, Braham invited her to enter first through the side entrance. 'Twas an appreciated opportunity, for she could now turn away from him and muster up the courage to continue this delusion that she was indeed the person he had hoped in.

Chapter Fourteen

Braham sat near his aunt, holding her frail hand while Minnie cleaned up the bedside table strewn about with empty bottles, powders, and several handkerchiefs. Daisy tended to the pillows propped behind Aunt Myrtle, and Josie sat on the bench at the foot of the bed, looking paler than even the dying woman.

While Daisy continued to recall memories of her mother to Aunt Myrtle, Braham leaned over and whispered, "Miss Clay, are you well?"

She nodded.

"Dear one, come closer." Aunt Myrtle patted the side of the bed where Daisy tucked her snuggly into the bedcovers. "I hardly know you, yet you've been such a help, haven't you?"

"I've hardly done a thing." Josie spoke as she had on the bridge, weak and uncertain. "Only what was needed to help Miss Young."

"You've got a deft hand, Miss Clay," the young apothecary affirmed. "It would have taken me twice as long to prepare the soothing salve."

"Tell me." Aunt Myrtle's voice was hoarse, and her eyes were bright with moisture. "Is my nephew a good manager at the mill?"

Braham chuckled, relief flooding him. "I see that you are still business-minded, even in this confined state."

Aunt Myrtle gave a brief smile but began to convulse with another coughing fit, the wild nature of it having been the reason that Minnie and Daisy had sent for him.

Miss Clay stood immediately, tending to Aunt Myrtle with the steady hand that Braham had witnessed during the factory accidents. A certain calm settled upon the beautiful woman as she helped. She was swift in positioning his aunt, unwavering in her soothing tone, and so concentrated on aiding her through the episode, she did not pay attention to Minnie, who had come up behind her with a fresh tray of tea and Miss Young's prescribed mixture.

"Miss Clay, if you would please step aside?" Minnie was short in her demand. She must have realized it, for she bit her lip and gave an apologetic look to Braham.

"Excuse me." Josie gently laid Aunt Myrtle against her pillows as the fit subsided. The poor woman was completely exhausted. Her eyes remained closed. Long folds of skin hung from her cheek-bones, creased around her mouth by the pulls and tugs from her coughing. Josie slipped behind Minnie, who was carefully holding the teacup to the spent woman's lips.

"Aunt Myrtle, please, try and drink." Braham sat beside her on the bed, wondering if she was indeed asleep.

A moan came out of her blue lips. She wagged her head back and forth. "My Bible."

"May I read to you?" Josie asked.

Aunt Myrtle stopped her movement and opened her eyes. "Please."

Braham opened the bedside drawer nearest to him and handed Josie the Bible he'd first learned from as a young boy. It was leather bound, near-pristine, with the gold engraving "Bates" in the corner. A red ribbon hung from between the pages. Josie used great care as she set it on her lap. Her fingers ran over the engraving, and upon using the ribbon to open the book, she shifted her gaze to him. Her eyes were seas, deep with trepidation—or was it longing? He expected that the same look crossed his face when he sat beside his uncle, wanting to soak in every last moment and longing to be the true blood relative of the man. It was a look of knowing and desir-ing all at once.

What was it that Josie Clay longed for?

Braham shuddered. He might not understand what Josie desired, but they all knew the fate unfolding on the white sheets and embroidered pillowcase. A wave of emotion cinched Braham's throat, and he begged his mind to remain here and not flip back to all the wonderful memories of his care under Myrtle Bates.

Josie's head dipped over the scriptures, and she read with a clear, steady tone. "O lord, thou hast searched me, and known me. Thou knowest my downsitting and mine uprising, thou understandest my thought afar off. Thou compassest my path and my lying down, and art acquainted with all my ways." Her lips pronounced peaceful words to the withering woman. Aunt Myrtle's chest was calm as it fell and rose.

No more convulsing.

She was listening.

"Excuse me," Minnie said, standing at the door with a platter. "This came for you."

Braham looked back at Josie, who was turning a delicate page, then gathered the envelope from the tray and stepped into the hallway.

He broke the wax seal and unfolded the letter, reading:

Mr. Taylor,

Your guardian's will explicitly states that you shall be the sole manager of the factory, unless death or an act of God halts production. If you are excused from your position unwillingly, then Mr. Gerald Bates Jr. will surrender his right to the trust furnished by his father at the time of the signing of his will. The amount of the trust is substantial. The loan against the factory has yet to be paid off. Gerald would benefit more from the trust than the profit from the sale.

You have nothing to worry about, dear boy. You are a legal ward, and as valuable as any other blood relative of the man. The late Mr. Bates held you with the utmost and highest regard.

M. Williams

Thanksgiving invaded Braham's heart just as he heard Miss Clay speak the well-known words, "I will praise thee; for I am fearfully and wonderfully made." He tucked the letter in his coat pocket, saving it for the next business encounter with Gerald. Gerald would return from Boston tomorrow after escorting Bellingham back to his estate and, no doubt, dabbling in the societal habits of his pampered colleagues.

Daisy met Braham at the door, wiping her hands on a towel. "She's put the woman to sleep. I've asked her to come by and help me on Sunday. You might be in need of a new employee, Braham—Miss Clay would make an excellent partner for me." She gave a sly smile and stepped back with her arms crossed. Daisy spoke in a more pleasant way to him than she had in years. Miss Clay was a marvel at more than healing the sick.

Aunt Myrtle expelled soft snores, yet Josie continued reading, "Search me, O God, and know my heart: try me, and know my thoughts: and see if there be any wicked way in me, and lead me in the way everlasting." Silence encapsulated the bright room at this noon hour. The clink of Daisy's mixing tools sliced up the lingering memory of the pretty reader's voice. Josie's lips were clamped tightly shut while she stared at the book in her lap. Without looking around to see who watched, she clasped Aunt Myrtle's hand and closed her eyes. Her mouth moved, barely so, and her brow was rippled in a sea of wrinkles.

Braham should not continue to stare at her in this moment of pure innocence and obvious beckoning of the Holy Spirit, yet he dared not look away. She was an angel beside his aunt, an intercessor who might be asking for something unattainable, but whose faith shone as brightly as the faith his aunt had once shown him. Braham was certain that Josie's presence was not happenstance but the very act of God directing the mill girl's every step to the bedside of his dearly loved aunt.

Anger seared Josie's throat as she tromped away from Braham's wagon. He'd walked ahead of her to ready the mill for the afternoon shift. Josie stopped beneath the old elm, glad to be alone these last few minutes before the courtyard filled with the other workers. They had skipped the two meals and the shift in between. But hunger was her least concern. She balled her fist and pressed it against the rough bark of the tree. Her knuckles whitened as she stared through boiling tears. She was Judas. Instead of sitting at a banqueting table as betrayal brewed, she'd sat on the bedsheets of a peaceful bedroom, reciting holy words. Yet it would not be long before she'd turn over that sweet lady to the bloodthirsty men who waited for her.

Mill girls began to file out from the boardinghouse. Josie swiped at her eyes, plucked some wild daisies that sprouted along the boardinghouse wall, and fell into step just next to Sally and Liesl.

"Where were you, Miss Josie?" Liesl plunged her arm in the crook of Josie's.

Josie just waved her daisies, swallowing hard as she outright avoided the question. "It is a beautiful day, isn't it?"

"Skipping meals will not bode well toward the last hours of work," Sally warned. "It's not worth it to me. Even with the glory of early summer's bloom all around." She plucked a flower from Josie's hand and stuck it behind her ear, giving a playful smirk.

"Ah, so you reap my treasures with a full belly." Josie's own stomach growled loudly, and all three girls fell into laughter.

"It is good to laugh, isn't it?" Liesl squeezed close to her. "My oma would say it is good medicine."

Josie's smile remained wide, a sure remedy for her recent anger. She was grateful for the cool breeze and the refreshing company.

Leaving behind the sunshine for the boxed rooms of the mill was unfortunate. The windows were hardly second best in offering views of the glorious day. Each pane was covered in a thin coat of cotton bits, showcasing only a hazy view of the cobalt sky and paper-thin wisps of clouds. As the hours went by, the muted sight agitated Josie, while Sally's prediction came true with a constant grumbling of her stomach. Josie's head became fuzzy as the windows darkened, and she leaned back on the wall, the room fading away and her body slumping down to the floor.

She was not sure how many minutes passed before she woke to a voice calling, "Miss Clay?"

Her eyes fluttered open but could only make out a blurred familiar figure. No matter how many times she batted her lashes, everything remained unfocused. "Braham?" She spoke his name before her senses righted themselves. The feel of his name on her lips was a comfort in itself. She squeezed her eyes shut then opened them again.

Horror filled every inch of her heart.

How could she have mistaken Braham for the silver-haired man whose wild eyes and pointed features sharpened in her recovered vision?

"Dr. Chadwick?"

He stood above her while she lay helpless. Were these past weeks a dream? Did she relive the terror of a mistaken death all over again? Or perhaps she was still ill, and the doctor was only here to help?

Dr. Chadwick stepped out of view again. Josie moved her wrists, assured that she was not bound. Perhaps she was waking from a nightmare. Perhaps there was not one speck of graveyard dirt on her conscience. Relief melted into sorrow for the fabrication of that kind factory manager. He had been a bright spot in all the dark twists and turns. She sat up, not feeling ill at all.

Where the yellowed glass of the doctor's cabinet might reflect her image, there was only a papered wall with a ticking clock. And instead of the usual off-putting smell of poorly cleaned utensils and bedsheets, a savory aroma of roasted chicken and biscuits teased her empty stomach. Dr. Chadwick retreated from her bedside. The man she'd longed for in these short seconds stood behind the doctor.

Braham Taylor was not a figment of her imagination.

She was lying on the settee in the boardinghouse parlor. A warm breeze poured in from the window next to her.

"Miss Clay, your former employer arrived just as you fainted." Braham knelt beside her, blocking out every other thing from view, extinguishing the monstrous man from her sight. She absorbed Braham's kindness. He was a shield for a moment—a comforting balm warding off the terror of facing her near murderer. If she could, she'd take Braham by the shoulders and keep him there so she'd never have to face that horrible man again.

Shivers erupted from her torso, and gooseflesh crawled down her arms. Her teeth began to chatter, yet sweat pricked her forehead. "Please, do not leave me," she whispered, her throat so thick with anxiety that she could barely make a sound.

Braham explored her face with the deepest concern. His fingers brushed her brow, and he fixed his gaze upon her lips. "Miss Clay, are you not well?"

"I—I think I fainted because I haven't eaten—" A throb spread across the back of her head.

"See here, I have some tea from the maid." Dr. Chadwick was unavoidable as he loomed behind Braham now. "Sir, if you would give us just a moment, I can help Miss Clay recover enough to tend to the business that brings me here."

"Certainly." Braham stood up and nodded to the doctor. "I must return to the mill. Please, Miss Clay, take the rest of the evening off. Your wages will be waiting for you in Miss Clyde's office." He gave a slight smile then stepped out of the room.

At the abrupt shut of the front door, Josie jumped. She was left alone with the doctor.

"Here you are." Dr. Chadwick handed her the cup of tea. She could not bring it to her lips. She only stared at the sage-colored liquid.

"Why are you here?" she seethed.

"My, my, instead of the complacent murmur of my assistant, I find the growl of a cat." He chuckled. From the corner of her eye, Josie watched him stride over to the cold fireplace. He thrummed his fingers against the mantel.

Josie's bitterness mixed with grief. She'd once considered this man a mentor. She'd admired his knowledge and enthusiasm in finding cures and caring for the sick. She'd valued him more than he valued her, in the end. The glint of his knife was an angry memory.

Josie stood, the teacup shaking in her hand. With a large gulp, she allowed the tea to do its trick. She was steady enough. Dr. Chadwick's back was to her, his sharp shoulders much too narrow for his unruly mass of hair.

"You have not answered my question, Dr. Chadwick."

"Miss Clay, as you know, my supply has dried up as of late." His fingers stopped moving. "Alvin seems to care more for business here in Gloughton than keeping his bargain with me."

"Sir, you also know my father's trouble."

"And what of my trouble?" he barked. The usual flush of anger crept along his cheeks with spidery edges.

Josie narrowed her eyes. "Forgive me, but your leisure time spent at the table is hardly a concern of mine when my father's very life is threatened."

The doctor's lip curled. "And if I happened to lead the authorities to your father, perhaps I'd end his misery."

"Dr. Chadwick." Josie's voice wobbled. "I am no fool. Alvin has visited you. You are well aware that your sloppy work has left much evidence against yourself."

"I see that Alvin has not been up-front with you, has he?" He snickered.

Josie clenched her teeth. "What do you mean?"

"He will do nothing to me," the doctor sneered. "Not with the amount of money I withhold from him."

Alvin had hinted to the fact that his meeting with Chadwick had not gone well the night of Harry Garnett's funeral. Josie swallowed back bile. Of course money was more important to Alvin than her father's safety.

"I am at the mercy of Alvin too," she admitted. "Believe me, I want to get this over with." Weariness fell heavy on her shoulders. She feared she might faint again. "I do not know when he will provide what you need."

"Then you and I are alike in that." His disheveled eyebrows prodded upward. "I have a plan that will get us out of this arrangement quickly."

A warning rang in Josie's ears—a cry against the knife plunging into her chest. "I will do nothing criminal—" She clutched at her waist, not wanting to use the exact word that pressed upon her brain.

Murder.

"No, no, we shall not go there again." He waved his hand and then ran it through his mop of hair. "I might reconsider my threat to your father for a price."

"What are you saying?"

"You work for wages that are to be sent to your father, do you not?" He thrummed his fingers together.

"What would you have me do?" Josie bristled at the answer she knew was coming.

He stepped closer, clutching at his coat. "You will give me your wages. I shall return them to your father when he gives me what I need—and that which will give you reprieve from this messy business."

"What of my father then? His farm, his well-being—" Josie grimaced. "His life is threatened by those men and our swiftness in supplying for them."

"But if you do not give me his wages, his life will be found out by more moral creatures." He pushed out his lip mockingly. "I'll make sure of it."

She balled her fists so hard her nails dug deep in her palms. "If anything, I should be the one to call on the authorities and have you locked up for good. I've seen the secret room where you've desecrated souls. I know your thievery."

"Ah, but, you turn me in and your father will go as well." He gave a wicked smile. "You see, the web is taut, and plucking one thread will bring down the whole lot."

Josie hung her head and swallowed a sob.

"Just think, one less worry for your dear father." Dr. Chadwick spoke in a soothing tone. "If we act quickly, he'll not notice the delayed wages." He reached out his hand to her, and she stepped back.

"Will Alvin comply?" She could barely get the words past her lips. Dr. Chadwick's blackmailing tactic was not toothless, because of that wretched Alvin and his lust for money.

"My dear, it is up to you to convince him." Dr. Chadwick caressed his bearded chin. "Beg him to act quickly. It is the only way to save your father. It is your father's debt or his freedom, Josephine. 'Tis your choice."

This was unbearable. All was lost, it seemed. "I will collect my wages this evening. Where will you be?"

A wide, unapologetic smile shone beneath the doctor's hooked nose. "I shall have my dinner at the tavern. I will wait for you there in my carriage at half past eight."

Josie's chest tightened. She prayed her father would find some relief and that the wages would return to him quickly.

She marched to the door. "Get out."

"I see your work as a mill slave has bankrupted you of manners." He laughed lazily as he walked to the door. Before stepping outside, he turned and said, "In case you were wondering, I am close to discovering the greatest cure of all." He placed his hand on Josie's cheek. It was cold, lifeless, like the bodies he craved. She pulled her head back and glared at him. His lips parted then smacked shut. "Your mother would have benefited from such a cure. It is a shame someone like you balks at such efforts."

Josie winced, remembering the stiff body of Harry Garnett being roughly handled by Alvin as he wrapped him in burlap and slung him over his shoulders. The man was treated like nothing more than livestock at market. No dignity was given to the creature who had once breathed the same air as he did.

"There must be a different way," she muttered.

"There is not," Dr. Chadwick declared in a singsong voice,

shaking a finger by his ear and nearly hopping out of the house. "Good day, for now." He crammed his hat on his head and disappeared out of sight.

Josie leaned against the door and began to weep. There was nothing to be done but pray for death to come quickly to poor unsuspecting souls.

That was the only way out.

Chapter Fifteen

The glass reflected Braham's figure—his disheveled hair, unbuttoned collar, and the slumped shoulders—a visible sign of the unseen grief that weighed him down. He stood at the window beside Aunt Myrtle's bedside. Her slight breaths were barely detectable as she slept. All was quiet at this late hour. An unwanted calm. He turned to sit in the chair next to her. The creak of the floor sent a chill up his spine.

On her bedside table, the candle's unwavering flame saluted the woman who'd been Braham's steady light all these years. All he could do was pray—not for the aunt who was certainly ready for her meeting with her Maker, but for peace for his own sorrow at losing the last of his family.

Footsteps grew louder in the hallway, and Braham wiped his eyes quickly, straightened his collar, and folded his hands in his lap. When the door ached open, the flame stumbled with the push of air then wobbled upward to find its posture again. Minnie stepped in, holding a small tray with a vial and handkerchief. Her mouth fell open, and she took a step back. "Oh, pardon me, sir," she whispered. "I—I was just bringing her next dose."

"At this hour?"

"Yes. It's round the clock, sir."

"I doubt it is wise to wake her." Braham grimaced at the thought creeping in his mind. *No medicine will do her any good now.*

"The physician that visited from Boston on Tuesday said it should be administered for her comfort." Minnie's eyes were lowered to the tray. It rattled in her trembling hands.

"You are not in trouble, Minnie." He sighed and stood up.

"Thank you, sir. Mr. Bates seemed very certain that the doctor was one of the best. I just want to follow his orders." She continued to the bedside, unaware of the sting of her explanation. Gerald's help disguised his apathy toward his aunt's well-being otherwise.

"I am going to take a walk."

"At this hour?"

"I need fresh air. Please, let me know if anything changes."

"Yes, sir."

Braham left the room, closing the door quietly behind him. He shoved his hands in his pockets, trudged downstairs, and stepped out into the cold night air. The breeze from earlier had picked up, inducing a low moan as it whipped through the stable window.

Braham strode down the dirt drive, kicking the pebbles with the tips of his boots. He should be thankful for Gerald's help in sending the doctor. Gratitude was difficult to dig up though, when Braham suspected his help had less to do with caring for their aunt and more to do with finding her favor at this final hour. He deflated his lungs with a long huff and dug his hands deeper into his pockets.

Braham began to run along the orchard. The wind became icy against his skin. Yesterday's sunshine did nothing for the late hour. He felt its sting in his chest. The moisture clung to his shoulder blades.

Time was slipping quickly now, and he must end this feud once and for all. He turned up to the main house. One solitary candle lit a window. It was the late Mr. Bates's study. Gerald had returned, no doubt readying papers to sell the factory to Bellingham.

So be it.

Braham could work for anyone. All he wanted to do was work.

He patted his front pocket. The folded letter crinkled against his chest. He would keep this by him as if it were the very proof of his existence.

In a way, it was.

Once he passed through the main house gate, he paused, placing his hands on his knees and catching his breath. Fatigue crept into his joints. His eyes burned with sleeplessness. He'd never rest until all was settled. Everything was abruptly coming to a head upon Aunt Myrtle's death. She was the last person to care about the orphan boy who'd found favor in his master's eyes. His aunt was the last person who'd favored Braham at all.

Yet he knew that was not entirely true as he recalled Josie's flushed cheeks and blue eyes, intent on keeping him by her side in the parlor this afternoon. She'd asked him to stay, but that doctor seemed competent enough. Regret had followed Braham all the workday long, knowing that he'd abandoned her to that stranger because of his own obligations to the factory. His incessant desire to protect Josie earlier today fought against his good sense, even now, with the looming house casting its moon-bound shadow upon him. The favor of a factory worker was little in comparison to the family who had made his life worth living. Even if that single worker proved to be a beautiful soul like Josie Clay.

Braham quietly entered the house using the key that Gerald had demanded he was undeserving to obtain. He lit a lamp and traipsed through the dark halls of the place. Light shone from the ajar study door on the second floor. Braham set his lamp on the table in the hallway then entered the room, prepared for the confrontation.

Gerald's head lay atop papers on the large mahogany desk. Soft snores rustled the feathered quill with each breath. Braham considered slamming the door shut to awaken the oaf but thought better of it. He should just leave. Deal with Gerald tomorrow. Curiosity drew him closer though, as he eyed the writing just beneath Gerald's hand.

Blood pounded in Braham's ears. He waded through a palpable silence as he approached the desk. The flowery script was difficult to read upside down, but Braham managed to steady himself by planting his hands on the desk beside Gerald's splayed hair. The snores quieted and Braham's every joint locked in place. He glared at the back of the man's head, waiting for the slightest movement to signal his waking.

The wind battled against the window. Braham took a slow step backward. Gerald gave a long, deep sigh and seemed to settle back into his rhythmic snoring. Assuring that he was indeed asleep, Braham did not move for several seconds. He stood with one foot pressed back, his palms melding with the wood surface, and his fingertips pressed hard near the dark ends of Gerald's hair. If Braham were a child still, he'd be tempted to tug hard at those locks of the cruel person who slumbered. Gerald had often been found kicking at slaves and mocking Braham and other indentured family members. He probably controlled the plantation the exact opposite way his kindhearted father would have approved.

Anger gripped Braham in that quiet moment, wondering what tyranny played out at Terryhold now, with this beast in charge.

He pressed his shoulders forward and looked, once again, at the letter beneath Gerald's hand.

> *My Dearest Doctor Brown,*
>
> *I appreciate your short but successful visit to my aunt. I do hope that you found the other matters satisfactory, and will give a good word to the board. There is nothing I would rather do than serve you and your committee with the utmost satisfaction and efficiency. As you know, my fiancée has discovered a rather useful tool, if you will, to aid in the cause. While the funds are no longer at my disposal since my property remains unsold, the discovery makes up for it. I am confident we shall be able to provide the goods for the community at large.*

Braham reread it to be sure. This had nothing to do with the factory, it seemed. Except, perhaps, Bellingham had backed out on the deal. That was a relief. What was this business though? Gerald was well connected in Boston with many intellectuals—Harvard professors, lawyers, doctors—all belonging to some sort of society or board.

What surprised Braham most, though, was the discovery of a fiancée. Gerald was not one to share his affairs with Braham, yet such an announcement would not be easily hidden around here.

Braham slipped away from the sleeping man, wondering at the business that really was none of his concern.

He crept into the hall, perplexed and a little ashamed at his snooping. Perhaps Gerald couldn't care less about Braham and his position at all. He may have just spat out his usual hatred in front of Bellingham because that was what Gerald had always done. It appeared that the true matter at hand lay in an exchange of goods— maybe cotton or cloth.

As he stepped back into the night, he felt as though the wind might carry him away. His resentment had brought him to this place, and now he left it knowing that he was only a cog in the grand scheme. A cog that was a permanent fixture, thanks to his uncle. The hoot of an owl skipped along the branches of the rustling tree above him. The crunch of his soles on the ground sounded a steady pace. He breathed in the smell of grass and green and sleeping flowers, trying to find peace.

The matter of Gerald's disdain for Braham eclipsed the surprise of a hidden engagement, yet Braham could not shake the twofold sorrow that filled his heart. As he turned toward his home, he spied the orange glow from his aunt's room, regretting losing an hour by leaving her alone—one less hour with her that he'd never revive again. He continued up the drive and thought about his uncle and his goodness.

While to his uncle, Gerald and Braham were adopted cousins, Gerald only thought of Braham as the man who ran the factory. He would never be the family member that he'd been under his uncle's care. No, Braham was nothing to Gerald. And, while Braham cared little for the ways of such a pompous man, Braham could not deny the disappointment that came from a hopeless death of his uncle's dream for them, proven by the very fact that Gerald had not even announced his news of a future wedding.

Josie plucked the fine teeth of a rosemary branch, her knees sinking into the earth. The weak morning sun unfurled its rays upon her ivory skin. Her past two nights were restless after handing over her wages to the horrible Dr. Chadwick. She could not manage to fulfill her interview for the next newsletter edition on Friday evening. Last night, she only pretended to be asleep beneath her bedcovers while her roommates read by candlelight. All the while she prayed and worried that she'd made a mistake.

The tiny green leaves between her fingers released a spicy aroma that reminded her of Mother's sachet. A songbird began to sing beyond the wall. Josie tipped her head up and closed her eyes. The soft brightness through her lids was cut off abruptly. She opened her eyes. A shadow swallowed up every bit of light, and she turned in haste.

Alvin stood above her. The rosemary fell from her palm. Josie scrambled to her feet as the leaves scattered on the ground.

"Didn't mean to frighten you," Alvin said.

"You did not," Josie remarked. "Why are you here at this time? I expected you later—after church today."

"Taking care of other business." He kept his squinty eyes on the kitchen door. Fran's noisy preparation was underway.

Josie could not look at him much longer. Her bitterness brewed faster than the tea in Fran's pot. "I'll not discuss this business with you here." No, not here, in this blessed patch of life. Let one place have no memory of these ill-doings. This garden had become her sanctuary. Josie brushed past him and went through the gate. She waved at him to join her beyond the wall as she hurried to the edge of the canal.

When he came up beside her, he unfolded a document. "I see you're making yourself known around here. But I wonder about this Mistress Mystery." He waved the freshly published newsletter. "The town's not onto you, are they?"

Josie snatched the page away and found the article to which he referred:

Mistress Mystery Sighting:

She skims the grounds of Gloughton Mill,
slips in and out like cotton dust.
Give us a clue, miss, if you will,
as to what you wish to hide from us.

'Twas about Audra. She'd forgotten the verse. "It is not I they speak about." But sadly, she could see how she might fit the same riddle. Her interview was just beneath it. She shoved the page back to Alvin's hand. Josie did not have the stomach to read through her reminiscent words about Mother's garden, her fondness of healing, and her philosophies of tending to the sick.

Josie was not who anyone thought. She was the same as Audra.

"How could you risk my father's life for a lump of money?" The question had rolled in her mind as she tried to sleep last night.

"What?"

She threw a sharp glare at him. "You didn't give Chadwick the ultimatum you promised."

Alvin furrowed his brow, keeping his eyes lowered. "I doubt he'll do anything. He's too distracted by his experiments." He squatted down and scooped up some water, splashing his face. He'd not shaved in quite some time. Josie imagined his hands pricked with the sharp stubble. "Honestly, it is a waste of flesh to provide for Chadwick."

"But you must, that is the only way—" Josie bit her lip, ashamed at her stance.

"His work will get him nowhere." Alvin gave her an apologetic shrug. "He's in an insignificant village, with little apparatus to truly learn much from his dissections."

"So, you do not care that he might call the authorities? Do you not care at all about the mess you've dragged my father into?"

"Care?" Alvin spat into the water he'd just washed with. "I saved you from that clumsy doctor's knife."

"It will do no good if he is caught," Josie snapped. "There's no doubt you will go down with him." She bore a look at Alvin. "You must appease the doctor."

He shifted from one foot to the next then walked away. "Your doctor will get his body." He flipped up his coat and sat on a nearby bench.

This man, enjoying the refreshing water and still morning air was unmoved by the topic at hand—proof that his soul was bankrupt by his deadly bargains.

Josie tipped her chin in the air and approached him briskly. The news with which she would melt his cool demeanor sat on her tongue. She lowered and sat next to him. "The doctor has my wages now. You and my father will not get one penny, until the doctor receives—"

He leapt to his feet. No apathy now. Every muscle in his face was pulled taut, and his eyes bulged. "You gave him your wages?" He grabbed at his chin. "What about your father?"

"It was for him. Dr. Chadwick promises to keep quiet now." Josie shot up, leaning in and narrowing her eyes. "Give him what he wants, Alvin, so my father can get his money."

"You are a foolish woman!" He swatted at the air between them and began to pace along the canal. "What a disloyal wretch you've become." He wagged his head.

Josie clenched her fists, resisting the urge to push the man into the water. She marched up to him and yanked at his arm, turning him toward her. Emotion stabbed at her throat and eyes. She feared all that she would pour out into this quiet morning might be louder and stronger than any steam loom. "Disloyal? You've turned my father against all that is good. The moment he escapes debtors' prison, you drag him into this business."

Alvin licked his lips and spoke quietly. "He is a good man. It is not what you think."

She stared at him. What could she believe anymore? It didn't matter now. Whatever it was, Dr. Chadwick had been correct. Alvin seemed to be worked up enough to finally make good on his promise. "The quicker you repay Dr. Chadwick, the less threat my father has to deal with."

"I did not expect this from you, Little Josephine Clayton." His face relaxed from his frustration.

"Expect what?"

His gurgling chuckle irritated Josie's ears. "You—to turn against your father for your own desperate need of a corpse."

Josie's stomach turned. "That is not it at all—"

"Oh, isn't it?" He adjusted the cuffs on his dirty work coat, seemingly pleased with himself.

Josie shook away the guilt. "Will the next body go to Dr. Chadwick?"

The sound of mourning doves answered before Alvin. He fiddled with his coat, gazing across the canal at the sleeping village. Any moment, the bells would signal the first call to church. But first, she needed to be assured that Alvin would cooperate. He began to walk leisurely along the canal, kicking at debris with every other step. Josie took quick, short steps behind him to keep up. He turned his head slightly and said, "Do you know why your father began in this business?"

"What?"

He paused then annunciated each syllable. "Do. You. Know. Why?"

"You turned him onto it with your desperate need for money."

"Well, that is the pot calling the kettle black, isn't it?" He chuckled again then faced the canal, arms crossed over his chest. "No, your father, fool that he is, wanted to take your mother to the city— to some doctor who could help her find a cure. When I discovered this business was lucrative, your father was desperate enough to help. Oh, he'd never go on runs with me while your mother was alive, but he would give me the cart as payment, and as long as he kept food in my belly and a place in his barn, I'd give him part of the earnings."

"You did this while you lived with us?"

"Aye. It was for your mother, of course. But she died. The past two years have been difficult—what with your father kicking me out and then you falling ill." He slid his eyes in her direction, a crease between his eyebrows. "The day I found you with Dr. Chadwick was the day we returned from New York. Your father had been desperate for money, for your cure, and he begged to be a part of it." Alvin bit his lip. "And I needed the help. Some help he was."

Josie's chest was tight with this news. Her buried grief was dug up with Father's exposed secret. "Why are you telling me this—"

"Because you are a fool to give your wages to that doctor, when all your father has wanted was to keep his land, and to one day have you return to him."

"I did it for Father. I do not want him to go to prison," Josie mumbled, her throat squeezing tight.

"Even if Dr. Chadwick could find law enforcement who aren't paid off by body snatchers, I doubt they'd come seek out your father. Your greater concern is the men harassing your father until we've paid up."

Josie's heart plunged down. "You do not think Chadwick's threat is valid?"

"Like I said, he must motivate the right do-gooder to charge your father. Corruption is a standard around New York cemeteries. Why do you think we went there?" Alvin sighed. "But now, what to do with your ridiculous agreement with that doctor?"

Movement distracted Josie from the guilt of complicating this predicament. Just past Alvin, she saw a figure turning from the bridge. "We must go."

She pushed past him, praying it wasn't Braham. She did not want to lie to him anymore. This man was not her father's farmhand. He was her father's demon.

As she drew near to the garden gate, the person appeared from behind the promenade of trees lining the canal. Her stomach sank. Audra's hair flamed from beneath her hood, and she waved frantically at Alvin while she approached Josie. "You, wait," Audra demanded with a pointed finger at Josie.

Josie swallowed hard, despising taking orders from this woman.

Alvin rushed over to them both. "What is it?" He searched Audra's face with an intensity Josie had never seen from the man. His eyes sparkled vibrantly, and his mouth was set in a genuine readiness to smile. He looked at this woman with nothing less than adoration.

Audra's attention skipped across Alvin's face with an uneasy acknowledgment. She then stared at Josie. "I've just come from the Bates house to visit my sister. Mr. Taylor would like you to know—" She frowned. "His aunt is dead."

Chapter Sixteen

Braham walked the minister to the side entrance of the church, thanking him for arriving at his home at such an early hour. The man's prayers were the last words to echo through the room before Aunt Myrtle's final breath.

"She would not have had it any other way." Braham dipped his chin as Reverend Lively shook his hand. "I'll credit you for her peaceful departure."

"Ah, you should credit Someone greater than I. I am only acting in obedience." He winked then patted Braham's shoulder before disappearing inside the church.

Braham stuck his hands in his pockets and looked around as he shoveled air in his chest. Everything seemed dull—the green leaves were gray, the crisp air was flat. He may have never felt as alone as he did this day. His belonging was null and void as the last two Bateses breathed their last. All family was gone now—at least the family who wanted him around.

He stepped into the main street, not feeling like attending a church service. Something about these past days irritated him. Everything had gone so quickly. Why had he been so caught up in the factory when Aunt Myrtle was so close to the end?

Braham hit the side of his cart. His horse whinnied. "Sorry, boy."

The church bells began to call to the waking village. The church attendant emerged from the arched door and began to sweep the porch. Braham hurried up onto the bench, not wanting to be caught by the steady stream of folks heading to church. Yet, there was one person who did not know about his aunt.

No matter how much he did not want to face the woman, he had to let her know. Braham turned down Mosgrove Way and stopped along the wooden fence. The high gabled roof and ivy-covered brick cottage was smaller than he remembered. He approached the door, and the scent of medicinal potions hung in the air as if a cloud of the stuff permeated through the walls. He slowed his pace when he heard muffled voices. The voices grew louder, and before he could slink back and avoid an encounter, the door opened.

Miss Young gaped at him, her eyes red and a handkerchief to her mouth. She dropped her hand. "So, I am the last one to know?"

"What do you mean?" His every muscle stiffened as usual around this woman.

"Even a mill girl knew about Aunt Myrtle." She stepped back, and Josie appeared. "A simple mill girl! You sent Audra to tell her and not me?"

Braham only stared at Josie. "Miss Clay? I—I didn't expect—"

"Pardon me, Mr. Taylor," Josie muttered as she stepped through the doorway. "I was collecting an elixir for little Liesl, the bobbin girl." Her glassy eyes wobbled as she approached him. "I am so very sorry for your loss." An uneven flush spread across her cheeks, and she began to weep in her arm as she pushed past him.

Miss Young rolled her eyes and crossed her arms. "She's a sweet thing, but I don't know why she is so upset over a woman she hardly knows." Daisy sniffled and picked at the lace trim of her handkerchief. Her lip trembled, and she also began to weep.

"Grief is grief," Braham snapped. "You of all people should know that." He spoke harsher than he should, but Daisy had the same coldness as Gerald. Just like they had made Braham feel the size of a fly at times, Daisy's words had painted Josie as insignificant and unworthy.

He spun on his heel and ran down the path, catching the gate just before it slammed shut behind Josie. She hurried down the lane.

"Josie—Miss Clay?"

The woman paused then turned her head. "Please, sir, I apologize for my outburst. It's just. . .just so much." She continued at a quicker pace. Before she got to Main Street, Braham caught up with her, placing a careful hand on her arm before she turned the corner.

"I am so very sorry for your loss." Josie held a handkerchief to her mouth, her long lashes lowered beneath the shadow of her bonnet.

"Thank you." Braham pressed his lips together, the word *loss* spinning like a bobbin in his heart. "I am sorry that you only spent these last days with her. I believe you two would have been good friends."

She caught a sob in her handkerchief. "You do not know me at all." She finally looked at him. Her blue eyes were tinged pink, clouded with anguish more than sorrow. "I am only a mill girl, as Miss Young said. It is all I want to be." Placing her hand on his arm, she leaned in. "Truly. I want that more than anything in the world. But—" She pressed her lips together.

"But what?" He laid his hand on hers; his pulse sped up past the grief. With Josie by his side, his loss was not seared by loneliness. She was the only person left whom he might depend on. The only person with whom he had been himself. "You are more than an employee, Miss Clay. You have become a friend to me."

A smile barely tipped at her mouth's corners but then dropped into a frown. She shook her head slowly as she pulled her hand away from his. "Oh Braham. If only I could be your friend." She placed her gloved fingertips on his cheek. "That is a wish that can never be met." Her eyes filled with tears once again. "Please, do not follow me." She brushed past him, leaving him just as alone as he ever was.

Josie ignored the women gawking at her as she passed them on their way to church. If she was questioned, at least she had good reason. Poor little Liesl had an ailing stomach, and Josie would care for her this morning with the elixir she and Miss Young had made. Josie had nearly made it across the canal before she was stopped. But it wasn't a mill girl who caught her attention. It was her father.

He stood beside the rail of the bridge. His hands fiddled with the old pocket watch that his own father had given him, and his shirt was missing a button at the crest of his wide belly. He was disheveled like a man would be without the care and attention of a woman. Her throat ached, and she ran up to him. She threw her arms around his neck and began to cry in the coarse fabric of his work coat.

"Oh, my dear Josephine." He pushed her away gently, a firm grasp on each of her shoulders.

She dabbed at her eyes with her handkerchief. "Father, you are here. You look well." His nose was pink and his cheeks filled with color. Yet his eyes held no cheer. They were dull, drooping with worry.

She swallowed past a lump in her throat. "How is the farm—"

His grip tightened, and he pulled her toward him. A thin layer of perspiration glistened across his forehead.

"Father—" she shrieked. His fingers pierced through her dress like dull knives. He let go and wrung his hands, a low groan erupting from his now trembling lips.

"I fear they have taken my wits, Daughter." His wild look frightened Josie.

She rubbed her arms and leaned against the bridge railing, not looking directly at him. "What have they done?"

"They mark each day that passes without a body with a bloody stake at the door." He wiped his forehead. "They have stolen my feed and my stored vegetables too."

"How dare they!" Josephine straightened up and looked around for Alvin. "This is enough, Father. Where is Alvin—"

"Alvin told me what you did," he blurted. "Is it true, Josephine? Does the doctor hold both my freedom and your wages for ransom?"

"Oh Father," she exclaimed, gathering together his shaking hands. "I had little choice. Alvin is ignoring the bargain he made with Chadwick."

"Josephine, listen to me now." He licked his lips. "You must not agree to anything without Alvin's guidance." His reprimand knifed at her guilt—and her resentment. "Anything. He knows more than you or I—"

"How could you have depended on such an income, Father?" Josie cried out. "All this time, we've been tied to that man and his wicked ways. And you hid it from me—and my mother."

At the mention of her mother, her father's shoulders drooped, and his bushy eyebrows tipped up. "It was for her," he mumbled.

"Well then, just as you've told me before. There are consequences for our actions." She bristled at his excuse. "And now look where we are."

"Well, you've added salt to the consequence, haven't you?" He licked his lips and wiped at his forehead again. "I fear the creditors will return."

She opened her mouth to speak, but her father continued, "Now we are at the mercy of that doctor more than ever. You must do well tonight, Daughter."

Her stomach soured. Josie was suddenly aware of the bottle in her pocket. She might need the elixir for herself. At least she'd been as forthcoming with Braham as she possibly could be. There was no possible way they could be friends. Not when Dr. Chadwick would receive his dear aunt's body just across the bridge from his beloved factory.

Her father shifted his weight and sighed.

Lord, give me strength.

She walked past him. "Come, we'll have breakfast, and I will gather some provisions for you to take home."

She was stuck between two men—one whom she'd loved all her life, and one who stirred something inside her she'd never felt before. Her loyalty to one was an inevitable choice at the expense of the other. How could she choose between affection and her very own blood?

Josie waited for him to catch up and hooked her hand on his elbow. "This will soon be over, Father."

The lantern swung from one hand, the lilacs hanging in the other. People abandoned the graveyard one by one as the darkening sky drank up the light of day. Soon, only Josie, Braham, and his servant were standing alone beside the coffin. Josie raised her eyes to the moss-covered tombstones in the older part of the cemetery. To her surprise, Alvin stood on the steps of the Gloughton tavern across from the cemetery's main entrance. She had expected that he would not appear until the light had been extinguished.

Braham let out a jagged sigh. "Come, let us return home, Minnie. She's to rest." He shifted his weight, turning to Josie. "I thank you for coming. . .even if—" He lowered his head. Josie's heart slumped at the distress she'd added to this man on Mosgrove Way. She'd convinced herself that ending their friendship was for his good. And it was, especially after hearing and seeing her father's despair.

"Please, forgive me for my behavior yesterday morning, Mr. Taylor. This is your time to grieve—not mine." There could be nothing between them. He would want it that way if he knew what was about to happen.

After a quiet that shook with tension, Braham spoke. "Will you join us for supper, Miss Clay? Not for me, but for my aunt? She would want you there." His face was pale, his eyes weary. Josie's heart tightened. She wanted to comfort him. If the outcome were different, her greatest desire would be to comfort this man.

"Please, Mr. Taylor. I'd like to stay here awhile longer." She began to shiver.

Braham tilted his head. A question flashed in his eyes. "Come now, you are cold. It is time to go." He took off his coat and wrapped it around her shoulders. Its warmth instantly relieved her shaking. This would not do. The longer they delayed, the worse this evening would drag on.

She put the lantern at her feet and returned the coat. "I would like some time to pray."

Josie did not lie. She was desperate for peace.

"Very well." Braham nodded to Minnie, and they began to leave, stepping away from the halo of the yellow lantern. "Do not stay too long," he called out in the gloomy dusk.

Please don't leave me.

Her soul cried after the man who had captured her heart. From the corner of her eye, Alvin slithered down to the bottom step of the stoop, his full body waiting just beyond the streetlamp. She stood in the lantern's glow while he was hidden by darkness.

This man made her heart recoil.

Yet he was the door to her family's freedom from this work. She ground her teeth and tried to soothe herself with a fragrant inhale of lilacs and soil. So much life filled her senses as she preyed on death. She remembered her mother's lessons on the different parts of the plants that were useful. Josie treasured the time spent among Mother's dried herbs, still emitting the aroma of growing plants yet useful in their lifeless stems and withered leaves. They would bring healing and goodness.

Bile filled her throat.

Josie's eyes blurred as she stared at the wooden box at her feet. This deed would be abhorred by those who loved this woman. Braham would be disgusted at such a crime. It wasn't worth it, was it? For what? Money, a farm? Was there no other way?

The lantern's flame flickered, yet it continued to cast a steady safe haven for Josie and Aunt Myrtle's grave. The light was literally a lamp at her feet. Her heart leapt. She nearly smiled behind her black veil.

Her spirit filled with the knowledge of the only way now.

"Wait!" she called to Braham, who was just beyond the cemetery gate.

He spun around. "What is it, Miss Clay?" He turned to Minnie and motioned for her to go ahead. Josie left the lamp and rushed over to him. Alvin shrunk back up the steps and beneath the dark overhang.

Holding her lips as perfectly still as she could manage, Josie whispered to Braham, "Please, don't leave me." She could not think fast enough, but once the gravedigger arrived and she extinguished the lantern, she'd never face Braham again. Perhaps not even her own self.

Josie returned to the gravesite and knelt on the cool earth.

Braham followed, crouching beside her. "Why must you stay?" The same skepticism simmered in his stare as the first night they met. She had pushed him away earlier today, and now he put up his own guard. That was wise of him.

"Please, sir." She folded her hands in her lap and spoke quietly, "I worry."

"Worry?"

"In my village, there were thieves in the night." A sharp breeze cut through her and bumps pricked her skin. She leaned close to his ear. "Body snatchers."

Saying the words strangled her throat. She was a deceiver through and through. The lantern's flame swelled though, and the heavens seemed to shine bright with stars.

She was a child of light, not darkness.

Braham examined her with a serious look. He asked, "What do you mean—"

Josie put her finger to his lips. "Shh. If there are thieves about, they might be listening." She moved her hand away quickly, the supple warmth of his mouth lingering on her skin.

Minnie called out, "Sir, the carriage is waiting."

Braham's attention on Josie was as vibrant and steady as the lantern's glow. A new energy emanated from his pitiful state of mourning. Without looking away from Josie, he replied, "Go home without me, Minnie." He slid his finger along his collar, and his Adam's apple bobbed. "Miss Clay and I shall pray together."

Josie turned to the gravesite, biting the inside of her cheek. Braham neared her. Her nerves frenzied now. Her rebellion against the devious plan sparked intrigue. The handsome Braham Taylor was beside her. She was not alone, and the flame would continue on, brightening the night she had dreaded these past weeks. There might not be another chance again, with the terrible network's threats more pressing than even withheld wages. But for now, she'd deter the chance of bearing shame every time she saw Braham Taylor. With him, her conscience would remain as white as snow. No, there was no deceit now, just a blooming comradery—a praying partnership.

Before they could bow and pray, the gravedigger approached with his spade. A pipe hung from his lips. After his word of condolence, they stood to give him room.

Braham took her hand and they sat together on a nearby bench. The lamp rested in plain view beside a tombstone. Its yellow glow bounced from the stone to the blades of grass and gently lit up the profile of the man beside her.

The dirt thumped against the box, and the spicy smoke from the pipe mingled with the scent of disturbed earth. Braham did not release her hand but held her tight. Josie lowered her head and prayed, sensing God was nearer to her than He had been in a very long time.

The thumps of soil continued. Her heart fell more and more prostrate.

When Braham's arm brushed hers she looked up. His cheek glistened with moisture. The off-putting incense of the smoking man carried upward to the heavens, racing Braham's prayers to the footstool of the Lord.

Josie continued to pray, tightening her grip on Braham's hand and ignoring her accomplice beyond the fence who was no doubt fuming.

God would make all things right in this night when darkness plotted. For this one foiled grave robbing, light would prevail.

Chapter Seventeen

Braham opened his eyes to the graying dawn. His arms were wrapped around the sleeping Josie Clay, droplets of dew shimmering on her black skirt. Her head was tucked between his shoulder and neck, and her soft breaths warmed his skin. A mourning dove sang out over the graveyard. The residual sorrow from yesterday's funeral sat thick in his throat, soothed only by the perfect fit of the girl slumbering by his side.

He should wake her before anyone found them. The sun would be up soon. But when Braham caught the freshly laid grave at his feet, he tightened his embrace. Without Josie Clay, he'd be left cold and alone. He could sit like this forever.

She moved in his arms and sighed. Her hand clutched at his lapel. He took her dainty fingers in his own, squeezed his eyes and prayed.

"Braham?" Josie sat up, and as he'd suspected, a chill replaced the warmth. Sleep kissed her face, just as it had that morning he found her in the garden. "How long have we slept?"

"I do not know. Perhaps an hour?"

"The grave!" She withdrew her hand and rose to her feet. She crouched down and fiddled with the lantern, which was cold and dark. "The candle is melted." Josie fell to her knees, smoothing the top of the dirt with her hands. "Does it appear disturbed?" Her face was fraught with desperation as she bounced her attention between Braham, the lantern, and the grave. She collapsed, weeping, on top of Aunt Myrtle's grave.

Braham remembered her concern about grave robbers. He'd read about their activity in Boston and the laws in place to thwart them. Several arrests were made, yet bodies still went missing. Resurrection men is what they called the robbers. A lofty term for such a morbid business. This was Gloughton, a sleepy town far from cities and bizarre criminal activity.

He lifted her up by the shoulders. "Miss Clay, I do believe all is safe and sound. We were not asleep for very long." A streak of dirt marred her cheek. He took out his handkerchief and wiped it gently. "Please, don't cry—" A weak smile formed on her lips. He wanted to bundle her up again, hold her close and forget their surroundings. Beside the bench lay the lilacs she'd brought to the graveside.

A shudder went through his frame as he gathered them and placed them on the fresh soil.

"There, it is done," he muttered.

An agonizing moan sounded from the far end of the cemetery.

They both froze, their eyes locked in question. Again, a painful outcry echoed across the yard.

"Wait here, Josie." Braham started for the gate but did not get far without Josie joining him. She hooked her hand around his arm, making it impossible to resist her accompaniment. As they carefully walked between the crooked tombstones, Braham looked over his shoulder, bidding farewell to the lady who'd given him a home. Josie caught his eye, her brow muddled with distress.

"She's at peace, I know it." He gave her a reassuring smile and squeezed her close to his side. She looked away. All he could see were the golden curls along her back.

When they left the graveyard, the silver of early morning gave way to a pale yellow sunlight, washing the gabled roofs of the village's Main Street shops and Josie's profile in a soft glow.

The quiet morning was interrupted with spitting and coughing followed by another long groan.

"It's coming from the side of the tavern." Josie pulled him that direction.

"Allow me," Braham said, taking the lead. He did not know what they might find, and he would not risk any harm coming to her.

At the corner of the brick building, a man was curled up like the frond of a fern, his head tucked beneath his arm and his knees to his chin. His body shook with labored breathing. Each exhale ended with a moan.

Braham rushed over and knelt beside him. "Sir, let us help." A waft of ale mixed with the metal smell of blood induced Braham to gag. The man slid his arm from his face, exposing a large black eye and a swollen lip. "Man, you need a doctor."

"I need my horse," the man muttered.

Josie rushed up, her face nearly green. "Alvin?"

"You know him?"

"It. . .it is—" She bounced a look from Braham to the man who was now trying to sit up. "It is the man who brought me here."

"Your father's farmhand?"

She barely nodded.

Braham immediately helped the man up.

"Careful," Alvin said gruffly. "My ribs are barely holding together." His slight chuckle ended in a groan. Josie also assisted. Together, they got the man on his feet.

"What happened?" Josie asked.

"What do you think happened?" Alvin sneered, spitting to the ground in front of him. "I got on the wrong side of the wrong man." He glared at her for a moment.

Anger began to rise in Braham. He'd always felt uneasy when he spied this fellow, and he could see he was a brute up close. "Miss Clay, I will take him to Daisy. You go home and get some rest."

"I am coming with you." She slid a wary look to Alvin. "I can help. Besides, you are needed at the factory more than I. If it takes too long, you can leave, and I will stay." She did not say it as a suggestion but as a fact.

Braham bit back a smile, once again awed by her confidence when it came to helping the injured—even the scoundrel that neither of them welcomed in Gloughton.

"What happened?" Josie whispered in the small room behind

Daisy's kitchen. Both Daisy and Braham had left. Daisy was calling on a neighbor, and Braham left half an hour before to ready for the workday. Josie held a bowl of water in her lap and dabbed at the nasty cut on Alvin's head with a fresh cloth.

"Someone did not want me to snatch a body last night. Simple as that." He squirmed, but Josie remained persistent in cleaning the wound.

"Did the man know about the body?"

He narrowed his eyes at her. "Why else would he pummel the devil outta me?"

She lifted her brow. "Doubt he did that."

"You're probably right." He laughed then winced. "Although, I've proven myself more of an angel on your part."

Josie ignored him. "So, this person did not want you stealing bodies."

"Not last night, he didn't." He twitched. Who else was about, knowing this underhanded business plaguing these rural parts of Massachusetts?

"It was wise to leave Myrtle Bates be." Confidence soared within her. "I work for her family. It would be difficult to face Mr. Taylor if we'd gone through with it."

He curled his lip. "Is that why you took your time? I waited and waited, and you just sat by that blasted grave."

Josie stood up, careful not to spill the water. "It was for the best, wasn't it? If that man didn't want you snatching last night, imagine your condition today if you had." She dropped the rag in the bowl and set it on the table beside his bed. "Who was that man, Alvin?"

Alvin's nostrils flared, and he answered, "His face was hidden from my view."

"Then how did he know your business?" Whoever the suspect was, Josie felt lighter than she had since her days before the fever had taken over her body. Aunt Myrtle's body was safe. And it wasn't even because of Josie's own efforts. The woman was blessed beyond her life. Josie's heartbeat sped up as she considered Braham. She would not have to hide her face from him like she had expected to do after being part of stealing Aunt Myrtle's body. A flutter in her spirit wondered if there was a divine hand in all of this. The one person who held her as they slept began to take hold of her heart in a fierce, unrelenting way.

Alvin curled his lips again and glared at her. "I do not know, but he knew who I was."

Fear slithered along Josie's confidence. Someone else lurked about, knowing Alvin's ties—and probably hers—to this business? "We cannot do this here anymore, Alvin."

"What are you suggesting? This is the only way. We have a factory filled with accidents waiting to happen."

All Josie's elation from saving Myrtle's body deflated.

"My father is running out of time. He said that the creditor is closing in on him." Josie's mouth went dry. "We must get the money from Dr. Chadwick."

Alvin slammed his fist on the wall, rattling a shelf of empty jars and bottles. "Thanks to you." He turned his head away from Josie. "Leave me."

She slunk out of the room, a heavier weight than before pressing down on her. She was still desperate for bodies. Saving Aunt Myrtle only delayed her father's freedom.

Who was she now, this Josie Clay? It was no longer the hungry spider dragging her into the web. She was the one feeding it and asking for it to continue on its wicked path of desecration.

What else could be done though, when her father would suffer in the end?

Before Braham reached his office, Miss Clyde spoke without looking up from her ledger. "Mr. Bates is waiting for you, Mr. Taylor." Her condolences at the funeral yesterday was the kindest she'd ever been to Braham, and yet it was the least heartfelt word he'd received that day. Even Gerald, whose tall figure now shaded the mottled glass of his office door, was at least kind to Braham. Yet he still had not mentioned the lost deal with Bellingham or his engagement. No woman sat by his side in the front pew of the church.

Braham entered, and Gerald turned immediately.

"Good morning," Braham said as he hung up his coat.

"As good as it can be." Gerald stood with his hands behind his back in front of the large window framing the lifeless workroom on the other side of the glass. "I am heading south."

"I see. And Bellingham?"

Gerald straightened his cravat. "He is. . .out of the picture."

"Will you sell?"

"Not anytime soon." He cleared his throat. "However, I will return at the first word of another accident. My father did not expect girls to nearly lose limbs and life when he put you in charge."

Braham bristled. "Perhaps we are both managing delicate businesses, Gerald. I daresay Terryhold is not accident-free, from what I remember." He swiveled on his heel and positioned himself behind his desk, ready for the man to storm out. But he did not. He only gave a slight laugh and tucked his hat under his arm.

The women began to take their places at the looms.

Gerald approached his desk. "I would take care, Mr. Taylor. I am the only Bates left. Loyalty is rather limited from beyond the grave."

The sorrow was fresh, yet Braham would not show emotion to this man. "We could go about this differently, Gerald. We will never be family, but we can at least be civil to one another."

Gerald tossed his hat on the table and splayed his gloved hands beside it. He winced as he leaned closer, gingerly removing one hand.

"Are you hurt?" Braham asked.

Gerald narrowed his eyes. "As if you'd care," he snorted. "Do not expect this arrangement to be anything more than what it is. I shall find another owner for this blasted place in due time. And in that case, we will be rid of each other. But in the meantime, you can stop trying so hard. You'll never be more to me than that ridiculous boy in the cotton rows."

Braham's fatigue was melting away any guard he should keep up with this man. Anger rushed along his spine. "Why do you hate me so much?" His pulse pounded in his veins.

"Don't be a fool," Gerald snapped. He stood up straight and cradled one hand in the other. "Up until his last breath, my father wasted more time on you than anyone else. I'll do anything I can to cut this ridiculous tie I have to the servant who stole away my inheritance."

"You don't want this inheritance!" Braham waved his arm at the factory all around. The man's glaring eyes glossed over. His scowl softened along his cheekbones, pulling his mouth downward and his brow upward. Braham understood what he meant. Inheritance was more than money and property—even to Gerald Bates.

Braham realized that the man in front of him, the beast who'd squish any living thing to prove his worthiness, was driven by more than just his pride. His father's attention meant something to Gerald, and Braham had been a distraction.

"I—I am so grateful for the opportunity your father gave me—" Braham's voice was lost as the machines began to rattle the windowpane. Gerald swiped his hat from the desk, his face ever stoic. He turned without another look at Braham and left.

Braham sank into his chair, defeat cloaking him.

Before he could straighten his thoughts, Miss Clyde knocked on the door, pushing it open without waiting for permission. "The bobbin girl is not here, and neither is that Miss Clay."

A guffaw came from behind Miss Clyde. Surely Gerald was marking their absences against the manager who'd stolen his father's affection.

Fran wrung her hands as she followed Josie into the front of the house where she hung up her things. "Liesl's been moaning and groaning all night. Her stomach is worse. Where've you been, by the way? You know Fawna will report you for missing curfew. And all night?" Fran's brow furrowed with concern. "Josie Clay, I expect your excuse to be more wholesome than it seems."

"Do not worry, Fran. I was tending to an ill man at Miss Young's." The whole truth would be impossible to believe. Guarding the grave of the late Myrtle Bates? Waking up in the arms of Braham Taylor? Her belly flipped. She would never forget her lashes fluttering against his soft coat and her whole self in an embrace so secure that no ill predicament could touch her. She had awakened to a dream.

Fran followed her up the stairs to check on Liesl. The little girl was asleep in a tangle of covers. Sweaty strands of blond hair pressed against her pallid face. A pot sat beside her, its vile contents tainting the air with sickness.

Josie reached over and felt the girl's head. "Good. She is not feverish. She must have some stomach malady. The elixir from before is not strong enough. I must return to Miss Young's for a special extract. I shall take care of this." Josie took the pot and found its lid, placing it quickly atop. "Get the child a fresh pot. I shall return soon."

Josie dashed downstairs and grabbed her cloak and bonnet then stepped into the courtyard. Besides the noise chugging from within the factory, everything was quiet. Not even a bird made a sound. She hastened across the bridge and passed by the graveyard, thankful for the undisturbed plot piled with fresh dirt. It was strange that Alvin had been demanded to leave it be when this business had so filled his time. A thought flitted in her mind—had he made it up? Did his trouble have anything to do with the body last night?

What would Alvin hide from her at this point, when everything seemed so easily confessed from his tongue of late?

Ahead of her, a familiar man bounded past the tavern, his long coattails flapping against his racing legs. He had a tall top hat and a pristine white collar. He turned to tip his hat at the blacksmith working in his yard, and she recognized his profile. She was certain it was Mr. Bates, the owner of Gloughton Mill.

Josie tried to manage the distance between them. Mr. Bates continued on her same path, eventually turning down Mosgrove Way. When he turned up Miss Young's path, Josie ducked into the shadow of the alley behind the shops along Main. She should not hide from him.

Even though she sought help for an ill mill girl, she should be working. And besides the mill's rules, Alvin was still there. She would rather not be questioned about her acquaintance with the ruffian, especially in his condition.

After a half hour, Mr. Bates left the cottage in a frantic state—more frantic than his determined procession down Main. He rushed to the road and looked up and down, forcing Josie to slip into the back doorway of the closest shop so she would not be seen. Once he passed the alley, she stepped out of the shadows and hustled to Miss Daisy's cottage.

Daisy was quick to help Josie. Together they gathered the ingredients for a stronger elixir. The young apothecary worked diligently to mix the extracts needed to soothe Liesl's stomach. While Josie ground some colic root, she asked, "Is Alvin gone?"

"He left shortly after you."

"Do you think he was well enough to do so?"

"He appeared anxious. I could not stop him." Daisy shrugged. "I believe the ale probably wore off and he wasn't as injured as he seemed. It's a good thing he was gone, though." She gave a pained look at Josie. "He missed quite a quarrel between me and my former—" She shook her head, as if whatever was on her tongue was too much to expel.

"Mr. Bates?"

"You saw him?" Her voice was laced with expectancy, but then she frowned. "He is leaving town, once again. The reason we could never be together. I love Gloughton, and he loves anywhere but here."

Daisy turned from the worktable and began to sort through her many jars on the kitchen shelf, sniffling as she worked. Josie considered revealing that Gerald Bates appeared distraught when he left—a doubtless sign of his perplexed devotion to Miss Young—but before she could decide if mentioning it would be beneficial, the outside door creaked open.

Minnie stepped inside, apparently not noticing Josie or Daisy until she turned to place her basket on the table. Her mouth fell open. She volleyed a look between them both. "Oh, hello, Daisy. . . Miss Clay." She scrunched her nose. "I—I would think you'd be at the mill."

"Were you looking for me?" Josie asked.

"No, not at all," Minnie said, fiddling with her lip. "That is why I am surprised. Didn't expect to see you." She gave a timid smile, once again looking over at Daisy.

"What can I do for you, Minnie?" Daisy lifted a jar, batting lashes that glistened in the shaft of sunshine pouring from the open door.

"I just thought I'd return the bottles used for Miss Myrtle." She took out several green-tinted bottles. "God rest her soul."

"Here." Daisy handed a couple of them to Josie. "Wash these up, and we'll use them for Liesl's remedy."

"Who is Liesl?" Minnie asked.

"A mill girl. She's come down with a stomach ailment," Daisy explained as Josie began to pour some heated water into a basin. "We're coming up with a good remedy." Daisy brought more bottles to Josie. "The batch is large. We'll need to fill several bottles."

While Josie washed the bottles, Minnie offered to make some tea. She clicked her tongue as she hung a kettle above the fire. "The old woman is gone." She sighed. "I do not know what to do with myself on this first day without her."

Josie watched her as she gathered the tea leaves. Grief set in her every feature except when she looked over at Daisy. Even though the young apothecary did not pay Minnie any attention, it appeared

173

that the servant was examining her. Perhaps she was longing to discuss the death of her employer and the change in her own duties. She must feel displaced now. Even so, Minnie did not realize that Daisy was feeling just as abandoned—her thoughts were no doubt ricocheting about a broken heart.

Chapter Eighteen

Delivering the elixir to Liesl was met with obstacle when Josie entered the boardinghouse. In the sunny parlor, a frantic Fawna waved her arms about, demanding, "This will not do! This will not do!"

Sally and Sarah were huddled near the cold hearth, each with a pot in her lap, the same distress as Liesl's in their miserable faces.

"They are as sick as dogs and need to take this to their room." The matron was nearly as green as the sisters. "Mr. Taylor followed these two over from the mill. He's concerned about them—" She looked Josie up and down. "But mostly for you." A flash of intrigue lit up her face. "He mentioned something about an occurrence early this morning?"

"He and I found an injured man in the village—" Josie winced. She quickly continued, "Mr. Bates left me to tend to him at Miss Young's and no doubt wants an update on his condition."

Josie bounced her gaze from the woman to the poor sisters leaning on each other, moaning.

Fawna placed her hands on her hips. "Well?"

"Well, what?"

"The man's condition?" She smirked.

"Oh, he is gone now. Just fine." She spun toward the sisters. "Come, ladies, let us get you to bed. I have something that will help soothe your bellies." They set aside their pots and gingerly stood.

"Fawna, please have Fran make up some fennel and peppermint tea. I will settle these two." She led the way to the stairs. "Oh, and bring some fresh pots, just in case."

When they reached their room, the sisters and Liesl were not willing patients at all. She had to convince them that their stomachs would handle the elixir, having handled little else all morning.

Finally, it was administered to each woman, and they settled on their pillows, anxious for relief.

Josie sat back on her side of the bed. Her head was clouding with exhaustion. No matter how contentedly she had slumbered in the comfort of Braham's embrace, she had little sleep altogether. Each ill roommate dozed off. Josie closed her eyes and joined them.

The sound of the dinner bell aroused her too soon. Late afternoon sun flooded the feet of their beds, and the rumbling of women in the dining room carried up the stairwell through their opened door. She slid off the bed, checking Liesl's forehead, once more grateful that she had no fever. The two sisters slept soundly.

What plagued this room of women? Had they passed along a sickness to each other? Would she be next? After a short prayer and doctoring herself with ointment on the bottom of her feet to ward off disease, Josie decided to go downstairs and grab a bite to eat before administering the last of the stomach remedy.

She passed by the dining room. If Fawna had said one word about Josie's whereabouts this morning, then she was sure to hear an earful from Molly O'Leary, who'd be thrilled for a new story. Josie's heartbeat sped up. The people of Gloughton were just a word away from discovering Josephine Clayton behind this exhausted mill girl.

She descended the steps into the kitchen. Fran's back was to her while she stirred a cauldron of soup. Before looking at Josie, she declared, "Audra, I'll have you wait on the next batch. It's nearly ready."

"It is me." Josie sank down on the bench at the table, resting her heavy head on her fist.

The cook turned and gaped at her. "Oh, pardon me." She returned to her task. "How is little Liesl? I heard two more are ill."

"They are all my roommates." Josie shook her head. "Pray that I don't fall ill. Yet, I do think the elixir Daisy and I concocted will soothe any discomfort."

"That is good." Fran poured some fresh soup into a bowl and

handed it to Josie. "You have the healing recipes, I have the hearty ones." She winked and returned to the fireplace.

"Good evening, Miss Clay," Braham called from the garden doorway. His silk voice was a delightful remedy for Josie's weariness. Her heart leapt as if they had been apart for too long and were now reunited again. Yet it had only been a few hours.

"Mr. Taylor, it is good to see you." Her voice rang high from the reaction he induced. She mustn't get carried away. Her job was not complete. She dipped her head and said, "I apologize for missing work today."

"Come." He waved her toward him, glancing over at Fran with a curious look. "Let us talk in the garden."

Although he was worn-out from a near-sleepless night, he had no desire to return home just yet. Gerald had unearthed insecurity in him. Braham's home was not his own but willed to him from two deceased relatives. Furthermore, this mill position was an undeserved gift, not an earned right, as far as Gerald was concerned. Braham's aching exhaustion collided with the fact that he was unwanted. There was not one person who would miss him if he passed by the Bates estate tonight and never returned. The thought of that terrified Braham. Enough so, that he dreaded facing the gate to the lonely house beyond the orchard. This garden would do for now, as long as Josie was with him.

"You do not know that I have stake in this garden, do you?" He cocked his head, giving Josie a playful look. He strode over to the vegetable patch where his rhubarb flourished since the factory first opened four years ago.

"You, Mr. Taylor?" She approached him, peering down at the patch. "Did you plant these?"

"I did. Helped the first months the factory was being finished." He squatted and combed the soil with his fingertips. "I don't mind gardening. There's a peace about it."

"Yes," Josie near whispered. She knelt beside him. "Cultivating life has a peace about it." Her mouth held a steady smile as she studied the plants. She caught his gaze. Her lips parted. Here they were again, speaking together as if they were the closest of friends, with not one care but the next crop of stew ingredients. He chuckled to himself, and she tilted her head in question.

"I do like talking with you, Josie," he explained. "Tell me, what is the most useful plant in this garden?"

"Useful?"

He held out his hand, and they stood together. "Yes, useful. What one plant would you have me plant in a garden at Bates estate?"

"Are you starting a garden?"

He shrugged. He had not considered starting anything at a home where everything had ended. Besides, a plot of his own would no doubt infuriate Gerald further.

Josie's teeth rested on her lip as she glanced around searching for an answer. He admired her thoughtfulness and pushed away his own cynicism. She was the perfect salve for his sorrow.

"I would have to say the elderberry." She nodded to an irregularly shaped shrub that sprouted in the corner by the gate. "The blooms won't come until midsummer, but they are creamy white bouquets." She clasped her hands together. "One of my mother's favorites." Her look turned serious. "But she always warned that the pretty bundles aren't fair warning to the poison of its other parts." She grimaced, staring at the plant still. "But when the blooms fade, they give way to its greatest treasure—the fruit. Useful in so many ways."

He watched her lips as she spoke. She caught him staring. Taking in a jagged breath, she walked over to the bench and sat down. "Is that what you came to speak about? The good and evil of a useful garden plant?" She smiled, her eyes flashing with amusement.

"Ah, no." He laughed, strolling over to take a seat next to her. He sat, aware of her warmth at his side, just like in the cemetery last night. "I wondered how those girls are. You were not around when I brought them here."

"The women are resting. Miss Young and I made an elixir that is sure to help them."

"And how is your father's man?"

"He is well, I presume. He was gone when I went back to Daisy's." She ran her fingers through the threadlike tufts of a dill plant then plucked a stem of lavender.

"He did not seem well enough to leave on his own. But I know Miss Young is nearly as good a caretaker as you are."

A blush bloomed on her face. A beauty through and through. "I would not worry about him." Josie swiped a loose strand of hair and tucked it in her bun. "But if the mill girls take a turn for the worse, Miss Young has more elixir for us."

"I will be sure to pay her for it."

Josie smiled and held the lavender to her nose. Chirping birds serenaded from beyond the walls. She offered her bit of lavender to him then plucked another. He breathed in the fragrance.

"I am glad that you are here, Josie—" Braham cleared his throat, shoving down the deeper truth behind his statement. "You are wise in healing. And have been very—"

Josie tilted her head and grinned. "Useful?"

"Yes, Miss Elderberry, useful indeed." He sat back with a chuckle then pressed his shoulder into hers. She smiled brightly, but a cinch of concern carved between her eyebrows.

"We have both dealt with much these past weeks, haven't we?" He softened his voice, saying, "Tell me, are things right with your father now?"

Josie lowered her head. "His situation only gets worse."

"I am sorry for that. I can imagine it is worrisome for you, being so far away." He grimaced. "It is difficult to be away from family, isn't it?" He swallowed hard past a lump forming in his throat.

"It is. And Mr. Bates left today, didn't he? He was leaving Daisy's when I arrived for the elixir. Daisy said he was heading down south and mentioned they were once in love. Both of them seemed quite disturbed."

"Interesting. It has been a few years since those two were together." The memories would be harsh now that Aunt Myrtle was gone. Even though Gerald had stolen Daisy's friendship, it was during a time of abundant life—when Aunt Myrtle and Daisy's mother would sit on the porch with tea and fans while they instructed Braham and Daisy to fill basket upon basket of apples for market day.

Life was simple then.

"Perhaps Gerald needed some relief for his hand," he guessed. "He appeared to have hurt it when I spoke with him today. Coddled it like an injured animal." He sighed. "The man only sits at his father's desk when he's not filling his gullet at the tavern. I cannot imagine how he managed to hurt it."

"The tavern?" Josie's eyes widened. "Where we found Alvin this morning?"

She searched Braham's eyes with a growing intensity.

"You don't think that man of your father's crossed paths with Gerald?" Braham considered the fists swinging. He had encountered Gerald's wrath as a boy. No matter how proper the man appeared, finding oneself on his wrong side was a dangerous place to be. "I cannot imagine what he would have to say to get Gerald that upset."

"I am sure it was not him." Josie stood up, tossing the lavender into the mounding plants. "I better get up to the girls. Pray that they are on the mend."

Before Braham could say another word, Josie disappeared through the kitchen door.

Josie gathered up her soup and bread on a tray as Fran insisted and took her dinner into the empty dining room. She had no desire to eat. Her stomach churned like the waves of soup sloshing against the bowl's edges. Had Mr. Bates discovered why Alvin was prowling about Gloughton last night, and in doing so, defended his aunt's corpse with his fists? Hadn't Alvin mentioned the man who'd affronted him was trying to stop him from stealing the body? Of course, Gerald Bates would defend the very corpse of his aunt! But then, why not turn Alvin in to the authorities?

Josie slumped into a chair and held her head in her hands. The suspicion that chased her thoughts stabbed hard and fast like the spindle of a loom. She begged God that she was wrong. Alvin was in rough shape, perhaps just coming out of a loss of consciousness this morning. Had Mr. Bates left Alvin, assuming he was dead?

Mr. Bates might not turn over Alvin's body to the authorities if he'd presumed he killed him. Had he run from the crime to escape possible charges?

Poor Braham was surrounded by more than resurrectionists and posed mourners. His only relative left might have attempted murder.

Josie stirred the soup, considering all other possibilities. But, regretfully, she was stuck in her own worry. If her suspicion was correct, and Gerald knew who Alvin was, and if he ever told Braham, then she would be found out soon enough. To have to answer to Braham about such a thing as this crushed Josie's hope in any kind of friendship with Braham.

Josie sniffled, the aroma of garlic from the soup teasing her appetite.

She had some time left.

Nothing had changed really, except that Aunt Myrtle's remains were safe. Josie must demand that Alvin describe the person who assaulted him last night. She would have to wait until he returned to Gloughton. At least Mr. Bates had headed out of town.

Josie walked beneath the shadow of a secret, one that would astound any kind, upstanding soul. And one person in particular fit that description every waking hour she had spent with him and the short slumber they'd shared together. Braham Taylor was oblivious to who she really was, and as she cleared her place from the table,

Josie's tears fell on her tray, mourning the dwindling chance that she might deserve such a man as him.

She took the tray to the kitchen and tidied up. Fran must have retired for the evening. Josie headed back to her room to check on the girls, but Molly appeared to be waiting for her at the second-floor landing.

"Miss Clay, would you consider another piece for our newsletter?" She leaned on the banister. Josie had one foot on the first step up to the third floor and the other on the landing.

"I—I do not know. I am busy tending to my roommates, who are ill."

"Ah, this would be a short interview. Nothing as tedious as reciting those Latin names of herbaceous plants." She smirked. "It would be a simple set of questions."

"Questions?" Josie noticed that a few other ladies had appeared behind Molly. Their arms were crossed, and they looked as though they were hanging on every word.

"There's a rumor going about, and you are at its center." Molly slid her arms along the banister as she neared Josie. "A few villagers have seen you with that man who visits often. They suspect you are both scheming."

Josie's mouth went dry. "Wh—what has been said?"

Molly shrugged. "Just that he's lingered about here, saying he's waiting for you one too many times."

"But he's my father's hand. He informs me on how my father is doing."

"He's at the tavern most nights, rattling off about the woman he's to marry." Molly leaned in and whispered, "Most are saying it is you."

A mass of auburn curls caught Josie's attention, and she knew the woman Alvin must have referred to. Audra glared at Josie with a look that warned more than wondered.

Speaking loud enough for all to hear, Josie continued up the stairs saying, "It appears to me that gossip has bred lies. The man is twice my age. There must be some other woman he speaks of." She slid a look at Audra, who had stepped away from the group. "Good night."

What choice might Josie face when everything was over? Would she be a welcomed mill girl, sending her wages to her father, or would all of this scheming mark her among the villagers, giving her no reprieve in this second chance at living?

Chapter Nineteen

The next morning, Braham arrived to a bitter scene on the factory's main floor. A third of his girls were missing, and Miss Clyde was frantic as she assigned certain women to several looms at a time.

The chomping noise of the machines rattled Braham's nerves as he chased the woman down an aisle. "Miss Clyde, come here this instant."

She spun around, wringing her hands. "Mr. Taylor, the women are ill. They are bound to their beds with nothing in their stomachs but a foul bile. Miss Fawna has enlisted the help of that Miss Clay, and they are doing their best to get the girls back up for work. I fear we will lose much productivity. Mr. Bates will be furious."

Braham grit his teeth. He swiveled on his heel and headed to the boardinghouse. The maid took him to the parlor. He waited for Fawna Jamison but kept an eye on the doorway for Josie. The disheveled matron dragged herself down the stairs, dark shadows encircling her glassy eyes and her arms wrapped around her waist.

"Are you not well?" he asked.

"I am fine, but I have faced much this past night. I fear my sympathetic heart is wreaking havoc on my own belly." She laughed weakly and collapsed onto the couch. "There are ten girls in their beds, and Miss Clay is off to acquire more medicine. Her roommates are on the mend, so we are hopeful it is helping."

"That is good," Braham said, pride blooming his chest for the stunning Josie Clay caring so diligently. "Get some rest, Miss Jamison. I trust Miss Clay will be successful."

He left the house, glancing toward town as he crossed the courtyard. When he reached the doorstep of the factory, Miss Clay hurried across the bridge. She carried a basket carefully in her arms.

He descended the stairs and ran over to assist her. "Is it as fragile as that?" He smiled as he strode up to her. She was pale but returned a genuine smile just the same. "Here, let me help." He took the basket from her arms.

"Careful," she warned. "They are corked, but already one has leaked as I walked."

Bottles clinked as he held the basket against his chest. "Your roommates are well?"

"Yes, I do believe it is a short-lived malady." In the bright sunshine, she put her hand over her eyes as she looked up at him. "How will the factory manage with so many women missing today?"

"We'll manage," he said. "A couple days will not cause too much suffering. This time of year, our cotton supply is limited anyway. And fortunately, it is Friday. The women will have Sunday to recover as well."

Josie marched to the garden gate instead of the front door and held it open for him. He passed through, hesitating as his arm brushed hers. He glanced down at her.

She did not look directly up at him. "You are a good manager, Mr. Taylor." Her lips were as red as a summer strawberry.

"And you are a good friend." His whisper moved a golden strand of hair from beneath her bonnet.

She lifted her eyes and searched his. Her color returned to her cheeks. "This is the least I can do. You are too kind," she muttered, dropping her gaze to his lips but shifting her weight as if she would abandon him in this tender moment. He'd not let her. Without considering any consequence, he leaned over the basket between them and softly pressed his lips on hers. She kissed him back, the sweet taste of peppermint tempting him to linger longer than he should. His chest exploded with warmth, and his heart thrummed, knowing that this woman was more than just a mill girl to him. What had life been before she'd arrived to Gloughton? Josie sighed softly. If this basket wasn't between them, he'd wrap his arms around her. The woman who'd arrived at the most inconvenient time weeks ago was filling up a space in Braham's heart that he hadn't realized was empty.

He gently pulled away and pressed his forehead to hers. Her eyes were closed as he whispered, "Josie Clay, where would we be without you?" He kissed the tip of her nose.

Her lashes fluttered, and her sapphire eyes grew round. She shook her head and stepped back. "Oh Braham, please, do not think so much of me. I am—" Pushing past him, she took the basket from his arms. "Please, do not follow me." She walked away quickly, the bottles clinking with each footstep, adding to his aggravation.

"You are what?" he called out.

She did not stop but continued into the dim kitchen. The sound of bells stopped him from following her inside. 'Twas eight o'clock, and his duty to the factory must not be delayed any longer.

While the factory remained quiet at the noon meal, Braham chose to stay in his office instead of returning to the empty Bates estate. This would be the first day since he began at the factory that he would not dine with Aunt Myrtle.

He unfolded a napkin that held a hard piece of bread, some berries, and a block of cheese. This was not much different than the rations they'd received on the plantation. Yet, even during those days, he was never as alone as he was now.

Josie's recoil at his kiss soured any contentment he had found in working today. He ate with little zeal until he could not take another bite. He pushed away from his desk and headed outside.

The day had no chill about it. Braham rolled up his sleeves and soaked in the sunshine. He took long strides across the courtyard to the bridge and then strolled beside the cemetery fence, keenly aware of the distance growing between himself and the garden—and Josie.

Without considering his next step, he turned into the graveyard and soon found himself standing over Aunt Myrtle's grave. Beside hers, Mr. Bates Sr.'s tombstone read "Loving Father." If Braham had any say in the arrangements that day months ago, he would have included "Uncle" as well. He could nearly hear Gerald snarl, "More loving uncle than father."

Braham sat on the bench where he and Josie had spent the evening and took in the peace of this place. Soft billowy lilac flowers hung over the fence close to his aunt's grave, dusting the air with their perfume. Dappled light danced upon the resting places of the many graves—a promise of life even amid eternal slumber.

Peace found him at last in the tranquil day. He regained his appetite and decided to finish his lunch before the factory started up again. Bidding farewell to the souls who made him the man he was, he returned down the path to the bridge and walked in haste toward the red-bricked building.

The girls filed across the courtyard. He fell back and waited. Audra and Josie were the last to leave the boardinghouse. He ran up behind them, wondering how the ill women were faring. The two women seemed to be in deep conversation. Braham slowed his pace.

Josie's words were close to begging. "You've got to let everyone know you are with Alvin. I do not want any more attention than I've gotten already."

Audra turned to Josie. Her lips barely moved as she spoke. "I am not any longer. Broke it off that night of the funeral. Probably why he went off like he did, drunk as ever, getting himself in trouble."

Josie gaped at her. "You know—" She saw Braham and swiveled toward him. "Mr. Taylor. I did not know you were there."

He gave each woman a cordial grin. "I apologize for sneaking up on you. It appears that I am running a bit late."

Audra tucked an auburn strand into her bonnet and stepped aside. "Well then, you better go ahead of us. You have more at stake than we do." She smirked. "What with running an entire factory and all."

His throat tightened. Audra and her sister, Minnie, had seen Braham rise from the poor orphan down south to the businessman in Gloughton. He never cared for Audra's biting intentions hidden in seemingly general terms around unknowing folk.

Audra feigned knowing more than she should as a simple factory girl. Perhaps because she was another soul saved by the late Mr. Bates. Minnie and Audra were scooped up as children—orphans needing a place in this world—and assimilated to the Bates household as well-cared-for servants. Neither of the sisters had received such a rise to position as Braham. Every remark from the elder sister, Audra, was laced with bitterness. Braham had won more favor than she ever would. And, unlike Braham, who'd gained the elder Bateses' attention when he arrived at Terryhold, Audra did not receive one bit of attention from Mr. Bates or Aunt Myrtle. Aunt Myrtle despised the thought of raising girls and assigned Minnie to household duties and ushered Audra to the factory floor as quickly as she could. Even if Audra was never kind, Braham did feel sorry for her. He ignored her attitude toward him as best as he could.

"Miss Jennings, you may go ahead. I must ask Miss Clay about the absent women today." He motioned with a wave of his arm, trying his best not to scowl at the woman. She stuck her nose up and strode away. He was perplexed by the conversation he'd overheard. Audra had been seeing Alvin?

Well, that might explain another reason why the man kept showing up around Gloughton.

A thread of sympathy for that man, caught up in Audra Jennings's heartstrings, wound its way into Braham's thoughts before he caught Josie's quizzical look.

"Well?" He clasped his hands behind his back. "How are the patients?"

"I have given each woman their portion. I expect their stomachs will have settled by this evening."

"Good." He rocked on his heels, wondering if her embarrassment earlier had to do with the rumor she'd mentioned to Audra. He had not heard such a rumor. "I want you to know that rumors around here are just that—rumors. Most folk do not take them to heart—" He swallowed hard. "I do not take them to heart. If that is why you were so upset—"

She folded her lips together and smiled. "Thank you, Mr. Taylor." A sorrowful lift of her brow spoke more than her words. He wondered if she regretted their last encounter, yet the gloom that filled her eyes made him suspect there was something deeper perplexing her. Why was she adamant that Braham thought too much of her?

He tried to gather words that would keep her close and not cause her to run. But Josie's sadness turned to serious consideration, and she said, "Of all the folks here in Gloughton, I am truly thankful that you do not take any rumor to heart." She placed her hand on his chest, reached up on her toes, and kissed him on the cheek.

Before he could say or do anything, she left his side for the second time today.

Fawna was frantic, once again, when she met Josie in the foyer at the end of the day. "You must come quick. The women are worse than before."

Josie did not catch her bonnet as it fell to the floor. She left it as she rushed up the stairs. "I administered the elixir myself. How could they be worse?" she exclaimed.

"They've been sleeping the afternoon away."

"That is good. They need rest."

"Yes, but now they are awake, saying their stomachs are on fire." She was at Josie's heels. "Perhaps we should call for a doctor. The closest one is twenty miles away. We would have to ask Mr. Taylor to hire the fastest messenger."

"That might be a good idea." Josie was thankful Dr. Chadwick's reach was not as close as the nearest doctor. She hurried to the rooms on the second floor. The ladies were in much pain, holding their stomachs, perspiration glistening on their foreheads.

"Here, try some more. You must try." Josie held up a spoon of the elixir to Molly O'Leary, whose face was screwed up tightly as she groaned.

"Why should I trust you?" Molly gave Josie a hateful stare. "Trust me?"

"You took offense to my sharing the rumor about that man. Audra said you were livid. How do I know that you aren't playing a trick on us with poison and not medicine? I've heard of such a thing."

"I am not that kind of person," Josie snapped. "Besides, Audra exaggerates. We all know that." Why would Audra stir up more gossip? She was the person who had been with Alvin. Did she use Josie to take eyes off her? Josie pushed away the dread of Audra sharing more than lies about her but the very truth.

Molly kept her weary eyes on Josie. She was not well at all. Josie softened her tone. "I promise, Molly. My roommates are well enough to sit up and read without an ounce of pain. They benefited greatly from this elixir. The apothecary even helped."

Molly glowered, gasped, and jerked her body forward. "Please, make it stop."

Quickly, Molly gulped the elixir down. She pressed her head against her pillow and began to breathe in and out, long and hard.

Josie placed the back of her hand on Molly's forehead. "You have no fever. That is good." Molly turned her head away and closed her eyes, continuing with her hard breathing.

After Josie gave the elixir to the rest of the women, she checked on her roommates. Their bright eyes and rosy cheeks shone from behind their books. Josie wished she could show their good health to the ill women and bring them a little hope in their recovery.

After a tense evening helping the girls, Josie retired and fell into a restless sleep. In the middle of the night, she was shaken awake.

Fawna's eyes were wide beneath her bed cap. "They are worse even still. I've sent for the doctor, but I doubt he will come in the middle of the night over aching stomachs. Is there nothing we can do now?"

Josie sat up. "I will get Miss Young. Perhaps she'll know better than I." She dressed and hurried out into the midnight hour.

Creeping about at night did not frighten Josie as much as it had as a child. Even though the owl's hoot shook her nerves, and her boots echoed sharply between the buildings of Main Street, she was not afraid. Perhaps being part of such dark schemes as she had been stole away the fright of being surrounded by it. The thought horrified her. She prayed the rest of the way to Miss Young's.

Please, Lord, let no darkness come upon me. Show me Your light.

She recalled the lantern at her feet that brightened her decision at Aunt Myrtle's grave, and the security of Braham's embrace during that pivotal night. She lifted her fingers to her lips, unable to hold back a smile. As she continued down Main, recalling Braham's warm breath on her skin and the taste of his lips on hers, her head fell back and she gazed up at the star-filled sky with a quiet laugh of wonder.

Her reflection in a shop window caught her eye. She rolled her eyes at herself, but her smile remained. How she wished she hadn't walked away from him at the garden gate yesterday. The regret had niggled at her as she ate the noon meal. And then in the courtyard, he tried to assure her that he thought well of her regardless of rumors. How could he be so caring when she had turned away from him hours before? Josie had melted right there in the courtyard, just the same as when he kissed her. That kiss would never be forgotten. No matter how uncertain the future might be for Josie Clay, she'd coddle that moment like a treasure, hidden away for only her to wonder at when the world grew dim. She'd stolen some goodness for herself during this grim season—or more accurately, Braham had offered it to her in the sweetest of ways. Josie almost believed she was toeing the edge of some certain providence with Braham Taylor's eager kiss and affirming words. Was she deserving of the attention at all?

A prayer burst in her heart that God's mercy would let it be so.

Josie turned down Mosgrove Way, now unaware of the darkness at all.

She knocked three times on Daisy's door before she opened

it. Once Josie was inside, she put down her lantern and untied her bonnet. "We must figure out something more to give the girls. They are complaining of pain."

"I do hope it's not catching. Perhaps they are ill with something bigger than we can soothe." Daisy fiddled with her braids as she led the way to the kitchen.

"I do not know, but we must try." Josie took to the mortar and pestle while Daisy lit the fire for the extractions.

As she ground the colic root, Josie considered all that had occurred. Molly had accused her of ill-doing without any evidence. A shiver passed through her. What if she *had* made a mistake and given them something harmful? However, the elixir had worked for her roommates. Sometimes a remedy could affect a patient differently than another though.

"Daisy," she said, "be sure that you check every item I include. You are wiser than I am in all of this. I do not want to make a mistake."

What if she already had?

Chapter Twenty

Josie arrived at the house with a new batch of elixir carefully made. Fawna was sitting on the top stair with her elbow planted on her knee and her hand to her cheek.

"How do they fare?" Josie tried to keep the bottles from clinking too loudly as she held her lamp in one hand and her arms wrapped around the basket.

"They are all asleep now," Fawna muttered. "I will not have this, Miss Clay. This is not a hospital. The girls who are well are worried about catching their illness. They must get rest, but their sleep is disturbed by the wailing of the others."

Josie sat beside her. "They seem quiet now." Only the clock in the common room could be heard ticking the early morning seconds away.

"They're exhausted. The ill girls have come down with the shakes." Fawna pulled at her cheeks and rubbed her eyes. "I fear the worst, Miss Clay."

"The worst?" Josie gasped. "No, they are not that bad off—no fever. Trust me, I've seen death. This is not that." At least, not yet. Josie grimaced but tried to remain reasonable. "This illness will just have to pass."

Fawna stood up. "How long?"

"Hopefully, they will be better by Sunday once they've had the elixir." Josie followed her across the hall to the nearest bedroom. She placed the lamp and basket of bottles on the sideboard next to the door.

Fawna put her ear to the door. "Nobody is stirring." She sighed.

"I will wake them and give them this—" Josie lifted a couple of bottles from the basket.

"No, you will not!" Fawna hissed. "They've kept everyone up

well into the night. We'll not wake anyone earlier than they must get up."

"But Fawna, we have to get them well—the sooner they take it—"

The woman held up her hand. "I shall give it to them in the morning. Go to bed, Miss Clay."

A door creaked open, and Audra appeared. "What is this? We are trying to sleep, you two."

Fawna shooed Josie toward the stairs, shoving her lamp in her hands. The matron then rushed over to Audra, ushering her back into her room.

Fawna gave Josie a sharp look and whispered with great force across the common area, "We shall wait for the doctor and see what he says. If they are not well by Sunday, then I am sending them home."

Josie gave a curt nod, disagreeing with the woman's drastic measure. "Please wake me when the girls are ready for their dose. I am certain they will recover nicely."

Was she sure though? She eyed the basket sitting in the dark hallway just before slipping up the stairs. The mixture was good. The three recovered women were proof.

Josie prayed for all to be well again.

But the morning came with another hand shaking her furiously awake. The maid Abigail stood over her. "Miss, the doctor's come and gone. All the girls are worse than ever."

Josie threw her bedcover back. Liesl was not there, neither were the sisters. "What is the time?"

"It is half past six. Mr. Taylor is down in the parlor with Miss Fawna. They want you to come there immediately."

"Why did they not wake me?" She hurried to get dressed while Abigail explained that Miss Fawna presumed the doctor would know better, so she let Josie sleep. But the man was befuddled by the girls' symptoms.

"Did they feel any better when they woke up?" Josie quickly pulled her dress on.

"No, they are weak. Can hardly speak."

"What? It is only a stomach malady," Josie exclaimed. Abigail turned her around to button the back of her dress. The maid quickly braided Josie's hair while Josie laced her boots.

They hurried down the stairs. As they turned the landing on the second floor, Josie spied the basket of elixir sitting where she'd left it last night.

"Abigail, did the women take the elixir?"

"I do not know. The doctor came just as they awoke."

Josie placed her hand on Abigail's arm. "Please, take it to them. See if you can get them to drink." The girl shook her head at first, but Josie insisted with a firm nod and a nudge for her to go.

"Tell Miss Fawna it was your doing, not mine," she whispered.

"Fine. She will want the girls to get better. Do not worry." Josie left Abigail and continued down to the parlor. Fawna was blubbering into a handkerchief while Braham paced the small sitting area.

Josie entered the room. "What did the doctor say exactly?" she asked. Fawna and Braham turned to her.

"He agreed with Fawna." Braham approached. She could smell the leather mixed with sunbaked cotton. His sleeves were peppered with cotton bits. "They must leave the boardinghouse."

"But why?"

Fawna barged between them, her eyes red and her lips chapped. "They're going to bring the whole house down, Miss Clay." Her nostrils flared. "That doctor said he doesn't know what it is—and with the epidemics plaguing other towns, all precautions must be made."

"This is hardly an epidemic," Josie uttered. "Look, you and I are not ill—and we've been closest to the women."

"I pray we don't fall sick," Fawna whispered in a shaky voice. She crossed herself as she walked toward the fireplace.

Braham lifted his shoulders. "We shall transport the women to my aunt's house. There is room, and they will not contaminate anyone—" He looked over his shoulder at the matron and then turned to Josie with a weariful brow. "Please, get them ready. I will have two carriages here by the morning break."

The matron expelled a loud sigh of relief and dashed across the room. "Oh, thank you, Mr. Taylor." Fawna took his arm and shook his hand. "Yes, get them to a safer place, that will do nicely. I shall get them ready right away." Her usual liveliness appeared in a flash, and she disappeared up the stairs.

Josie drew near to Braham. "Must we take such drastic measures?"

"There will be no harm in doing it, and I fear the other women will suffer." He cinched his brow and reached for Josie's hands. "Will you come and care for the women?" His secure grip on her fingers and the worry in his umber gaze hinted at a notion that this man, good in all his ways, depended on her now—even if it was to take care of others.

"Of course I will come." She smiled. "If you can spare one more factory worker."

"You are so much more than that to me." His eyes glimmered with as much determination as worry. An unspoken promise lay in his words. He thought only well of her. Whatever crept into Josie's mind was shoved aside right now. She chose to believe his wordless affirmation and become the woman she had always wanted to be, the woman who Braham Taylor believed she was.

Braham grew anxious as he turned down the lane by the orchard. He pushed up his sleeves in the warm afternoon and begged God for His sweet providence this Saturday and in the days to come. Gerald would now be informed. It was his factory, after all.

Braham hopped down from the cart and went through the kitchen door of his house. He nearly crashed into Minnie, who was reaching for a pot from the rack. "Excuse me, Minnie." He passed beside her.

She stumbled back and knocked into the table, the pot crashing to the floor. "Oh goodness, sir." She fell to her knees and gathered up the pot. Braham caught a small bottle rolling toward the hearth and handed it to her. She stuffed it in her pocket. "I am sorry. I've been helping Miss Clay all morning." She patted the pocket. "I guess I'm more tired than I thought."

"I am sorry for startling you," he said. "Thank you for helping Miss Clay though."

"Lunch will be served soon, Mr. Taylor." Cook came from the pantry with an armful of jars.

"Thank you."

Minnie was only a couple of years younger than Braham, but her timid posture, and even more timid countenance, made her seem like she had not quite blossomed to the full. Very different from her sister, Audra. Braham always thought that Aunt Myrtle should have allowed Minnie to join Audra at the mill instead of being a house servant. The work and independence might have helped her. It had obviously given Audra full opportunity to become a strong soul— whether for good or bad, Braham wasn't quite sure.

He stepped backward out of the kitchen, feeling as though he filled it up after such a racket. He passed through the dining room and into the parlor. An early summer breeze poured through the windows. The scent of grass and blooms freshened the place. Josie sat in the high-back chair by the empty fireplace, her eyes closed and her hair falling from a loose braid. She brightened up the room more than any summer bouquet or sunny ray.

He crept across the plush carpet and lowered onto the matching chair beside her.

"Braham?" she mumbled as her eyes fluttered open. "Forgive me. I mean, Mr. Taylor."

He gathered her hand and said, "Braham to you."

She gave him a sleepy smile then stretched her other arm up. "Are you home for the day?"

"I am." All his trepidation fled. He could not think of anywhere else he might find more assurance that all would be well than with this woman sleepily greeting him. "How are the women?"

Her smile fell and she leaned over, taking his hand in both of hers. "I am afraid they are fading. I don't know what to do." Her eyes filled with tears, and she began to weep. He gathered her in his arms and allowed her small frame to rest against him. When her crying subsided, she mumbled, "They refuse the elixir now. We still have half of it left. Daisy just went home to look through her mother's recipes. We are both perplexed."

"Should we call on your doctor? Dr. Chadwick? Might he help?"

She sprang from his arms. "No, that would be no good at all." Her face paled. "He is not a. . .very wise man."

Braham softened his tone. "Josie, do you escape these men—the doctor and the farmhand of your father's? I worry that they have harmed you in some way." The mere thought of someone hurting this woman lit his anger—just as it flamed when he was a boy and his own father's mistakes had brought on condemnation from the slave master.

Josie settled back in her chair. "They have wicked ways about them. I do not trust them—not as I trust you." She wiped her eyes.

"I understand," he soothed. "Trust is hard to come by. And even more difficult to gain once it's broken."

Josie's eyes widened, and she blanched. "In Ains—my village, I was surrounded by broken trust."

"I too have been haunted by it." He stood up, shoved his hands in his pockets, and strode to the window. The curtains flapped in the breeze. "I prefer to move forward, leaving the past as a closed book. Yet the man I must face does everything to keep that book pried open."

Josie sighed. "Moving forward for me is not nearly as comforting as looking back on a sweeter time. One with my mother. One without—" She closed her eyes and pressed her head in the chair. "Those men in my life. They do not let me forget my sorrows."

"We are the same in so many ways, Josie." He wagged his head as he paced along the room where he'd once found happy moments. It was strange to think on the sad ones before his time here, but they pressed on him as tension grew dense with the only Bates man left. "I have the same trouble with certain folk."

"Mr. Bates seems a proud man," Josie declared.

"So you know the man I speak of." Braham gave a dry chuckle. "He does not forget the story that brought us to this moment. Not one day passes that he might forget." He placed his hands behind his back. "My father found favor in Mr. Bates Sr.'s eyes, but he was not as trustworthy as he seemed. Father pretended to be someone he wasn't to gain a position with Mr. Bates. The slave master was livid, as he had expected to work alongside his cousin's man, not an indentured servant. Mr. Bates forgave my father, especially after hearing about our desperate beginnings on that ship from Ireland. That man was filled with as much compassion as his son is filled with animosity." Braham sighed and ran a finger along a small painting of Terryhold on the mantel. "Mr. Bates was not around much, but the slave master was. He used Father's lie to inflict torture on every person acquainted with us." Braham swallowed, squeezing his eyes shut. His best friend Howie and the rest of the slaves—the cruelty inflicted upon them still haunted him. His throat burned. "I have often wondered if Father was satisfied to die in that final beating, knowing all the blows others had suffered for him."

Josie reached her hand to him, compassion rounding her blue eyes. "I am so sorry, Braham."

He squatted down in front of her, placing his hands on the arms of the chair. She cupped his cheek, and he continued, "The one thing I've struggled with all this time is that I was almost relieved when Father died."

Josie cocked her head, waiting for an explanation.

"We were all free of his mistake."

"Was it so?"

Braham winced, shaking his head. "Free from the slave master? Yes. Master Bates was proud from a young age though. He'd torture the slaves in his own way. I was thankful to come here when Mr. Bates decided to build a factory."

"The factory has been a good escape." Josie folded her hands in her lap. "For both of us, it seems."

"It is good—between Gerald's visits." He stood and held out his hand. "I also pray mightily, hoping that my friends in Georgia are well. Mr. Bates Sr. is the one person I've seen allow trust to grow again. He fired the slave master after my father revealed what was happening. That was the reason for his last beating."

Josie took his hand. "The late Bates sounds like a wise and grace-bearing master."

"He was." Braham led her to the dining room. "And just."

"I crave justice," Josie said. "It is not often found and is usually crowded by all the darkness."

He pulled out a chair for her. "If that farmhand or doctor returns, and justice must be served, you must tell me why—"

Her weary eyes dulled. "I can only say it's for the wicked ways of the heart—justice is not to be found on this earth."

Braham observed her as they placed their napkins in their laps. He tried to believe her when she spoke, but she withheld her gaze.

He wondered what deeds poured from the hearts of these wicked men.

Chapter Twenty-One

Sunday was a quiet day. Daisy and Josie had tried a new elixir, but many of the women refused to sit up and drink. The young apothecary left after dinner, suggesting that the doctor must return. Along with calling for the doctor, Braham had sent a messenger with a letter to Gerald, reluctantly so. He hardly slept that evening, awaking with a start at three o'clock. He crept downstairs, a foreboding in his spirit weighting him with every step. He was relieved to find Josie boiling a kettle in the kitchen. She could not sleep as well. They spent the early morning sharing a pot of tea by the fire.

Josie Clay was fast becoming the one person in the whole world whom he wanted to share his life with. But telling her that did not seem possible right now. Not with every other corner of his world pressing in on them. What would the future hold?

On Monday evening, after a day of making up for the lighter workforce, Braham hoped to return home to a doctor with decent news. He stopped at the bridge when he saw Daisy and Minnie waving at him. He wondered if they bore word, not from the doctor, but from Gerald. In that regard, decent news was out of the question. His throat tightened. What would the young Bates accuse Braham of, now that he had a third of his women needing to be replaced?

"Good evening, ladies." He tipped his top hat as he pulled his horse to a stop.

"Perhaps you should get down from there, Braham." Daisy's voice was clipped, her usual stoic face pulled down in worry. "I am afraid we have some terrible news." She looked at Minnie, who only dipped her head, hiding her face.

"What is it? Is it the girls? Miss Clay?" Fear gripped him as he considered that Josie might be struck by this horrific illness.

"It does have to do with Miss Clay," Daisy replied. "Minnie, show him what you found."

Minnie slipped her hand into her apron pocket. "Mr. Taylor, I was in Daisy's kitchen when Miss Clay mixed the elixir. After they left, I noticed this bottle and its spilled contents on the floor. A mouse was eating crumbs coated in the powder. I picked up the bottle and stuck it in Daisy's cupboard since I wasn't sure where it belonged. When I turned around, the mouse was dead."

Braham took the blue bottle and held it up to the dying sunlight. "This is not the same bottle you dropped the other evening?"

"No sir, that was green," Minnie mumbled. There was a small amount of powder left at the bottom of the bottle. "What is it?"

"I believe it is arsenic or some sort of poison if a mouse was killed so instantly. I have never handled the stuff before," Daisy remarked. "I am glad Minnie put it where she did. I would have never found it. Minnie brought it to me today when she heard that the women hadn't healed yet."

"Wouldn't the women have perished the same as the mouse?" Braham exclaimed.

"Depends on the amount used. If it's given a little at a time—a small amount in each dose—then it could prolong death." Daisy grimaced. "Arsenic is known to create havoc on the victim's stomach though."

Braham ran his hand through his hair beneath his hat. He shoveled in air and tried to think clearly. "There is no reason to believe this was Josie's intent."

Minnie nibbled on her lip and glanced back and forth between Daisy and Braham. Daisy nodded as if encouraging the timid woman to speak. Minnie licked her lips. "Audra said that a Miss O'Leary even accused Josie of mixing the elixir wrong on purpose." She swallowed hard. "To hurt her."

"Well, that is absurd. Miss Clay would never hurt a soul."

Daisy shrugged her shoulders. "I am not sure, Braham. That man whom you two brought in seemed rather suspicious. Gerald had been looking for him on his way out of town. Said something about him stealing. And then he told me he would catch him on his way down south."

"Stealing?" Was that why the man was so beat up? The only thing that Gerald might protect was his own possessions. Braham remembered Alvin being around the Bates estate that first night Josie arrived. Was he there for mushrooms, or Audra—or was he a thief? "The wicked ways of that man have nothing to do with Miss Clay. She has only helped us."

Minnie spoke up, "All I know is she has every bit of control of who might perish by her so-called remedies. And Daisy said that this poison would do that very thing." She reached over and took the bottle from Braham. Even with her shoulders straight and her head tilted in confidence, her timidity seemed to tug at her lip with a twitch.

"The evidence is poor, ladies," Braham asserted. His stomach was heavy. "However, I will ask Miss Clay myself. She is at the house now. Would you two like to come with me?"

Daisy opened her mouth to speak, but Minnie spoke for them both. "No, sir. We are to market." She slid her arm in Daisy's. "We are to collect the goods for a hearty broth for the ill women. That's what Cook demanded."

"Very well," Braham said, climbing on top of his cart. "Do not worry, ladies. I am certain Miss Clay is as innocent as each of you. We will get to the bottom of this, and all will be well."

As the cart rolled away, he left his confidence behind. Everything that Braham held dear was crumbling. Gerald's fury was soon to find him once he received word that Braham might need to hire more women, and Josie Clay might have caused the very demise of Gloughton Mill.

He prayed for truth and goodness all the way home to the Bates estate.

Audra blocked the door that Josie was trying to get through. "Like

I told you, this is much more complicated than you might think. Everything is going according to plan."

"According to plan? The girls are very ill. We must help them." The clock on the papered wall ticked seconds like pinpricks in her ear. Time was not to be wasted now. The women were fading just like Josie had seen her mother pass in Dr. Chadwick's care.

She would do everything in her power to keep them alive.

A dagger of doubt twisted in her heart. Was she working against her father in doing so?

"Ah, but think, if you let them be, you might finally get that corpse for Dr. Chadwick."

Shame flooded her as Audra spoke aloud the ominous doubt in her determination to heal. The dagger faded though, and anger rose like a fire inside her. This woman knew Josie's darkest secret. Exactly what else did she know? Josephine Clayton was not a posed mourner for the thrill of it, as Audra had seemed to be.

"Did Alvin tell you the whole story, Audra?" Josie's voice shook. Audra cocked an eyebrow—either out of challenge or surprise. "I do not take stealing the dead lightly, like some might." Josie leaned forward, her arms tight across her rib cage. "That is the very last thing I want to focus on right now. If someone is ill, my allegiance is to healing. Even if it means my father—" She swallowed hard, thinking of her crippled father waiting for the doctor to release his wages.

"Your father going to debtors' prison is the least important consequence. Others are waiting, aren't they?"

A storm of anguish whirled through Josie. She remembered the fear in her father's eyes.

"We will figure this out." Josie spoke through her teeth. "But for now, I must go to Daisy's. We need to try—"

A thud from outside had both women stiffen. Josie looked out the window, but the lowering sun glared from behind the stables, blocking any view.

"I must go," Josie muttered, trying to pass by Audra, but the woman only leaned back on the nook's doorjamb with her arms lazily crossed.

"Don't bother, Josie. Just think, by the end of the week, you'll have a body to that silly Dr. Chadwick, and possibly the rest that you need. Everything will work out just fine."

"What do you mean? The girls need the elixir."

"Do not be ridiculous. I know that you poisoned them. This is all a good show, Miss Clay, but let us be honest."

"I did nothing of the sort!" Josie crumpled onto the kitchen bench. Molly's suspicion haunted her thoughts. "I don't think I mixed it wrong. I—I am always very careful."

Braham hurried through the front door, not wanting to mess with the stable just yet. He took off his hat and coat and followed voices from the kitchen.

He stopped when he heard Audra's sharp question, "Did you not mix the elixir for the girls, knowing that death would provide you exactly what you need?"

He held his breath, praying that the answer would come from anyone but Miss Clay.

"I only thought of helping them when I mixed the elixir." Her gentle tone seemed pure, innocent. But Audra's mention of death as Josie's commodity kept Braham hidden in the shadows, hoping that Josie would secure her innocence before he had to interrogate her further.

"You are desperate to get a body to the doctor you work for, aren't you?"

"Please, Audra, do not speak so loudly."

Braham's blood rushed to his ears. What did she mean? Josie had mentioned that the doctor was a wicked man. He pushed against the wall, trying to make sense of—a body? What was this?

"That is the whole reason you left Ainsley and came to Gloughton, is it not? Alvin told me everything before I chose to leave him for good. I don't know how you do it, Josie Clay." She sniffed. "That whole grave-robbing business is too much for me. I would rather die than continue such a charade. It's why I ended it with that Alvin. Who wants to marry such a person?" Braham stepped closer.

Grave robbing?

Josie had said she was worried about grave robbers the night of Aunt Myrtle's funeral. Braham stumbled back and caught himself along the chair rail. Was it a ploy? He caught Audra's eye as she stood against the opposite doorway. A thin smile broadened on her lips, and her gaze fell on Josie, whose back was to him. "We are very thankful that you did not steal away that sweet Myrtle Bates. I heard that Mr. Taylor stopped you from going through with your plan."

Braham burst into the room. "What is this about?"

Josie swiveled in her seat and stood. "Braham—I mean, Mr. Taylor, please—" Her ivory skin had not one tinge of pink to it. She was pale, bloodless. Perhaps heartless, if any of what he heard added up to her guilt.

"Tell me," he barked. "What was your intent for my aunt?"

"No, I refused—I couldn't go through with it—" She lunged toward him, her small hands clutching at his. They were cold. He withdrew his fingers. "Please, Braham!"

His mouth went dry, and every beat in his chest pounded harder than the one before. "You—you stayed after the funeral for. . ." He grabbed his mouth, his fingers shaking against his jawbone.

"I insisted you stay with me because of what I told you." Her lip quivered as she spoke. All her color was back, and she seemed as adamant to convince him as she had been the day Amelia hurt her arm in the factory. "I knew if you stayed, your aunt would be safe."

"But you are in a plot with the doctor, are you not?"

She lowered her eyes, and her shoulders began to shake. No sound came from her, but he could see the tears fall to the floor.

"You poisoned the women for, for—"

"Bodies," Audra spat.

Braham shot Josie a look. She lifted her shoulders. "I didn't poison anyone," she cried. "At least, I didn't mean to."

Braham sank to the bench and leaned his head on his fists. "Miss Clay, do you wait to steal a body?"

"It is not as it seems. I was forced into it. I needed to supply Dr. Chadwick before—"

"I cannot believe this." Shock whirred through Braham's body. "When you first came to the factory, I wondered about your associations. Everything you've been to me seemed good and pure, but everything you've hidden has erased it all." He turned from her, unable to focus on this person he'd been so close to loving. "Please leave. You are no longer an employee here."

"I am not the person they want me to be. I do not want to be a part of it—I—I—"

"Go," Braham shouted and left the room. He cringed at Josie's sobbing outburst and her footsteps running from the kitchen. The door slammed shut.

How could he have been so foolish? From the very beginning he was not sure about that man who had brought her here. Even Aunt Myrtle had warned him about a woman who'd show up for a job at such an hour as twilight.

It was all clear to him now. That mill girl was not the bright light in his life of loneliness. She was a stranger to him. He wished he had never hired Josie Clay.

Chapter Twenty-Two

The warm breeze whipped against Josie's skin, mixing her tears with droplets of sweat. She had been found out, and while she expected to burn with shame, she was at least free from hiding her terrible purpose from Braham.

At each turn in the road, she would stop, catch her breath, and then weep in her arm, praying and begging forgiveness. No matter how much she resisted, Audra's mention of being desperate for a body was not entirely true—she'd wanted far more than one. Josie's desires assumed that the outcome was indeed deaths and robbings.

As she turned toward Gloughton to gather her belongings, she noticed Daisy trudging down her lane from the market square, both arms carrying baskets.

"Daisy, wait!" she called, her voice hoarse from crying.

Daisy spun around and waited, but as she did, she kept looking up and down the lane, as if she were in enemy territory and any moment a creature would pounce upon her.

"What is it?" she seethed as Josie drew close.

"Please, I want you to know that whatever happened to that elixir, I did not mean for it to."

"I believe it was arsenic in the little blue bottle we found," Daisy snapped.

"I only deal with herbs and plants. I do not own one ounce of arsenic."

Daisy narrowed her eyes.

"You have to believe me." How did she become the center of blame when she was only trying to help? Minnie appeared ahead on the road but stopped when she saw them. "Minnie was there when we were making the batch. Could she have accidently put the wrong ingredient in the rest of the elixir? The first elixir we made did nothing but help my roommates."

Daisy frowned. "I had never seen that bottle before. Minnie said she found it where you were preparing the elixir."

"I have no blue bottles. Only green." She pulled an ointment from her pocket. "See."

Josie shoved it into Daisy's hand. "You must believe me." Minnie continued to glare from the top of the hill. "Maybe she isn't telling the truth, Daisy. I have never even seen that bottle before."

"Why should I trust you, Josie Clay? I've known Minnie since she was a young girl. I've known you for a few weeks."

"You do not need to trust me. I am leaving—going home to be with my father until his time is up." Josie did not deserve trust anymore. She only wanted to do all she could to help. "But I will tell you what I know about ridding the body of poison. You must go to the Bates estate right away and help those women." Daisy began to turn away from her, shaking her head. Josie clutched her arm and leaned in, widening her eyes. "It is absolutely necessary that you do, Daisy Young. Not one of those mill girls must perish. You are the only one left to help them."

"Josie—"

"You'd better speak with Audra also. She's convinced that I poisoned the girls too."

"Do you think Minnie did this?" Daisy muttered.

Josie shrugged. "I do not know what she would have against me or the mill girls. But the poison found its way to the girls, and now it's up to you to save them. I have a long journey home."

Daisy nibbled on her lip then said, "Very well. Tell me what to do."

As Josie explained, she looked over to the hill. Minnie was gone.

Braham sat at dinner not having any appetite at all. Audra had explained how she'd found out about Josie. When Alvin had confessed his business with corpses, Audra was shocked and broke it off with him the night of Aunt Myrtle's funeral. She had also discovered that Josie was waiting for Alvin in the graveyard. Audra had immediately warned Gerald, and Gerald used his fists to make sure that Alvin and Josie's plan would not go through.

Braham stirred his stew, not seeing it. Audra's story played over and over in his mind. Although Audra was not usually trustworthy, everything she said added up. Everything, except the fact that Josie had begged him to stay with her. She did not want to be alone that night, and she did not want to run the risk of grave robbers. It was not a ploy. Was it a change of heart?

He slammed his fist on the table and groaned. How had Josie Clay become part of such a scheme? And why would she injure so many women but save his elderly aunt? He was wrong. Something didn't measure up at all. The goodness he saw in Josie far exceeded the accusations being made against her.

"Braham?" Daisy stood at the dining room entrance. She had been upstairs helping the women for at least an hour.

"Come in, Daisy. Would you like Minnie to get you some?" He lifted his spoon and let its contents pour back in the bowl with a slosh.

She shook her head and took the seat directly next to him. "I must tell you something."

"What is it?"

"I do not believe Josie intended to poison the women."

"I am having a hard time believing it as well," he confessed. "But what about the bottle?"

"If it was not mine, and it was not Josie's, the only person who possessed it—"

"Minnie?"

"Yes?" Minnie said as she brought a basket of rolls into the room. Daisy and Braham just stared at her. She slowed her pace.

"Where did you get that bottle, Minnie?" Daisy asked.

"I told you, it was on the counter near where Miss Clay washed the other bottles." Her teeth rested on her lip, and the corner of her mouth twitched just as it had done early that afternoon.

Braham stood up and walked over to the maid. She flinched but faced him. "Minnie, are you certain?"

Her eyes widened, and she looked over at Daisy.

"Josie had never handled that type of poison before," Daisy explained. "And she insisted on giving me the remedy to flush it out of the girls. I just don't see why she would want to hurt them."

"Minnie, would *you* want to hurt the mill girls?" Braham furrowed his brow, wondering if her timidity was actually a sinister disguise. But the maid began to fiddle with her fingers, took in a deep breath, and fell into a dining room chair, crying like the child she seemed to be.

Daisy rushed around Braham and took Minnie by the hands. "What is it, friend? What happened?"

"I—I shouldn't have done it. I knew it was wrong." She took a folded napkin and wiped her eyes. "But Audra promised that I could finally leave this place if I did."

"Audra?" Braham seethed. "What does she have to do with it?"

"She has everything to do with it." Minnie slumped back in the chair, letting out a long sigh. "I swore I'd never say anything, but seeing the effect of the poison on the girls has haunted me every night. At first she tried poisoning the soup Fran made. Audra even offered to help serve it that evening. But Josie's first batch of elixir actually healed some of the girls, so I put the poison in the rest of the elixir." Her chin wobbled. "Audra was so desperate and scared me into it." Minnie glanced at the kitchen door. "The stew in there is contaminated as well. Audra made sure of it before she left." Minnie grimaced. "Audra has promised some men terrible things, Mr. Taylor." Her voice shook. She leaned over and searched the room with a frantic gaze until fixing her eyes on him again. "Bodies. She needs bodies, Mr. Taylor, and she used Josie to cover it all up."

Braham arrived in Ainsley at the break of dawn. His distress induced an urgency that stole his breath away.

Audra had been the biggest culprit of all. Unfortunately, she had disappeared. Not even his factory overseers and the hired night watches could find her. Minnie had mentioned there was a meeting occurring in an undisclosed location. The body snatchers were preparing to provide a whole caravan of bodies, and Audra was on her way because she was the network's southern-based spy.

Had she arranged for that body snatcher to take Aunt Myrtle's body?

Braham ground his teeth, disgusted by it. No doubt Audra would have little conscience in doing so, with Aunt Myrtle paying no attention to her these past years. Thank the Lord for Gerald's interference.

Braham was perplexed by the whole thing. According to Audra, Gerald had defended his aunt's body. If that was true, an uexpected pride for Gerald fanned in Braham. There was some decency in the younger Bates after all. He must be informed of the Jennings sisters' involvement in this morbid circle of crime. Especially since Audra was ever after his affections.

Unlike her sister though, Minnie was a fragile thing through her entire confession, increasing sympathy more than anger. But the fact that she had been convinced to help in such a scandal forced Braham to keep her in the constable's custody indefinitely.

Audra had done one helpful thing in all of this. She had mentioned the name of Josie's village in the conversation that Braham had overheard. Now, Braham must find Josie and discover if she had any clues as to where Audra might be.

Ainsley's main street was nothing more than a cluster of houses and shops on one side of a green, and a church and short building on the other. The building sat beside a graveyard. A sign hung above the door, swinging in the warm morning breeze. Braham stood directly beneath it and read, OFFICE OF DR. CHADWICK.

Was the doctor behind that door now, conversing with Josie on their next move—the next grave they would stake out and desecrate?

His heart sank at the thought of the beautiful healer being a part of this business. He could not bring himself to face her or that man just yet. He slunk away from the place and found a seat on the steps of the church. Josie had recoiled at the mention of the doctor and Alvin. Yet she was the same as them, wasn't she?

Before he could even utter a prayer, Dr. Chadwick's door opened, and a hunchbacked woman shuffled onto the porch. She carried a wooden box and a candle near its wick's end. She blew it out with thin lips and then tossed the candle into the shrubbery lining the graveyard fence.

She was muttering to herself when Braham approached her as she slammed the door shut.

"Do not bother, son," she crowed when she saw him. "The doctor's abandoned us for good. Says he's got plans in Boston now." She adjusted the box on her hip. Piercing clinks of glass and metal made a clatter.

"Actually, I was not looking for the doctor."

"Oh, really?" Her gray hair frizzed from beneath a black scarf around her head, and she wiggled her large bulbous nose. "Surely you aren't needing me?" She cackled. "However, I am out of work now and could use a good master who'll let me cook and clean for him." She smiled, showing a gap of missing teeth. "Are you in need of a house servant, sir?"

He gave a weak smile. "I apologize, but I am not in need of a house servant." Although Minnie might have to forfeit her position now. "I am actually looking for someone who used to work here." He cleared his throat. "Do you know where I might find Miss Josie Clay? I believe she has returned to Ainsley."

The woman considered his words then shook her head. "No, there's nobody by that name. I am the only employee of Dr. Chadwick's." She sniffled. "Or was."

"I do believe Miss Clay worked here a few months ago."

The woman continued past him, adjusting the box and causing a ruckus in the early morning quiet. "Nah, the only person who worked here before passed away. Poor Josephine." She clicked her tongue then turned to him. "Who'd you say again?"

"Josie Clay?"

"Ah, I see your confusion. Josephine Clayton is the girl who was here. Not Josie Clay. Pretty close to the same name though." She seemed amused. "Josephine Clayton died, just like her mother, only two years later."

"Her mother?" His mouth went dry.

"Yes, she was a wonderful herbalist. The best. Josephine assisted Dr. Chadwick and had quite the knack for remedies. God rest her soul." The woman continued to walk away. "I live only round the corner in the small cottage by the brook. If you change your mind and need a servant, do not forget me," she called over her shoulder as she wobbled down the path.

Braham stood, frozen. Did everyone in this village think that Josie was dead? "Excuse me." He ran up to the woman. "Please, where is Miss Clay. . .Clayton's home?"

"Her father's farm is just east of town. Though he's not kept it up. I do believe they took him away already. Debtors' prison in Ashton."

Braham resisted dropping his mouth in shock.

Josephine Clayton was the same as Josie Clay. And she was considered dead by all she knew.

Chapter Twenty-Three

J osie stared at the notice in her hands. She was too late. Father had been taken away. But the bloodied wooden stakes she'd found by the front door suggested that he was better off behind the walls in Ashton than facing the torment of the network's men.

She sat at the small wooden table in the kitchen, alone, watching the flames devour the stakes. She should not even be here. The house was no longer theirs. But she had a key and nowhere else to go.

The house was in disarray. Dirty pots and pans filled a washbasin. The floor was in need of a good sweeping, and Mother's curtains were encased in cobwebs that shimmered in the early sunlight.

She found some bread in the cupboard and nibbled on it, wondering how she might save her father. One thing she knew for sure, she would never turn to crime again. The look in Braham's eyes bore a hole through her heart and cloaked her in disgrace. He did not just seem disappointed, or even horrified. He'd looked at her the way she felt about Alvin. He had been disgusted.

"Lord, I am not the same as Alvin. Please, forgive me."

As she walked through the house of her childhood, she reminisced in the times when her mother lit up the room. The parlor, where they spent the most time, had a big hearth in its center with shelves on either side holding jars and hooks tied with hanging herbs for drying. Father never cleared it after Mother passed. Josie ran her finger along the shelves, reading the Latin names on the labels. She could almost hear her mother's voice in her own.

"Mother, how I miss you." She wiped her cheek. How could everything crumble at the last breath of the woman? She had been the life of this home, the person who gave Father a reason to continue on and thrive after his injury hindered his work around the place. Mother was the one woman who treated Josie as someone to value and not someone to spite. The village girls would never include her in their circles—at first because of the enamored attention their beaux would give Josie, but then when she grew interested in medicines and ailments she appeared out of step with the usual duties of girls her age. Mother had often reminded Josie that she was exactly who God made her for a reason.

When Mother died, Josie's joy had transferred from the shadow of her mother's knowledge to applying that knowledge in the very best way—helping the sick. Her mother was right. If she had found acceptance in the midst of gossiping women, she'd have missed a grander purpose.

Josie marched out the front door, only slightly hesitant when she thought of the creditor appearing to arrest her for trespassing. She hurried down the steps and across the garden to the small grove of trees atop a rolling hill. In the bright morning, her mother's grave lay as peaceful as the day they buried her. The fine stone cross marked it handsomely, and the pretty lilac shrub had grown nicely over the past two years. Mother had given Josie the lilac seedling when she was sick. The shrub was spectacular now.

Josie smiled to herself as she recalled Aunt Myrtle's graveside being guarded by established lilacs. Fear and horror had trapped her memory in Gloughton. But now she remembered her mother's wisdom.

The flower was a symbol of first love, and Mother told her to always remember her first love—the Christ, the Creator and Comforter. Josie gently lifted a bloom to her nose, inhaling the sweet fragrance. "I have not forgotten You, Lord. But where are You in all of this?"

She'd lost Braham and her father and her reputation among the mill girls. But she had saved Aunt Myrtle's body, hadn't she? And her father's imprisonment had given her courage to wipe her hands clean of his debts to the network. They could not touch him within the walls of the debtors' prison.

Hadn't she prayed for God's deliverance from this work after Harry Garnett's snatching? But instead she'd lost everything. Was that truly God's plan? He seemed close in the memories of her mother, but the darkness was too thick to understand His way now.

Josie sighed, plucking the young lilac bloom. She turned from her mother's grave. A man stared at her from afar. She flung down the bloom and trudged toward him.

"Alvin Green, what are you doing here?"

He leaned against the barn. He'd slept there many nights as a grave robber posing as an innocent farmhand. Josie stopped a few feet in front of him with a hand on her hip.

"I still rent this place from your father." His bruises were green around the edges, covering the left side of his face. His lip was still swollen.

"Did you not hear? He's returned to debtors' prison."

"Oh, no, I did not." He grimaced, lowering his head. "At least the network can't harass him anymore."

"And I refuse to help anymore, Alvin. I will find my own way to get him out this time." Josie felt much less confident than she sounded. "We'll leave Ainsley...everyone thinks I am dead anyway. Those men can't harm us if we leave—" Josie stepped back. Alvin just stared at her. Would God protect them if they left? Had He already? "Alvin, you must go before that creditor returns. I just want to collect some things—" She swiveled on her heel but did not take a step. Swallowing away tears that pricked her eyes, she could only wonder where she would go next.

"Wait," Alvin mumbled. She turned to face him. He'd never appeared so disheartened before. His face was drawn down in a sorrowful look, with eyes as watery as hers probably appeared. "I have decided to stay here and help your father. Not much for earnings, but at least it's honest. I cannot manage to stay in the network. Not now—" He wrung his hands. "That Audra Jennings has played me for a fool."

"She said that she broke it off with you." A pang of sympathy for Alvin surprised Josie. But the man before her did not seem to be the scoundrel she'd encountered before. He was deflated, broken not just by his wounds from his beating but by the cunning Audra Jennings, the same person who revealed all to the man who'd awakened love in Josie these past weeks.

"Well, she is closely connected with the business, and I will never be able to face her again."

"She told me she was done with it, said it was a horrible thing to do. . ." Josie's voice trailed as she recalled Audra's unapologetic demeanor when she had assisted in that first grave robbing.

"Not Audra Jennings. She is in it deeper than any of us, for she has found her pot of gold. Will murder for it."

"Murder?" A sick feeling rushed through Josie. Her last conversation with Audra grew loud in her mind. She had spilled so much just before Braham walked in. Now, looking back, Audra had her eye on the hallway the entire time. Josie even looked over her shoulder twice to see what she was looking at. Did she know that Braham was listening? "Who would she—"

"There is a need for a large number of bodies, and she was willing to provide them for the chance of a life of luxury." He leaned back on the barn wall. "I could not be part of it. So many innocent women." He shook his head.

"Innocent women?" Josie gasped. "The poison!"

He wiped his forehead with a handkerchief. "She was fine with letting me go. I daresay she was relieved." He stuffed the handkerchief in his pocket. "Do not worry about your father, Josie. Dr. Chadwick has released your wages and his debt to me. All can go to your father. He can get out of debtors' prison once and for all. It is the least I can do." He began walking toward the barn door.

"Wait. Dr. Chadwick? Did you give him a body?" A sour taste sat on her tongue.

"No, I gave him something better." He shook his head. "I took him to the head of the network that supplies an entire medical society. Well, I gave him the clues to reach him. I do not know the head of the network myself." He rubbed his neck. "Dr. Chadwick has moved to Boston to share the wealth with colleagues." He snickered but then slumped his shoulders and disappeared in the darkness of the barn.

Relief for her father's situation and anger at Audra's wicked hand warred in Josie. She ran to the house. She must return to Gloughton. The women were dying, and Braham thought it was her fault. Even if he was disgusted by her own association with body snatchers, she must at least let him know that she was not a murderer. She must at least let him know that there was a murderer in his midst.

When she got to the porch, Braham was there, waiting.

"You are Josephine." He stared at her, his sable eyes as intense as the sunshine.

Her heart leapt at her given name on his lips. "I am."

"And you are considered—" He cleared his throat and frowned. "Dead?"

Whom had he spoken with? Any townsman would have told him the story, she was sure. But now he must hear it from her. Would he ever forgive her for what she had almost done?

"I was very sick. Everyone thought I had died. Even Dr. Chadwick. I—I was actually buried."

Braham gaped at her. He stepped closer, searching her face—perhaps for a lie?

"It was awful, Braham." Her voice shook. "I awoke beneath his knife. He was going to use my body—" She reached out, longing for an assuring touch.

But he slid his hand behind his back. "The resurrection men." Confusion muddled his brow. "You were given to him by one of those men?"

"I was. And that man, Alvin, found me just before Dr. Chadwick tried to kill me. Because of Alvin's loyalty to my father, a bargain was made for my life." She lowered to sit on a barrel. "I did not have a choice—my father's life was being threatened. I took his place as an aide to Alvin. I didn't know Father was part of such a business until the bargain was made—"

Braham knelt down, running his hand through his hair. "I never heard of such a—a—"

"Wicked web?" Josie blurted. He nodded. "Trust me, that is what it is. I never wanted to be part of it. But so much was at stake. My poor father was being tormented night and day."

Braham sat back and hooked his arms on his knees. "And my aunt, you were going to—"

"I could not do it. I saw Alvin waiting, and I saw you, Braham. You loved her. I called you over and kept the lantern lit so that nothing could happen to her." Josie stood up, wrapping her arms around her waist. "You might not believe me, but I have found out more. I did not accidently poison the girls—"

"I know. You are innocent." He rose and stood inches from her. He searched the rolling hills in the distance as he spoke. "Audra and Minnie are the guilty ones." He turned to her, a hardness still in his gaze. "You must lead me to the place where Audra will meet the others."

She nodded and glanced over her shoulder. "Yes. I know how to find them, I think." Alvin had saved her once. Perhaps, if he showed them the meeting place, she could help him end that chapter in his life. She looked back at Braham. "But it will come with another price, I am sure."

"I'll not get caught up in any of that business," Braham retorted.

"No." Josie shook her head. "Of course not. Braham, I have also sworn never to be a part of it again." She searched his stoic look, trying to find one ounce of the tenderness he had once shown her. "But the man who knows where they meet will need protection."

He stepped off the porch, now looking in the direction of the barn. "Who is he?"

A thickness lodged in her throat at his coldness. How could Josephine Clayton convince him that she had wanted to do the right thing all along, but she hadn't a choice in the matter?

Braham stared at her as she whispered, "You'll see."

He wanted to trust her, to believe her good intent. The woman had been through so much, and now her father was in debtors' prison.

She reached out her hand, and her large blue eyes pleaded for him to take it. "This morning, I swore to myself that I would not follow through with my end of the bargain. And before you arrived, God answered my need." He bounced his look from her lips to her hand. "Please, Braham, follow me." She pushed her hand in the air between them. He took it. A slight smile grew on her lips. "I promise, we will end all of this. You'll see."

They walked across the yard deserted from any life that might have been contained in the empty coop, pigpen, and barn. When they got close to the barn, Josie let go of his hand.

She shaded her eyes, calling out, "Alvin? Please come here."

Braham stepped back and exclaimed, "You have that man here with you?" He was right not to trust Josie after all.

Josie glanced at him. "He is not as he seems. Not anymore, anyway. Trust me." She was as confident as she had been when she cared for the sick. He remembered her posture at his aunt's bedside. He remembered how Mr. Bates graciously trusted his father again. Braham took in a deep breath and waited.

The scruffy man appeared from within the dark barn. "What's he doing here?"

"He wants to find Audra, Alvin. She's hurt so many women. Can you help?"

His nostrils flared. "I do not want any part of it. I've done too much."

"You do not have a choice, man," Braham seethed, balling his fists by his side. "Where is Audra? Is she with you?"

Alvin narrowed his eyes. "That woman is nothing to me now." He scowled. "I may have done terrible things, but I am no murderer."

Braham leaned in and whispered, "Close enough." All his grief, all his anger, welled in his burning chest.

"Josie, I think this is a mistake," Alvin growled. He retreated to the shadows, his eyes remaining locked with Braham's.

Josie stepped between them. "Alvin, if you take us to the meeting place, we will not say one word about your part in it."

"Josie, I do not know about that—" Braham could not let the criminal go, could he?

"Braham, Alvin has sworn to cut ties with that lifestyle. He saved me and promises to save my father." She glanced between them. "Now I will give him a chance to start over."

Alvin wore the marks of his beating all over his face. Braham was certain it was Gerald's work. This man had planned to steal their aunt's body. Should Braham trust Alvin now?

"Braham, Alvin has made mistakes, but he also has a heart." Josie grinned at the man. "He's paying off my father's debt. We shall keep him here, and he'll work hard and honestly. Right, Alvin?"

Alvin gathered his lips together like an obstinate child but nodded quickly, looking away from Braham. "They meet tonight. We have little time."

"And then you will go to Ashton?" Josie asked eagerly.

"Aye," he said. "Your father will sleep in his bed by the end of the week, I guarantee it." Josie beamed at Braham.

"Fine," Braham said, unable to look in her eyes. He wished that Gerald would give him as much grace as Josie showed this man now. She was almost glowing at the resolution. Josie mentioned that she would tidy up for her father and left Braham and Alvin alone. Braham watched her. He could never let go of the feelings that lured him to love Josie Clay. Even now, his heart thrummed in double time at the sight of her. But she had been pretending all this time. How difficult would it be to trust her again?

Alvin cleared his throat. Braham turned to him. The man was several years older than he was. Alvin rubbed his jaw and looked toward the house. "She never wanted to be a part of it. The day I dropped her off at the mill, she begged for a different way. Even now, with her father in debtors' prison, she swore she was done with the business."

"You offered to help her father."

"After she said she was done."

"I do not know what to think anymore." Braham shoved his hands in his pockets.

"You love her, I can tell." Alvin snorted. "Trust me, I've felt the same as you look."

Did he refer to Audra? Poor fool.

"And you were okay with Audra's ways. How can I forgive Miss Clay for what she has done thus far? It seems unforgivable."

"Mr. Taylor, I do not know what you think, but the woman hasn't done anything. She was forced to clean up a grave after the robbing. She took her father's place. All because she loves the old fool." Alvin grabbed a shovel and some empty sacks from inside the barn door. "Trust me if you can—Josephine Clayton has a gift— she is an angel for the sick. Even when I was in the thick of crime the day that I found her with Dr. Chadwick, I could not let such a creature die."

Chapter Twenty-Four

Their ride was quiet. A tension sat between them. Josie was elated about her father's release. She could not contain her chatter at first. But Braham remained a statue, and he gave no indication that he listened to one word.

"Forgive me, I have rambled on." Josie clasped her hands in her lap. "I was trapped between helping my father and his terrible debts. Now, all of it has melted away." She turned her face to the fresh breeze streaming along the country lane.

"We have quite a feat ahead of us yet," Braham said. "I will be more at ease when Alvin follows through with the plan." He sighed. "But I understand your elation. All has worked out for you."

"And for you," Josie declared. "The mill girls are safe and will no longer suffer."

"Yes, but I will always have the burden of Gerald's distrust. He will use this incident against me, I am sure. I have yet to hear from him, and that makes me worry."

"I am sorry, Braham. You are a good manager."

"Gerald shall never find out about your part in this," he said in a bitter tone. "To know that his factory was caught up in such a scandal. . ." He shook his head. "We would both be out of work." He called out to the horse, and it slowed to a trot. "There was a time down south when several of the slaves had become ill. My father assisted some of the boys in their rows while neglecting his own." His jaw flinched. "Gerald was only twelve but noticed and told the slave master. The overseer of the place had my father watch two slave boys endure the whippings in his stead. That night, Father told me that watching two innocent children suffer was worse punishment than feeling the pain himself."

"That is awful," she muttered, trying to resist the scenario forming in her mind.

"You've taken on much yourself, Josephine." He turned his face toward her. Rounded brown eyes shone bright beneath his hat brim, offering a warmth she had not seen from him since he arrived in Ainsley. "Even with all the horrific planning that tied you to those wicked men and women, you continued to care for your friends. You became a friend to me."

"And you to me." She smiled. He brought the cart to a stop along a wooded embankment. The dappled light danced all about them.

"When you left Gloughton, I had never felt more alone, Josie— I mean, Josephine." He looked in her eyes. "I will be honest with you. When all was revealed, I never felt more betrayed than in that moment."

"There is no reason you should ever trust me, I understand that." Sadness welled up inside her. "Yet, even in knowing what you thought of me, all I wanted was to be everything you saw me do. That is the real Josephine Clayton. I want to help the sick. I want to pray with the dying." His nostrils flared, and he studied her lips as she spoke. He reached out and tightened his hands around hers. "And I want you to be with me through it all, Braham."

She felt as though her words were billowing between them, transfixing them in this moment like cotton dust hovering as evidence of the grander work upon the loom.

"I love you, Josie Clay," he whispered, leaning toward her without unlocking his trance. She met him with her lips against his, an unspoken acceptance of the love he gave her. Had she ever expected to find such a sweet reprieve from all her bitter circumstance? His breath was warm against her skin. His fingers left hers and embraced the hair at the nape of her neck. Loneliness would never invade her heart again. She would never be trapped by darkness. Every touch from Braham's sweet caress filled her heart with the brightest love she'd ever known.

A sharp, loud slap cracked the peace around them, and they

both turned to see what made such an unnerving sound.

Audra and Gerald sat on the bench of a carriage, one that did not seem sturdy enough for the bumpy country lane. Their horse whinnied and shook its mane. Gerald once again slapped the air with his whip.

"That is her," Audra declared, clutching the ribbon of her bonnet.

"I do wonder at this choice, Braham," Gerald snickered, but then his face grew red. "At first, I expected to have you replace each of those girls one by one, sharing with their families about a terrible illness that plagued our factory. But when Audra shared the scheming of this, this—" He sneered at Josie, scouring her with the ugliest of looks. "Witch," he spat out, "I decided that you might not be the man for the job after all. Such weak judgment of women, it seems."

Braham stood up, his fists clenched at his side. "What is this? Audra, you have fed him lies. We know it was you who poisoned the girls."

"Me?" She brushed aside an auburn curl and twirled it with her gloved finger. "Please, Braham, I am not the one who squirmed her way into the apothecary's trust, mixing up supposed remedies."

Gerald jumped down from the cart, and Braham did the same from his. Soon both men stood within inches of each other.

"Gerald, you must listen. Audra is caught up with body snatchers. She wanted to kill the women to provide. . .to provide bodies—"

Gerald bellowed with laughter. "Bodies? Who are you listening to?" He spun around. "Audra, it appears they are projecting the witch's intent on you, my dear."

She stuck her nose up in the air. "Absurd." The woman was just as cool as she had been the night in the cemetery. Josie scurried down the cart, running up to Gerald, who seared Braham with his hateful look.

"Please, you must listen, Mr. Bates—"

Gerald ignored her and seethed, "You are done at my factory, Braham Taylor."

Braham's nostrils flared. "You cannot do that. I have evidence from the executor—"

"Williams? Well, isn't that a pity. He passed away last week, and somehow, the documents in his office just. . .disappeared." He leaned close, snatching Braham's cravat. "You have no one."

Braham jerked himself away. He put his hands on his knees as if trying to catch his breath.

Josie interjected, "Mr. Bates, we have evidence that Audra is the one you must question. Her sister—"

"Minnie?" Audra screeched. Her mouth fell open, and then she brought her lips together in a crooked smile. "She's always been jealous of me. Remember, Gerald, the day your aunt chose me to go to the factory? Minnie cried for a week. Pathetic thing."

"You're coming with me." Gerald clawed at Josie's arm and forced her next to him.

"Stop!" Josie tried to wriggle free, but his grip was tight.

"Gerald Bates, you let go of her." Braham lunged at Gerald. But the man swung hard, hooking Braham in the stomach and knocking him to the ground. Josie screamed, Gerald's tight grip burning through her sleeve.

"I am surprised at you, Braham." Gerald kicked at him. "My father trusted you to be of sound judgment. Hiring this one?" He held up Josie's arm. "Well, I will have no choice but to replace you."

Josie felt as though she might faint. The pressure of his grip on her arm was causing it to go numb. Suppressing more cries to appear strong exhausted every bit of her. Gerald thrust her into the carriage, and they drove off. The last she saw of Braham was through the carriage window. He scrambled to his feet, disappearing in a cloud of dust.

Chapter Twenty-Five

Braham groaned as he tried to stand up. Gerald had knocked the wind out of him. The man had once again proven himself to be a brute, with just one swift blow. Fighting through the ache, Braham climbed up on his cart and tried to catch up with them. He must get to the town constable, and to Minnie, before that manipulative Audra convinced Constable James that Josie had poisoned the women. It would be even more difficult to convince the constable with Gerald there. How blinded might he be by Audra's story with the wealthiest man in the area standing next to her?

There was no doubt in Braham's mind that Audra may have found a way to Gerald's heart after all. She had satisfied him with the one thing he had hoped for—proving that Braham Taylor was unfit to manage the factory. Audra had used this twisted business of body snatching to frame Braham's newest hire.

Sweat ran down his elbows as the day heated up. He knew a quicker way to Gloughton and steered the cart away from the path. There were many days when he'd go hunting with his uncle while Gerald was away at school. This land was familiar to him. He continued through the fresh green countryside, praying for God to protect Josie.

The sun was hidden behind thick clouds when he arrived in Gloughton. He jumped down from his cart and ran up to Constable James's small brick house. As he knocked, he looked around for Gerald's carriage. Had they arrived here first?

The tall, lanky constable held the door open and greeted Braham.

Braham looked up and down the street once more. "Did Gerald Bates arrive yet?"

"Mr. Bates?" He motioned for Braham to enter. "No, sir. But that girl has been making a fuss all morning." He nodded to the locked door of the room where Minnie spent the night. "Wouldn't eat one bite of her food."

"I will talk to her. But first, I want you to know that Mr. Bates and Miss Audra Jennings will arrive and try to discount all we've been told by Minnie."

The constable shifted his weight and hooked his finger on his chin in contemplation. "Mr. Bates is a powerful man. He owns nearly all of Gloughton."

"But he has been tricked by that Audra Jennings. She is trying to frame a mill girl. That is what I am here to tell you. We have another witness to firm up what Minnie has told us."

"Who is this witness?" He sat on a stool and picked up his pipe and lit it.

Braham lowered to the bench across from him. "It is a man who was in business with Audra."

"Pah!" The constable widened his eyes. "And we should trust him over Mr. Bates?"

Braham knew it might be hard to out-reason the constable's allegiance to Gerald. Yet he also knew that the constable was a good man—an ambitious one too. "James, I will take you to the entire network." He was emboldened when the man pulled the pipe from his mouth and leaned in, waiting for more. "Didn't you once say you want to get on in a bigger city? Imagine what the authorities in Boston might think if the hired constable from Gloughton brought down a whole network of body snatchers?"

James tamped down his pipe's tobacco and relit it. A cloud of smoke rose between them. "When will Bates arrive?"

"Any moment now." Braham rose and went to the window. "I do not know what is taking them so long." His path was not that much shorter.

He went and spoke with Minnie, assuring her that all would be resolved, then stepped outside and looked up and down the street again. The sky was still gray, and the damp scent promised rain was on its way. A storm brewed in Braham's pit, and he ran out to his cart. His mind raced. He mounted and headed down Main Street.

Had he just wasted time sitting around waiting? What if they'd never planned to bring Josie here at all?

Josie clung to the door of the carriage as the rain pelted down. Gerald's loud shouting to the horse was barely heard. The day was nearly as dark as night. Where were they taking her? She'd never been this far north. Soon, the carriage slowed beneath a bridge, and the sound of rushing water took the place of the rain. She looked out the small window. A brook was filling quickly beside the road.

Many minutes passed. She wondered if they were stuck. Josie tried to peer toward the front of the carriage, but she could not see anything. The rain continued to pound. She pressed her head back, and just as she began to pray, the door flung open, and Gerald reached in and grabbed her.

"Where are we?" she shouted above the noise. But the man ignored her, pulling her along the bank. When they lost the bridge's shelter, he began to run, holding his top hat with his other hand. Ahead, she saw the flicker of a light in the midst of a wild wooded area.

This was not Gloughton.

Would she even have the chance to plead her innocence? The only assurance she had was that this man, while pompous to Braham, was considered upstanding by all. She prayed he would have the decency to allow her to plead before a wise counsel.

The light in the distance was actually a lamp hanging from Audra's hands as she stood beneath the overhang on a large porch of a barn. Her sly smile discouraged any hope. Josie doubted that any authorities here would care anything about Josie's side of things. Not with Audra Jennings around.

They entered the building, water from their clothes puddling at their feet. The odor of mildew soured the air, and cobwebs strung across every corner of the large room. Audra's lantern shone on old tools, broken wagon wheels, and parts of furniture piled up. The light offered nothing to Josie's path but dread.

"Where are we?" she asked again, this time her voice louder than the rain that drummed on the roof. Fright crawled through her veins as the light reached a corner housing a mouse nest and a pile of rotting apples.

"One might call it—your fate?" Audra cackled.

"Tie her up," Gerald barked. He pulled down a rope from a hook beside him and handed it to Audra. Josie tried to pull away as Gerald handed her to the woman, but he did not let go until Audra had secured Josie's hands behind her back. Audra tugged her like a prisoner to its cell, but instead of a cell, a large trunk. Gerald opened it.

"Wait," Josie cried out. "I cannot go in—"

"Ah, but you are small enough you can." Gerald grinned.

"But I thought you would take me to the authorities. Please, do not believe what Audra has said. There are others who know the truth."

Audra yanked hard on Josie's hair, causing her to yelp. "Others? Who?" she demanded at Josie's ear.

"Minnie. . .and. . .and. . ." She stopped herself. Alvin had been her biggest headache, but he was also going to help her. She would not share anything with this woman who had done so much harm. "And the constable in Gloughton."

Gerald shook his head and joined Audra in a hearty laugh.

"The constable? Isn't that where Minnie is?" Audra snorted. "He knows nothing but what Minnie has said, you foolish girl." She tied a handkerchief around Josie's mouth. It didn't matter if Josie tried to resist now. She had no chance to escape. Audra shoved her toward the trunk. Gerald reached over and scooped Josie up like a child and lowered her inside.

She would never be found here. A sob threatened to erupt, but she feared she would choke.

"We had better go. Boyles and Drake will meet us at sunset." Gerald looked at his pocket watch. "I cannot be late."

"Whoa there." Audra slid her hand along his chest and tweaked his chin with her gloved fingers. "*We* cannot be late. Remember, we are in this together. After this job, you will no longer have that puny Braham to worry about or that terrible factory. I can stop traipsing around, trying to set him up."

Josie's eyes widened and a guttural sound came from her pit.

Audra turned, the lamp shining in Josie's eyes. "Yes, you were a pest from the very beginning, Miss Clay. Constantly undoing my work as you helped with those injured girls. Every bolt I loosened, every screw I stole, you'd patch up the damage and leave Braham with little fretting." The lamp swung to and fro. Josie remembered the evening she thought she saw someone enter the factory. The light on the front steps—was that Audra? "And then your elixir for the soup." She rolled her eyes. Josie's pulse jolted. Hadn't Fran mistaken her for Audra when Josie had entered the kitchen the night they had soup? Audra had been helping serve dinner. A convenient task when she'd planned to poison the girls.

"It all worked out for the best, though." Gerald snickered. "A mass need, a supply at my fingertips, and a nuisance to finally get rid of."

Josie ignored the searing light and gawked at this man.

"Well, two nuisances." Audra nudged him. "That executor needed to go before you could really do anything about Braham."

Gerald stared at Josie, tugging at his gloves. "That was easy. When you are in charge of an entire operation that deals with the dead, what's one more?"

Josie's blood pounded in her chest, and her stomach churned as if she were going to be sick. Gerald Bates had just admitted to murder.

"I am just glad I have such a pretty spy to find the goods I need." Gerald turned his attention to Audra.

"The broth for the girls should be doing the trick, right about now." She kissed his lips. "Next week will be a busy one." He brushed her cheek and strode away.

Gerald Bates was not just a fool for Audra's flirtations, nor was he just the wealthiest man in Gloughton. He was the pot of gold which Alvin declared that Audra had found. He hadn't left Alvin for dead that night of Aunt Myrtle's funeral; he had only punished him for focusing on the wrong body. The one body he was connected to.

Gerald Bates was the man whom Audra was supplying all this time—Gerald Bates was the head of a business that thrived on stolen bodies.

Audra lifted the lamp and winked at Josie. Josie shook her head frantically, screaming against the gag. No, she could not shut her in. No!

Audra paused and called over her shoulder, "Shouldn't we just get rid of her?"

Sharp footsteps drew close, and Gerald appeared behind Audra again. "No, save her." He grunted. "In case we're one short."

Chapter Twenty-Six

Braham's chest tightened as he trampled down the bank by the brook that Alvin had mapped out for him. Alvin went ahead to be sure that nobody was on guard at the network's storage barn. He would stand on the porch with a lit lantern if all was well.

The constable and two of Braham's overseers were just behind him. They did not know how many men they might be up against. Braham feared the four of them were not enough. But he was more concerned about setting Josie free.

"As soon as we get Audra in our hands, we'll find out where they took Josie."

"And if she refuses to confess?" Constable James asked, clearly nervous about the sabotage. "I do not want to face Mr. Bates. He could strip me of my title and my home."

"Audra cannot refuse when we find her at the exact spot where she'll be waiting for bodies." Braham spoke through his teeth. "Alvin will help. Do not worry." Although there was a small niggle of doubt as he spoke.

That man better be as trustworthy as Josie claimed.

Braham had prayed over and over for God's protection on Josie these past hours. As the sun burned toward dusk, his hope for her return waned. How could he ever convince Gerald that Josie was only a cover-up for Audra's wicked ways? Braham worried that Gerald had gone ahead to Boston. There was no doubt that Audra would have convinced him to find more established authorities in a larger city than in the small home of Constable James. If Gerald released Josie to the police there, they would hardly listen to Braham, who had little worth next to a man like Gerald. He was even more respected in the high society of Boston than the small village of Gloughton. No, Braham did not stand a chance.

It all depended on the scruffy man he saw ahead. Alvin leaned up against an old barn hidden in the woods, striking a match to light a lantern.

Braham lifted a hand, acknowledging him as he walked up.

Alvin stepped back when Constable James came up beside Braham.

"Do not worry, Alvin." Braham turned and placed a hand on the constable's shoulder. "He knows everything and is here to help."

"Everything?" Alvin loosened his collar.

"If you are telling the truth." Constable James spoke deep and low. "Then you will have led us to the largest crime ever connected to our town." He stepped closer to Alvin, looking down his nose. "But if not—" He poked him in the shoulder.

"Hey there. I am a changed man. There is nothing so cruel in me as to murder innocent women." He crossed himself, as if assuring them by the sign of God that he spoke in honesty. Constable James gave a quick nod and stepped back.

"This is the place?" Braham asked.

"No. This is where we will collect the things needed. There are specific carts they use to make the exchange. Marked with a white canvas over the bodies. That way, they know who their men are in the dark of night." Alvin stepped over and unlocked the door. "Come on."

His lantern lit up the place. Nothing seemed usable. Everything appeared broken and tossed about. Alvin walked over to some sacks hanging on a wall and removed them, revealing a door. "This way."

"Men, be on guard," Constable James warned over his shoulder.

"I said he is trustworthy, James. He would never have taken us this far—"

A knocking sound came from beneath the window to Braham's left.

"Hold on." Constable James pulled out his pistol. The other men did the same.

"Alvin, are you certain there is nobody here?" Braham whispered loudly, crouching down with the others in a corner.

The knocking was firmer, and the sound of a muffled voice had all the men freeze.

"It's coming from that trunk, I think." Alvin ran over to a large trunk with rusted metal hinges. Another knock. "Someone's inside!"

Braham and Alvin tried to lift the lid, but it was locked.

"I don't have a key for this." Alvin spoke through clenched teeth as he tried to pry it open.

Braham looked around the room. He found a hoe. Lodging the metal end beneath the hinge, he began to try to pry it off. Alvin also grabbed a spade and did the same on the other hinge. Braham struggled to get the hoe to stay directly between the metal piece of the hinge and the wood. After a few tries, he pressed his feet against the wall and leveraged it with all his might. The hinge began to loosen.

He looked up, sweat blinding his view. "Alvin, is it working for you?"

"It is, I almost—" He grunted loudly, and a cracking sound echoed in the room. His spade flung across the floor. "It split the wood." He managed to break off the hinge with the heel of his boot.

Braham continued to work on his end, and he finally got the metal hinge off. Together, Alvin and Braham forced the lid until a loud snap indicated the locking mechanism was broken. Alvin held up the lantern. Yellow light flooded inside the trunk, revealing a person balled up like a kitten.

Braham could see a small blond curl against a face half covered by a handkerchief.

"Josie?" He carefully turned her by the shoulder. Her eyes were half-shut and her face was damp with sweat. A handkerchief prevented her from speaking, but sobs shook her small frame. "Oh no!" He quickly lifted her out, her body limp. All the men rushed up around them. Braham untied the gag, and Josie breathed deep and hard. He loosened the rope around her wrists then wiped away the moist hair that matted against her forehead. "Dear, sweet Josie.

What has happened here?"

Her breaths quickened. A panic flashed in her swimming blue eyes. "Braham." Her voice was thin, shaky. "Oh Braham. It is not what we thought."

"What?" He leaned back, uncertain as to what she meant, but sensing dread invading the stale barn air.

"They lied." She lifted trembling hands to his cheeks. "Gerald knew that Audra was guilty all along." She turned to Alvin. "Did you know?"

"About Audra?"

"No, about Gerald." Her nervous glance back at Braham forced the dread to sit heavy upon his chest. His brain reeled, trying to figure out what she meant.

Alvin lowered his head and kicked the trunk. "I had seen them about town together. I am no match against that man. Are they engaged?"

"Not that," Josie said. "He was your boss, wasn't he?"

"Boss? No, I've never worked for him." Alvin scratched his head. "At the factory?"

Josie shook her head. "No. Who did you answer to for the. . . bodies?"

"It is a secret network. We gather notes from designated places to find the drop-off location, but the person in charge is to remain hidden." Alvin stepped over and crouched down. "The note for this evening's location was in. . ." He gulped. "In the lantern hanging from the gate at the Bates estate. Come to think of it, many of the notes were hidden on those grounds."

That very first night, Braham had seen Alvin leave there.

Braham's jaw tightened. "What have you learned, Josie? What did we get wrong?"

She only stared at him, her eyes wide with pity. "He's part of it."

Braham fell back and sat on his backside, the pieces forming a horrific puzzle in his mind. It couldn't be. He ran his fingers through his hair. The letter to Dr. Brown—the goods to be delivered— "No, it can't be," he whispered.

"It is, Braham." Josie spoke quietly. "Gerald has been part of this the entire time. He is the one in charge of collecting bodies." She wagged her head. "He and Audra are working together."

Braham grabbed his mouth and tried to remember any evidence against such an accusation. But the man who'd hated him all this time had done nothing to prove himself innocent. In fact, moments flooded to Braham's mind—the secret whisperings between Audra and Gerald, the letter to the doctor, the targeted mill girls, the death of the executor of his uncle's will. . .Gerald was not a murderer also, was he?

"Audra and Gerald tied me up here, and that is when I found out." Josie's hand flung to her mouth, and her eyes filled with fresh tears. "Oh Braham, he. . .he admitted to killing your uncle's executor— Gerald is a murderer." Braham pulled her close and held her tight against him, trying to still his shaking body. A long groan threatened from deep within him. Josie rasped, "They were going to kill me if they did not have enough bodies—" Sobs racked her small frame.

Anger and disgust filled his gut. He pressed Josie closer to him, smothering his face in her hair, trying to will away the tears.

Once he calmed the current inside him, he looked up at Alvin. "We must get there quickly. This is coming to an end tonight."

Josie refused to stay at the barn alone, and the men agreed that they needed every single one of them to capture Gerald, Audra, and whoever else might be waiting. Braham's best overseer, Tom, went up to the road to retrieve a horse where they had left their carts. He met them at the back of the barn.

Alvin informed them that Gerald would be the one in the black cloak; his face would be hidden. Audra wore her mourning clothes at meetings like this. It was a disguise in case they were caught. She would play the part of a mourning family member, seeing that the body was transported safely to a family cemetery.

"They have never once been stopped or questioned," Alvin said as he led them through the back of the barn. "There's nobody along these wooded paths at the midnight hour."

Everyone but Alvin slipped inside the cart, lying flat on their backs. Josie stayed close to Braham, clutching at his hand by their sides, trying to forget the cargo that lay here last. She shook all over even though the night was warm.

"Do not fear, my love," Braham whispered, squeezing her hand. "We will be free of all of this soon."

"I am so sorry about your cousin," she muttered, resting her cheek on his shoulder as they lay close.

"Me too."

She could feel his body shudder against hers, and she wondered at his grief. "Will you be able to do this, Braham? You do not have to be a part of—"

"It must be done." He sighed. "There are many people he has hurt over the years. And now he has risked smearing my uncle's legacy."

She tried to see him in the darkness and could only make out his profile—a tightly closed mouth, eyes squeezed shut.

Alvin appeared above them with the white canvas in his arms. "Typically, we lay hay over the…goods…just in case we are stopped." He grimaced then cleared his throat. "But if we are caught by someone, there's nothing to hide anymore."

His shoulders slumped. The man had become a near hero now. Josie saw him in a new light. The yellow lantern that hung on a hook shone on the face of a worn-out gentleman—a man who had his heart broken by the woman he loved and who had left the life of crime because of an innate awareness for life. He had stopped his wayward existence because he wanted nothing to do with murder. Just as he had saved Josephine from Dr. Chadwick's table.

For the first time since her mother was alive, Josephine saw Alvin as a decent man, one who was loyal to her father and a friend to her. Now, as he took the lantern from the hook, she prayed that he would always be guided by a lamp unto his path and that darkness would no longer tempt him.

"Do not forget, I'll place the lantern at the edge of the clearing so you will see your way," he reminded them, then set it down to pull the canvas over the top of the cart.

"We will look for it," Braham assured him.

Josie nestled up against him once more and closed her eyes as the white canvas fell heavily on top of them.

Braham kissed her forehead. "You are safe, Josephine Clayton. This nightmare will soon be over."

The ride was bumpy. Braham's shoulders took the brunt of the movement as he was directly above a wheel. He lay between Buck Walters and Josie. Their lungs were filling with the mildewed scent of the canvas, yet he kept breathing deeply to calm himself in the tight space. His mind raced with the possibilities of how this plan might fail. By the time the cart maintained a steady pace, his grip on Josie was tight and sweat had covered his brow.

"Buck, if something happens to me, take Josie and hide in the woods, do you hear me?" His voice was barely a whisper, competing with the churning wheels.

"Aye, sir."

Josie clutched at his arm with her other hand. "I feel like I am going to fall off."

He slid his arm beneath the heavy canvas and embraced her as best as he could. "I won't let you, love." He pressed his cheek to her forehead. The edge of the canvas flapped up, revealing a bright moonlit sky along the crest of a hill. They had planned for Josie to lie at the very edge of the cart in case Gerald wanted proof of a body. Alvin would say a mill girl perished this morning—one who needed to be transported to her hometown. Josie would hold her hand perfectly still, allowing it to poke out from the canvas. However, the position may threaten peril before they even arrived to the meeting place. She seemed dangerously close to the edge.

"I should switch places with you, Josie."

"No, just hold me."

They could no longer speak when the cart slowed down to a creeping pace. Before it completely stopped, Josie rolled back to her position. The darkness was thick, but he could feel her breath on his neck. She squeezed his hand with a passionate grip.

"Do not fear," he whispered. Buck warned him to hush with an elbow in his ribs.

Alvin's singsong voice carried to them. "The mourn is done, the time is come. Never fear, we are here." The signal. He had mentioned at the barn that the secret code would be sung three times, and then he would be permitted to draw close to the bridge where he would meet the head snatcher.

Every breath beneath the canvas seemed to hitch on the silence that followed Alvin's hoarse verse. If the silence remained, then that meant that Gerald did not trust the delivery.

"Ho there, do you need assistance?" Gerald's voice traveled up to them, and Braham's shallow breath trembled. A final crumb of hope that they had got it wrong—that the cruel man was not as cruel as to profit from such a business—that small sliver in his heart dissolved, broadening his agony once more.

The cart began to move again. They headed downhill, Josie's side pressed against him, warm and delicate, his assurance that he was not alone and that love had not disappeared with his aunt's final word.

They came to a halt. He stiffened. His ears strained to hear beyond the rush of blood barreling through his body.

"Alvin, what are you doing here?" Audra's sharp tone was close. She must have stood right next to their side of the cart. "I thought you were done with this."

"Opportunity arose." Alvin chuckled. "I could not resist."

Braham's heart leapt and splashed into doubt. The man sounded smug.

"I've not heard from Minnie. Is this from Gloughton?" A knock against the cart rattled along their heads.

"Only one girl. She's en route to her hometown. Shame that robbers might meet us along the road." He chuckled at the story they'd come up with at the barn. A snort came from Audra.

Minutes passed. No word was spoken. He prayed that Josie stayed perfectly still in case they checked on them. They all waited for Alvin's signal. He was going to ask for a bit of whiskey by the fire before the exchange.

They waited.

But it did not come.

Chapter Twenty-Seven

I am going to get out and look," Josie whispered in Braham's ear.
He clutched at her arm. She froze, afraid that the movement was obvious. "No," he breathed out.

"They have not said anything for several minutes. Perhaps Alvin forgot the signal and is in trouble." She would slip easily from beneath the canvas and crouch behind the cart. "I will be careful, I promise."

Braham tried to hold her tight, but she wriggled free and slid away. She begged God to protect her as she carefully lifted the canvas, turned on her stomach, and dropped to damp mud.

The air outside carried a more pleasant smell than the dirty cart offered—one of lingering rain and quenched leaves. She crouched behind the large wheel and filled her lungs. Although the moonlight was bright, the trees were guards against it. Only a flicker shone several yards away. She squinted, allowing her eyes to adjust to the darkness. She could see a fire. An occasional figure walked about it. Unease crept up her spine, wondering what Alvin might be up to. Did he truly forget the signal?

"Hey there!" The shout shook the silence on the road ahead of them. Her heart stopped then regained its strength with erratic thumps. The voice was too far away to have been directed at her. She caught her breath and crawled around the cart, her dress dragging in the mud. She snuck to the front and could just make out another cart like theirs, the white canvas catching the moonlight. A lantern's light swung between two men—Alvin and a stranger—as they lugged a body into the wooded area. Several times Alvin looked over at their own cart. The glint of the lantern revealed his concerned brow.

"I haven't much time," the stranger grunted. "I need to get back before they get suspicious."

"I'm doing the best I can," Alvin snarled. "I have my own load, you know?"

"Knock it off, Alvin," Audra snapped from somewhere in the trees. "You've got nothing but time. Nobody cares where you are."

Fury stabbed Josie's heart. What a callous woman. Poor Alvin was facing her now.

Josie waited a few more moments. She heard the distant footsteps and listened carefully to be sure they didn't grow close. Reins snapped in the air, and the cart ahead wheeled away.

She took quick steps back along the cart and ducked behind the wheel. The fire flicker was no longer visible, yet the yellow glow of a lantern showed Gerald, Audra, and Alvin sitting with their backs to her, pouring cups of drink. The only way she could tell that Alvin had followed through with their plan was by that lantern he had placed at the edge of the clearing.

Josie carefully lifted the canvas. Although she could not see Braham and the men in the dark, she could hear their breathing.

"It seems that another one of Gerald's men arrived," she whispered. "Too bad we could not stop him as well. But I think Alvin has been stuck with Audra bossing him about." She reached in and found Braham's hand. "It's time that we go. The lantern is in place."

Braham pushed himself to the edge. "I want you to stay back, Josie. These past minutes were an eternity." His eyes caught the moonlight. They were wide with concern. He jumped down next to her then pulled her by the waist. "They might have seen you and—" He found her chin and lifted it.

"You needn't worry. I stayed close to the cart." She cupped his cheek.

"You are brave, I'll give you that." He gently kissed her. A shiver traveled through her. The nightmare was over, and soon the dream would begin. A smile threatened her lips as they pulled away.

She could not fully smile until this last scheme was accomplished.

"There now," Tom whispered behind them. "Let us get this over with."

Josie was thankful for the night hiding her blush. She slipped behind the men. Braham gathered some rope from the cart then held his hand up to her, insisting she stay back.

"I will stay behind you. I promise," she assured him.

The men crouched down with pistols in their hands and the constable leading the way. Josie prayed, keeping her word by staying behind them at a distance yet creeping forward slowly. She would not stay at the cart alone.

Braham pushed down the anger that erupted at the sight of Gerald's broad shoulders as he slung back whiskey beneath a black hood. The constable stopped just beyond the circle of light cast by the lantern. They were close enough to hear the conversation by the fire.

"Are you certain you won't miss this?" Audra reached behind Gerald and ran her hand across his shoulders.

"Why get our hands dirty if we have the money from the trust?" Gerald snorted. "There is no proof that my uncle put a stipulation on it. There is no evidence of the ward's part in the will at all." He wagged his head then chuckled. "If you could have seen Williams's face. He thought he was safe after I forced him to give me the money. Did not see what was coming—" He sniffed. "He died quickly. Easy and quick."

Bile filled Braham's throat. The heartless words of a murderer rang in the air, and it was from the one person he could call family.

Alvin stood up. The constable straightened his shoulders, and the others stepped forward with Braham. They waited for the signal.

"Oh look," Audra whined. "We've made Saint Alvin uncomfortable with all this talk. He only likes stealing the dead, not helping them along." She giggled, and Gerald laughed.

The constable flicked his head, and they crept up behind Gerald and Audra, who were still sitting. Alvin slung the rest of his drink in the fire, just as planned. The flames swelled then smoked.

"Watch it, man," Gerald reprimanded. "You'll put it out."

Tom lunged at Gerald and grabbed his arms. "What the—" He squirmed, trying to get free, but Tom was nearly twice his girth. He swiveled him around, revealing Gerald's befuddled face.

Alvin held Audra in a full-on embrace from behind. She screeched and hollered. Braham did what he was supposed to and waited behind the constable with the ropes to tie their hands.

"I never had a good feeling about you." Tom spoke through his teeth in Gerald's ear. "Your uncle was right to choose Braham over you."

Braham winced. The truth would hurt any son.

Gerald's face flashed with fury. He flung himself about trying to get free. Constable James stopped him with a pistol inches from his face. "You have just confessed to murder, Mr. Bates," he said, his hands shaking. "Tie him up, Braham."

When Braham stepped forward, he could not help but look Gerald in the eyes. "What have you become?"

"You cannot speak to me that way." Gerald glared. "What I provide is the chance of discovery. Doctors make the greatest strides with these goods. An entire medical society depends on me."

Braham recalled the letter to Dr. Brown. He shook his head. "But to kill for it. . .to do what you have done. Your father would be—"

"*My* father, Braham. Remember, he was mine," Gerald fumed. "A far nobler man than yours was."

Braham would not retort, not now. Even if the cruelty his father endured was, in part, due to this monger of greed.

"I just wanted to do the job I was entrusted with by *your* father. We could have been friends."

Gerald sneered. "Never. You are just a pathetic servant. You always will be."

Braham tied Gerald's wrists tightly. "I would rather be a servant than what you are. One day I pray that you will remember the footsteps you could have followed. And I hope that you get a second chance to deserve the title of Bates Jr." He secured the knot and stepped back, begging God that he would never forget to keep his word and pray.

With a sigh, he walked over to tie Audra's hands, but she hadn't stopped struggling in Alvin's firm embrace. She thrust her head back and hit Alvin in the face. He let go, grabbing his nose that gushed with blood. Audra ran toward their cart.

"Get her!" Constable James called out. Buck Walters took off after her, and Braham tossed the rope down and also tried to chase her down. A cry filled the night, and then another. His heart sped up as he realized it wasn't Audra's cry.

"Josie!"

The two women were on the crest of the hill. Audra had Josie by the hair, and Josie was trying to pull her down to the ground.

"Get off me," Audra shouted. She whipped her arms up, and Josie lost her grip. With a vicious shove, Audra pushed Josie down the slope. Braham lunged forward, but Josie tumbled down into the darkness. Before Audra could run, Braham was close enough to grab her and pin her down.

"It is over, Audra." Alvin came up and began to tie the rope around her wrists. "Go, Braham, check on Josephine."

Braham's chest constricted as he took careful steps, trying to make his way in the darkness. "Josie?" he called out.

He heard nothing.

Panic gripped him.

The moonlight brightened, and a few yards away, he saw her. She was crumpled in the same position he had found her in inside the trunk. When he turned her from the muddy earth, he noticed that a large rock jutted from the ground where her head had been. She appeared lifeless. "Josie," he whispered, gently shaking her. Her temple gushed with blood. He hooked his arm under hers, and as he stood up he threaded his other arm beneath her legs and lifted her against his chest. "Please wake up, my sweet Josie."

No matter how much he begged her to awake, though, she

hardly moved. Her eyes remained closed, and her breathing was shallow. The moonlight's cast on her skin heightened Braham's worry—she was more a ghost than a girl. She seemed more dead than alive.

He swallowed hard, trying to steady his staggered breaths. "We need to go. She is badly injured," he barked at the men who were loading Gerald in his own cart filled with evidence of his sick network. "Constable James, good luck in Boston. Alvin, drive us home."

He took long strides to the cart, passing up Alvin as he dragged Audra over to the constable. Braham was done worrying about them. The only thing that mattered was getting Josie help. After all they had been through, what would he do if anything happened to Josie Clay?

Chapter Twenty-Eight

Josephine Clayton batted her eyelashes in the bright warm light. A pleasant smell of lilacs filled the room, and she felt as though she lay on a cloud.

"Josie, you are awake." Braham's loving face appeared above her, and his soft lips brushed her forehead. If she had found her way to heaven, she would believe it now.

"Where am I?" She tried to sit up, but a pang gnawed at the side of her head. She sank back into the pillow with a wince.

"You are in your room. At your father's house."

"My father's house." A smile spread on her lips despite her aching head. "Oh Braham. He is home again?"

"Soon, my love. He will be." He tucked her hair behind her ear. "We ran into a terrible storm on the way to Gloughton. Alvin thought it best that we come here instead since it is not as far west as Gloughton is south."

"You will be just fine." Daisy appeared beside Braham. "Hit your head hard. There's an awful bump under that bandage."

"Daisy, what are you doing here?"

"We sent for her a couple days ago," Braham said. "She gave you a proper dressing. She's stayed with you each night to be sure you didn't need anything." He nodded toward a pallet beneath the window. "I've made a bed by the kitchen fire." He rubbed his neck and stretched out his back.

Josephine reached up and touched her forehead gently. She found the edges of the cloth. "How long have we been here?"

"Three days. You've slept quite a bit." Daisy straightened the bedcovers. "You are a stubborn patient. I have forced you to drink several times."

"I am sorry, I don't recall a thing."

"After all you went through, it's no wonder you've slept so much." Daisy frowned, her shoulders drooping. "I am the one who is sorry. I did not trust you, Miss Clayton. Minnie was my dearest friend. I did not expect her lies."

"I understand. It was hard for me to not believe that I had ruined the remedy. Audra is very convincing." Josephine gave a soft laugh. "Where is Minnie now?"

"She is going south again. Wants to start new—well, restart again. Braham sent her with the new manager for Terryhold." Daisy gave a weak smile to Braham then reached over and squeezed Josephine's hand. "And she is ever sorry for all she has done."

"She was coaxed by her sister," Braham muttered. "And Minnie had no family but that Audra. It is a shame. We both lost our only family this week." He pressed his lips together and sighed.

Josephine gave his hand a squeeze. While she'd suffered injury, this week had been hardest on Braham's heart. She turned the conversation. "Who is the new manager for Terryhold?"

"The most trustworthy man I know—my best overseer, Tom," Braham declared. "He will make the necessary changes needed to bring fairness to Terryhold. Especially for my friends. I plan to visit him down there soon."

"I am sure your friends down there will be happy to see you," she offered.

His eyes flashed with joy. "Maybe you'll meet them one day."

Her heart leapt at all the hope held in that wonderful maybe.

"I will finish cooking dinner. They will be here any minute." Daisy raised her eyebrows in anticipation then swiveled around and disappeared.

"Who will be here?" Josephine asked Braham, who wore a broad, flashing smile. "Father?"

A door banged shut at the front of the house.

"Come, let us see." He took her hand and helped her stand. Her legs were wobbly. She held on to Braham's arm and took slow steps. Her temple throbbed beneath the bandage.

The floor creaked in the exact places that it should. Her childhood home was second only to Braham's loving embrace as her favorite place to be. She had both right now. She snuggled close to his neck.

"She is probably sleeping still. . ." Alvin's voice carried from the front room.

Josephine turned her head quickly, a pang caused her to wince again. Her father leaned against the mantel by her mother's jars. Every crease in his face was lit by the streaming sunlight. He'd grown older. She hadn't noticed it before. Now, in the home where she had grown safe and sound beneath the wings of her mother and the hardworking provision of her father, she realized the time that printed on him. So much had changed since those days. Death had led them both down dark paths. Now, his crippled body stood beside fresh blooms on the mantel, just like those that perfumed her room. In this bright sunny place, all was righted. Although much had been lost, at least this was found—light had won in the dark places of this life, no matter how difficult the journey. She would never forget that.

"Father, you're free," she called from across the room.

He turned, lifted his hands, and strode over as best as he could. "My dear Josephine," he warbled with tears streaming down his face. "I was so stricken by my grief that I never rejoiced in your second chance at living." He cupped her face with his hands and kissed her three times on her forehead—just like her mother had always done.

"There was so much to deal with." Josephine spoke through her own tears. "It is finally over." She rested her head on Braham's shoulder, aware of the throbbing in her neck.

Her father regarded Braham. "Thank you for caring for her, young man."

"There is nothing I'd rather do more," Braham replied, squeezing her close to him.

Daisy called them in to eat. The savory aroma of rosemary and garlic promised a salve to Josephine's grumbling stomach. She leaned back on the chair, trying to eat without moving too much. By the end of the meal, she was tired and ready to sleep again. Yet more than the meal had satiated her. The conversation had filled her up. Alvin and her father discussed a plan to resurrect the farm again. Daisy had already begun to clean up around the house. Josephine would finish it when she was well.

"When will I return to the factory?" she asked as they all left the table.

Braham once again offered his arm, and she pulled herself up. "Do not worry, love. The cotton can wait. You must get well."

"Let me sleep a bit." She yawned. "Then I'd like to take you to meet someone."

He arched a brow. "Whatever you'd like, Miss Clayton."

She slept soundly, and when she awoke, the room was lit by the silvery light of morning. Had she slept through the night? She carefully sat up and found the floor with her feet. Voices carried from the other room. She tapped around the bandage on her head. Her pain was less, and she felt even more rested than before.

When she entered the front room, Braham was drinking from a steaming cup on the window seat while Daisy admired the jars on the shelf.

"I am glad you both are still here," Josephine said. They gaped at her.

Braham jumped to his feet and rushed to her. "You are well? We did not expect you to sleep through till morning."

"Do not worry, Mr. Taylor." She laughed. "Tending to the mill girls deprived me of sleep. I suppose I am just catching up."

"Does it hurt?" Daisy approached, eyeing her bandage.

"Just slightly." She patted Daisy's arm. "Daisy, you are welcome to take anything you think you could use." Josephine nodded to the mantel and shelves.

"But aren't they your mother's?"

"Yes, but she would like them to be used." Josephine sighed.

"She would like them to continue to heal others."

"Thank you, Josephine." Daisy glided across the room and began to search among the jars.

"Braham, can we go for a walk?" She held out her hand.

He took it. "You lead the way."

They stepped onto the same farm that appeared dilapidated and beyond repair just days ago. Now, it glistened with potential. The plans discussed at dinner came to mind. She could almost hear the new chickens from Wednesday's market, and the snort of the pig that Alvin would purchase from old Farmer Jamison. Hammering came from the barn followed by the voices of Alvin and her father.

She could not help but smile.

Braham placed her hand through his arm, and she stayed close beside him as they walked to her mother's grave.

" 'Belinda Clayton, loving mother and wife,' " Braham read on the gravestone. "A beautiful name."

"She was a beautiful woman." Josephine sighed.

The warm summer breeze lifted the brown locks from Braham's forehead. "Do you still worry about what she thinks of you?"

"What?" She tilted her head.

Braham slid his arms around her waist and pulled her close. "One morning by the fire, you said you were concerned about what she might think."

"My valley was pressing in on all sides then." She rested her head beneath his chin, relieving the ache from her wound. "Your words had been a comfort and a curse—look forward, you said, for there was no use looking back."

"I do not know if I still believe that. Not now that I have so much to look back on." He pulled away, and she looked up into his tender gaze. "Who would have thought that we would meet as we did, and that we would stand here as we are today?"

Josephine grinned. "My mother once told me that my passion would lead to my purpose. And just like hers, mine is helping the sick. Yet I believe God carved my path to something greater." She pressed her lips together, admiring this strong friend. All the medicine and herbs that she had so loved offered no match to the joy this man brought her. He was a salve to so much of her misery, her discomfort, her shame. He had witnessed her true self, even behind the mask of a secret. "Braham, my purpose was my path to you. Just as you said you prayed that immeasurable good would come to me that night in Fran's kitchen. It has—because of you."

"You are my greatest friend, Josephine Clayton." He furrowed his brow. "The closest person I have to family." Braham stepped away, the warm breeze gushing between them as he dropped to his knee.

The wind had little strength compared to the anticipation that flooded every corner of her heart. Braham's soft brown eyes danced with all she felt—a love so light, as pure as cotton, with not one strand of tangled web.

Braham rubbed his finger over her knuckle as he spoke. "Your father was hesitant to give his blessing, only because he wearied of the thought of having to visit Gloughton so often." His mouth tugged up at one corner, and he winked. "I told him, if you accept, we would visit him equally."

"Oh Braham," Josephine exclaimed, squeezing his hands tightly.

"Josephine, Josie, Miss Clay—" He smiled wide. "Miss Elderberry." They both laughed. "Will you marry me?" His teeth rested on his lip, and he searched her gaze as if he were not sure of the answer. How could he not be certain?

She giggled and fell to her knees. "Yes, of course, my dear Mr. Taylor. There is nothing I want more."

As Braham gathered her in his arms, Josie was certain that the nightmare had faded away, leaving only this dream filled with goodness, brighter than the morning sun and more constant than a lantern's shine.

Dear Reader,

I suspect you wonder what in the world is true about Josephine's tale. While Gloughton and Ainsley are fictional towns, there are several factual threads that make up such a yarn. The true crime of body snatching was more rampant than rare throughout history, and as I dug into research, I discovered how common this practice was amidst the 19th century medical community.

Because of the lack of medical advancement, doctors sometimes mistook a person as being truly dead, ending in the alarming outcome of "live" burials. These types of horrific mistakes, along with the desire for finding cures, led many doctors to hire body snatchers, or "resurrection men," to obtain corpses for research purposes. I was surprised to come across a case where several stolen bodies supplied an entire medical society, but more disturbing was the fact that some body snatchers would even murder for the chance of payment.

Outraged relatives of the deceased pressured officials for justice, and by 1815 in Boston, an act to protect the "Sepulchres of the Dead" passed, declaring body snatching illegal (see **www.truecolorscrime.com** for the actual act). Several snatchers ventured to New York to continue supplying doctors around Boston.

As precautions were made to protect gravesites, body snatchers would hire women to pose as mourners and keep watch for any obstacles that might thwart a quick retrieval. It is a very real fact that body snatching was not always a lonely business, but one that depended on a type of network.

Many other factual tidbits are laced in Josephine's tale. If you'd like to contact me or learn more about my books, sign up for my newsletter at www.angiedicken.com.

Thanks for reading!
Angie Dicken

Angie Dicken credits her love of story to reading British litera-
ture during life as a military kid in England. Now living in the
US heartland, she's a member of ACFW, sharing about author life
with her fellow Alley Cats on The Writer's Alley blog and Facebook
page. Besides writing, she is a busy mom of four and works in adult
ministry. Angie enjoys eclectic new restaurants, authentic conversation with friends, and date nights with her Texas Aggie husband.
Connect with her online at www.angiedicken.com.